# More Than I Dreamed

### *A Novel*

## Sandra L. Moreno

Published in the United States of America by Second Act Publishing, LLC

LIBRARY OF CONGRESS CATALOGING-IN-PUBLICATION DATA

Names: Moreno, Sandra L, author

Title: More Than I Dreamed

Description: First Edition

Identifiers: LCCN: 2025906034 | ISBN 979-8-9928380-1-5 (trade paperback) | ISBN 979-8-9928380-0-8 (eBook)

Scripture quotations are from the ESV Bible (The Holy Bible, English Standard Version®), copyright © 2001 by Crossway, a publishing ministry of Good News Publishers.

Cover design and illustration by GSB!ackburn Design

*For my mother—who always believed in me, even when I didn't believe in myself.*
*Thank you, Mama. I love you.*

# Glossary

"ah"—an appendage added to the name of someone younger than the speaker, a form of familiarity.

ahjumma—a married or middle-aged woman

aigoo—oh my goodness!

annyeonghaseyo—hello

banchan—side dishes that accompany Korean meals

byeonhosa—lawyer

eomma—mom

halmeoni—grandmother

hana, dul, set—one, two, three

Hangul—the writing system of the Korean language or the word for "Korean"

hyung—what boys and men call an older brother or older male friend

imo—maternal aunt

khamsamnida—thank you

makjang—Korean drama with an outrageous, over-the-top plot line

mijo—literally "my son," or a term of endearment for male family and friends

mija—literally, "my daughter," or a term of endearment for female family and friends

Nine-tailed fox—a creature in Korean folklore that transforms into a beautiful woman to seduce men, and eat their liver or heart.

noona—what boys and men call an older sister or older female friend

omo—oh my!

oppa—what girls and women call an older brother or older male friend

pali—hurry

samchon – maternal uncle

"-ssi"—a Korean honorific suffix like Mr./Ms.

unmyeong—destiny, fate

unni—what women call an older sister or older female friend

Ya!—hey!

# Prologue

*Dallas, Texas*
*2016*

She'd sworn she would never come back.

But as the Uber left Love Field Airport and traveled eastbound on Mockingbird Lane, Greer Garza stared through the side window from the backseat. Like all other cities, much of the scenery had changed over the last two decades, yet here and there, she recognized some familiar sites.

They crossed Preston Road and entered the Park Cities, composed of Highland Park and University Park, two cities within a city and among the most affluent in the United States. Wide, tree-lined streets framed modest mansions. The neighborhood shopping center housed a luxury car dealership and world-renowned designer boutiques. There were no dollar stores here.

Greer admired each of the elegant homes, just as she'd done as a law student. Then and now, she wondered about the charmed lives of those who dwelled behind those doors. But as they approached the intersection of Hillcrest Avenue in University Park, her breathing grew rapid, and her fingers gripped the edge of the seat. She had thought after all these years, she would be okay, but she was suddenly not so sure.

"Ma'am?" the driver said. "Do you still want to drive by the university?"

Her heart was in her throat, but she was determined to do this. She nodded and met his gaze in the rearview mirror.

He hit the turn signal and eased into the left turn lane, and the sound of each click pounded in her ears.

The light turned green, and as they turned left onto Hill-crest, Greer sucked in her breath as her past and her alma mater, Southern Methodist University, lay before her eyes. She had forgotten it was such a beautiful campus. Her fingers now splayed across the back seat window. Even from the peripheral street view, she felt like she had never left. Her intention had been merely to drive by, to peek from a distance, but she was intrigued. Like a siren song luring sailors at sea, it beckoned her to take a closer look.

She asked the driver to turn right on Daniel Avenue and pull into the parking lot behind her old dorm, Lawyer's Inn. She opened the passenger door before the car stopped, then hesitated before setting her right foot on the pavement. This was her last chance to turn back. She hoped she wasn't sealing her fate.

She followed the sidewalk that curved around Lawyer's Inn, which, according to a sign, was now called Carr Collins. Across the grounds sat the Tarleton Law Library. The academic buildings Florence Hall and Storey Hall flanked their sides. The four buildings formed a perfect square officially named the Law Quadrangle, but everyone called it the Quad.

As she reached the rotunda in the center of the Quad, the inscription carved at the top caught her eye: *Through vision, love and courage for his fellow man, Umphrey Lee left an enduring spiritual heritage.*

She shook her head. How had she walked past the rotunda daily for three years without noticing that? She'd possessed tunnel vision during those days. And talk about irony. Vision, love, and courage were three traits she sorely lacked.

She climbed the wide stone steps that circled the rotunda and gazed at the campus as déjà vu washed over her. Had a portal in time opened and allowed her to step back? Everything looked exactly as it had that first day she walked onto the lush grounds in 1989. Even the wrought iron tables and chairs on the Lawyer's Inn porch appeared the same. But where were the students? The Quad had always been brimming with students hurrying to and from class. Maybe the winter weather had driven them inside—or they hadn't returned from Christmas break yet.

She shivered, but not from the cold. Once upon a time, she'd naively believed destiny had brought her here and that all her hopes and dreams would come true. Instead, her dreams had shattered into a million pieces like fine porcelain, leaving her to wonder what had gone wrong—what *she* had done wrong.

To put the pieces of her heart back together, she'd left the past behind, buried in a metaphoric time capsule, never to be unearthed again. Mercifully, with time, her plan had worked, as the memories of her time here became so removed from the reality of her day-to-day life that she sometimes wondered if it had all been a dream.

Standing here, those memories came rushing back in vivid color, triggering a sensory overload. She squeezed her eyes shut against the sudden onslaught of emotions they produced. She could hear her friends and classmates talking and laughing and envision their youthful faces as clearly as if only a day had passed. She could almost smell the aroma of the food from the grill inside Lawyers Inn. And as she feared, sharp pangs of loss and regret cut through her.

She pressed her hand to her aching chest as her eyes stung. She had been so foolish. Why had she thought she could rewrite the present by denying the past? That time—the good and the bad—was gone, lost to her forever, and life didn't offer any do-overs. And even if, by some miracle, she could turn back time and do it all over again, would she have the courage to do anything differently? Would she get it right this time?

Her chest spasmed in a sob, and she began to cry.

# Chapter One

G reer hated weddings. Everything from the cringey "Today I Marry My Best Friend" invitations to over-bearing brides and the requisite over-hyped hoopla. Weddings were nothing more than a cliché-ridden celebration of that elusive emotion called love, and she found it exhausting. From personal experience, she knew that true love—that rare once-in-a-lifetime, until-death-do-us-part kind of love—only existed in love songs, Hallmark movies, and Korean dramas.

Yet despite her aversion to matrimonial ceremonies, she sat among the hundreds of guests at Carole Anne Connally and Donnie Colletti's grandiose wedding reception at the Dallas Ritz-Carlton Hotel. So far, this wedding was different from the ones she usually attended, and she had no complaints about that.

Perhaps it had something to do with feeling genuinely happy for the bridal couple. Carole Anne, one of her oldest and dearest friends, had found Donnie later in life. She wasn't a naive young girl with hearts in her eyes who gushed with empty, romantic platitudes. That alone was cause for celebration, but the presence of Charlie Bell, a friend of hers and Carole Anne's, added to the joyous occasion. A girl couldn't ask for a better plus-one, and with Charlie by her side, no one had interrogated Greer about her love life, or lack of one.

Their dinner plates had just been cleared when Carole Anne approached their table. The three met as first-year law students at SMU, a mere fifteen minutes from the hotel. Greer stood to greet her and offer her best wishes, and Charlie kissed the bride.

"You look fabulous, babe," he said.

Greer had to agree. Carole Anne, who'd chosen a floor-length coat of Venetian lace over a simple white gown, looked like Italian royalty.

"Why, thank you, Charlie. I want you to know that having you both here means a lot to me." She turned to Greer and smiled. "Gigi, do you mind if I steal you away for a few minutes? I want to introduce you to Donnie's grandmother, Nonna Maria. You didn't meet her since she didn't attend the rehearsal dinner. She's been watching you and would like to meet you."

Greer's Spidey senses tingled. "Donnie's grandmother has been watching me?" She gave Carole Anne a knowing look. "What are you up to?"

She laughed and batted her ridiculously long eyelashes. "Oh, Gigi, it's nothing like that! And I don't know why. She just asked to meet you."

Greer found this unconvincing and wanted to say no. She could say no, right?

"Oh, so Gigi gets to meet Grandma, but I don't?" Charlie teased in his booming baritone. "I see how it is."

Greer looked up at him, hoping for backup, but he lifted his brows and tilted his head toward Carole Anne, indicating that she should go with her.

*Traitor.*

Charlie abandoned them to get a drink, leaving her no

choice but to follow Carole Anne through the maze of tables. Along the way, Donnie's relatives from New Jersey called out to their new in-law.

"Hey, Carole Anne, how ya doin'?"

"Nice shindig!"

Greer stifled a laugh. She knew better than to stereotype, but this reminded her of the scene in *Goodfellas*. The one where Ray Liotta's character introduced his crew at the Bamboo Lounge. But this crew consisted of Donnie's uncles and cousins instead of Fat Andy and Frankie Carbone.

They soon reached Nonna Maria's table near the dance floor, where she held court surrounded by several of Donnie's aunts. Carole Anne made the introductions and explained that Greer would need to speak up. At ninety-two, Nonna Maria had difficulty hearing.

"Nonna Maria!" Carole Anne shouted. "This is my friend Gigi. The one you asked to meet."

Nonna Maria might be hard of hearing, but her mind and eyes were still sharp. She grabbed Greer's hands with her weathered ones and fixed dark eyes on Greer's face. It almost seemed like the old lady could see straight through to her soul. As she spoke in Italian, her tone partly scolding and partly sympathetic, Greer smiled nervously. She gave Carole Anne a side-eye, pleading for help.

"What's she saying?" Carole Anne asked one of Donnie's aunts, whom she'd introduced as Aunt Francesca.

"Uh, she's saying your friend here looks so sad."

Greer withdrew a hand from Nonna Maria's surprisingly firm grip and tucked her hair behind her ear. "Oh. That's nice of her, but I'm not sad. I'm a little tired, which must show on my face."

Nonna Maria spoke again, and Aunt Francesca continued to translate. "She's saying not to be sad anymore, okay? Don't ruin your pretty face with sadness. She says you should smile because you're still young, and something special is coming your way."

Greer caught her breath. Did Nonna Maria have special powers? Or had she given herself away? She thought she did a pretty good job of disguising her true feelings. So how did Nonna Maria know the biggest reason she hated weddings was because seeing all the couples made her feel like she was the loser in a game of romantic musical chairs? The only one left standing without a chair or, in this case, a partner. Not knowing how else to respond, she said, "*Grazie*," which she'd heard meant "thank you." She gave a slight bow of respect, hoping Italians, like the Koreans, did that too.

Greer excused herself to return to her table, but Carole Anne stopped her with a hand on her arm. "You know, Gigi, I'm glad Nonna Maria said something because I've been thinking it's time for you to get married again."

*And here we go.* Greer shook her head.

Carole Anne held up her beautifully manicured hand. "Now, just hear me out, okay? You're too special to spend the rest of your life alone. I know you feel discouraged because of . . . well, you know, and because of your marriage to that horrible man. Those relationships didn't work because those men weren't right for you, and you were never meant to be with them in the first place. But, Gigi, I can feel in my bones that it's time. Time to meet the *right* man, the one meant for you."

She paused and smiled as a dreamy look crossed her face. "I never thought I'd meet that special someone or get married again, and look at me now. I want you to know the kind of love I found with Donnie. So, here's the plan. When I get ready to throw the bouquet, I want you to stand in front of everyone because I'm going to throw the bouquet at you. Let's get you married, Gigi."

Carole Anne clapped like an excited child who'd just been told she was getting a pony, but Greer couldn't match her enthusiasm. Although thrilled that her friend had found the man of her dreams, she had no desire to participate in silly superstitious rituals, nor did she care to make a spectacle of herself in front of a ballroom full of strangers. With her luck, someone would post the picture on Facebook with the caption, *Desperate middle-aged woman rushes to beat young women to the bouquet.*

Thankfully, the dashing groom's appearance spared her from making a rebuttal. Donnie came to claim his bride for their inaugural dance and asked why they looked so serious.

Carole Anne explained her idea with lots of gesturing while Donnie—clearly smitten with his new bride—listened with admirable patience. Then he smiled, flashing his dimples. "Honey, while that's a great plan, why don't we let Gigi decide if she wants to catch the bouquet? She might not want to get married again."

Greer didn't know Donnie well, but she liked him already.

Carole Anne sobered. "Oh. Well, yes, I suppose that could be true." She considered that for a moment, and then her doe eyes widened. "But Gigi, you must get married again! I want you to be happy!"

The master of ceremonies' voice came over the loudspeaker, announcing the bride and groom's first dance. Fearful of being shamed on social media, Greer grabbed the red herring. "Hey, hurry up, you two," she coaxed, waving them toward the dance floor. "Get out there."

In relentless, true Carole Anne fashion, she opened her mouth to present her closing argument, but Donnie slid his arm around her waist and urged her to join him for their dance. He gave Greer a conspiratorial wink as he led Carole Anne to the dance floor.

Greer shook her head as she watched them dance, still unable to comprehend the absurdity of Carole Anne's plan, then returned to her table, where Charlie entertained the other guests. A tall, handsome Black man, he'd always had an infectious personality, and she had yet to meet a woman immune to his charms. As a successful criminal defense attorney, she had no doubt he used that charisma on juries.

"So what's going on with Caro?" he asked as Greer sat down. "Looked like you guys were having an intense conversation."

As Greer explained, he exploded with laughter. Everyone at their table and the surrounding ones turned and stared, but she smiled, having grown used to Charlie attracting attention years ago.

He shook his head. "Oh, that girl is nuts. I love you guys, but she's nuts. That new husband of hers has got his hands full. It's good that he's younger than her, but I hope he got a B-12 shot for tonight. He's going to need it."

They laughed at poor Donnie's expense, and Greer took a sip of champagne.

"So, speaking of catching the bouquet, are you seeing anyone?" Charlie asked. "Is there anything I should know?"

She nearly sent her mouthful of champagne flying across the table at him. She dabbed her lips with her napkin before answering. "No, I'm not, and please spare me the lecture. We can't all play the field like you. Besides, I'm content with my single status."

"Ha! I don't believe that for one minute." He looked her in the eyes with the candor of an old friend. "You gotta get back out there, Gigi. What's holding you back? You're not still holding a torch for that bonehead, right?"

"No! Of course not. That ship sailed years ago."

His expression turned suspicious. "Mm-hmm. Well, that

ship better stay lost at sea or shipwrecked somewhere, like the *Minnow* on *Gilligan's Island*. You understand what I'm saying?"

Greer rolled her eyes. She understood. They'd been having this same discussion for over twenty years. It was good that she hadn't told him about her visit to the campus. No doubt he'd get the wrong idea.

They began reminiscing about their outlandish adventures, belly-laughing at the foolishness of their youth. Thirty minutes later, they were recounting the night several of their classmates got arrested when Charlie suddenly stopped talking and looked toward the band. "'Volare'. Now we're talking," he said, snapping his fingers. "I must've danced to this song at every wedding I attended back in Jersey." He got up, grabbed her hand, and pulled her to her feet. "Come on, Gigi, let's dance."

When they reached the dance floor, he twirled her around, and she threw her head back and laughed. She'd forgotten what it felt like to have fun. After a couple of songs, the adorable groom asked to cut in. Donnie had wavy dark brown hair and blue eyes that twinkled when he smiled, and Greer could see why he'd swept Carole Anne off her feet.

After that, Greer joined the East Coast contingent in the Tarantella. Being a native Texan, she'd never danced to it before. At weddings in these parts, folks danced to the Cotton-Eyed Joe, a Mariachi band, or both. But she found the Tarantella a fun family affair. Everyone held hands and danced in a circle, just like in the movies.

She watched the bridal couple cut the cake, then stood in line with the other guests at the Viennese table and drooled over the selection of sweet treats like a kid in a candy store. She couldn't pick just one, so she finally selected a crème brûlée and a cannoli and boxed them to eat in her room, where she could change out of her dress, which suddenly felt too tight. Then she went to find Carole Anne.

Greer said goodbye and begged forgiveness for not staying for the bouquet toss. Donnie kissed her on the cheek, telling her he looked forward to getting to know her, and Charlie embraced her in a bear hug and yelled after her as she walked toward the ballroom doors, "Don't go breaking any hearts, girl! Don't do anything I wouldn't do!" He threw his head back in laughter.

Greer smirked. *Yeah, right. Fat chance of that.* Charlie had greater ambitions for her than she had for herself.

She stepped out into the ballroom lobby, and the sight of a young couple canoodling on the couch greeted her. *Get a room,* she wanted to say, but weddings did have a way of putting people in an amorous mood. She passed beneath the spectacular Murano blue chandelier and took a left, then hurried toward the gold elevator doors that would take her to the refuge of her room.

Once upstairs, Greer changed into pajamas and washed her face at the marble vanity in the spacious bathroom. She dried off with a thick, luxurious hand towel and studied her reflection. The hair around her face had begun to curl as it did at the slightest hint of humidity. Having grown up when Marcia Brady's and Malibu Barbie's board-straight hair was the standard of beauty, she'd always hated her dark, curly hair. Thank goodness she discovered keratin treatments five years ago, but she wished that would've been available when she was young. It would've spared her years of straightening her hair to fit in.

She supposed her features were not bad, though. Everyone said her brown eyes and smile were best, but she'd always wished for a smaller nose. She turned from left to right, looking for signs of wrinkles, and couldn't find any, but her skin wasn't as supple as it had once been. Was that why Nonna Maria thought she looked sad? Did her skin sag? She pulled the skin from her cheeks back toward her ears. Maybe she needed a facelift, a refresh, or whatever they called it these days.

She sighed and padded out to the room. Equipped with her crème brûlée and a spoon, she sat in the winged chair by the window and looked out over the night skyline with its tall buildings and sparkling lights. She'd once loved this city and cherished living here, but that was another lifetime ago.

Still, despite her initial reservations, seeing Carole Anne's happiness was worth the risk of returning. She chuckled at her friend's scheme to get her to catch the bouquet. Carole Anne and Charlie might have her best interest at heart, but a string of failed relationships and a bad marriage had proven that love and marriage were not in the cards for her. She couldn't say she was deliriously happy, but could anyone—married or single—say they were? Contrary to what others believed, she liked her life. She had her health, her parents, a successful career, her cats, and a love affair with Korean dramas. That was all the romance she needed at this point.

She smiled and ate a spoonful of crème brûlée. Two years ago, she discovered K-dramas while surfing Netflix, looking for something to watch during the summer hiatus. Like an addict, she became hooked after watching that first drama and searched for more. Everything about them fascinated her, and she couldn't get enough. The engaging storylines with twisting, turning plots, the heart-fluttering romances, and the soaring musical scores unfailingly moved her to tears. The lens of skillful cinematography perfectly captured the aesthetic beauty of Korea.

The ultimate appeal, of course, was the talented actors who could emote such depth of feeling simply from a look in their eyes or the subtle twitch of a facial muscle. It made for a heady combination that resonated with some unexplainable feeling deep within her. Now, everything on television seemed dry by comparison, and she rarely watched anything else.

Like soap operas, the dramas had their share of tropes, usually starting with a spunky heroine and a cold but swoon-worthy hero who had an "accidental" meet-cute when he saved her from falling. Then there were the requisite love triangles, misunderstandings and mistaken identities, wrist grabs, disapproving parents, and sometimes even amnesia. But the trope at the heart of every drama, the one she lived for, was the One True Pairing—when the two leads discovered they shared an entwined and destined fate, an unbreakable bond, and nothing could keep them apart.

Based on the social media comments, many netizens found this trope old-fashioned and cliché, not to mention unrealistic and sentimental. But strangely, despite her cynicism about love and marriage, she liked believing that two people were "meant to be."

Her Korean clients were ecstatic over her newfound interest in a slice of their culture. She enjoyed gossiping with them about the latest dramas and the handsome actors. She couldn't remember when it started, but she'd found Asian men attractive for most of her life. Yet, despite the attraction, she had bought into the stereotype that they were nerds who wore thick glasses and bad haircuts. The dramas had disabused her of this false belief. Not only were the men masculine, but most of them were profoundly handsome.

That said, *ecstatic* was not how she would describe the reaction of her family and friends. They were stunned and questioned what had gotten into her. Some teased her and attributed her interest to a passing midlife crisis. Others expressed open disdain. Their reactions were disheartening but not surprising. As a child who grew up during the Vietnam War, she'd been keenly aware of the negative sentiments toward Asian people.

When she was in the third grade, her aunt Judy had brought her Chinese American boyfriend to a family barbecue. Greer liked him. He was funny and not condescending, even though she was a kid. Her relatives had treated him kindly, but she'd heard their whispers, wondering how even someone as free-spirited as Judy could think of dating an Asian man.

Greer had gotten the message. As a result, she never breathed a word of her attraction to Asian men or her interest in the culture to anyone, not even her best friend. So, from their perspective, her passion for K-dramas had come out of nowhere. For the first time in her life, she dared to defy the accepted norms set for her, to color outside the lines, and her confession shocked everyone. But that was their problem. She didn't care anymore if her family and friends approved or understood. The first half of her life was already in the books. She would live the rest as she pleased.

Greer polished off her dessert, licked the spoon, and reached for her tablet, ready to watch the latest episode of a romantic drama. She settled under the bedcovers but paused before hitting the play button. In the hidden recesses of her heart, she wished she could experience one last adventure of her own—the "something special" that Nonna Maria talked about. But adventure required risk, and she could not, would not, dare assume the risk. She owed a duty to her heart to protect it.

Her hand fell from the tablet as the pillows and cozy comforter enveloped her tired body. "Please, God," she whispered as she drifted to sleep.

~

*August 1989*
*Southern Methodist University Dedman School of Law*
*Dallas, Texas*

The traditional collegiate red-brick buildings, tree-lined sidewalks, and immaculate grounds of the campus bore a striking resemblance to the small undergraduate college Greer attended in Virginia. However, she wasn't in small-town Virginia anymore, but in metropolitan Dallas, a city she'd dreamed of living in. Though only three and a half hours north of her hometown of Austin, a city with a weird, laid-back, college-town vibe, Dallas represented big hair, wealth, culture, and Neiman Marcus.

She had explored the campus when she first arrived. Still, this morning, as she and five of her fellow Lawyer's Inn residents trekked across campus to the university bookstore, she looked around again, searching for something she might have missed.

As they passed the Meadows School of the Arts, she noticed something akin to a garden—and what appeared to be an angel's wing—hidden between the buildings. She wanted to stop and check it out, but fearful of getting left behind, she made a mental note to come back later.

Greer and her friends had assumed they would be in and out in thirty minutes, but when they reached the bookstore, a long line waited to enter—as if the entire student body had decided to purchase their books that day. Once inside, there was barely room to move, and everyone kept bumping into each other. It took her group almost forty-five minutes to locate their books and another thirty minutes waiting in the checkout line. Finally, they left the bookstore at noon, when the temperature hovered around one hundred degrees.

She had put her hair up in a ponytail, but sweat slid down her face as she carried the heavy load of legal tomes. She blew air from the corner of her mouth to move the bangs from her eyes. Her arms ached, but she had to keep going. The fall semester would start in only two days, and they had no time to waste. The professors had already posted their reading assignments, and during yesterday's orientation, the 2Ls warned them that there was no such thing as a free first day like in college. They were first-year law students or 1Ls, and they'd better prepare.

To their collective relief, the fountain in front of the Cox School of Business appeared ahead, meaning they would soon reach the Quad in the northwest corner of the university. Now that they were close, the enticing aromas from the grill inside Lawyer's Inn wafted through the air, and Greer's stomach growled.

The guys at the head of their group hurried ahead, anxious for lunch. Only Charlie stayed behind to keep an eye on Greer and Carole Anne and keep up a steady flow of conversation.

"I was talking to some second-year students, and they said it's just like in that movie *The Paper Chase*. The professors make you stand up in front of everyone and answer questions, even on the first day of class," he said. "That's messed up. I hope I'm not one of the first ones they call."

Neither Greer nor Carole Anne responded, and he looked from one to the other. "You guys need any help? Those stacks of books are so high I can barely see your faces."

Carole Anne, a Fort Worth Southern belle, let out a genteel laugh, but she sounded out of breath. "You are such a gentleman, Charlie, and we appreciate your kind offer, but we're strong women, and we can handle it."

Unfortunately, her words were a jinx. After that proclamation of their feminine competence, the books tipped in Greer's arms and landed on the sidewalk.

"Gigi!" Charlie exclaimed. "Are you all right? Let me help you."

When Greer met Charlie four days ago, an instant camaraderie formed as they checked into their rooms; they went to dinner together in the dining hall, and he invited her to watch *L.A. Law* with him and the guys in the television room. He'd even begun calling her by the nickname used only by her family and closest friends.

Greer laughed to hide her embarrassment. Why was she always such a klutz? "It's okay, I'm fine. I got it. Y'all go on ahead." She hated feeling dependent on others.

"Let me take my books to the Inn, and I'll come back and carry those for you. Stay right here, and I'll be back." Charlie took off jogging toward the Quad.

Greer squatted down to gather her books and saw Carole Anne struggling, too. She stood back up, leaving her books in a pile on the ground. "Let me take some of those from you. I'll come back with Charlie for mine."

Carole Anne looked relieved. "Well, if you're sure you wouldn't mind . . ."

They laughed to ease the tension, and not just about the dropped books. They'd entered an ultra-competitive and cutthroat world where every man and woman looked out for themselves, so finding an empathetic friend was crucial for survival. Their rooms were at opposite ends of the third floor of Lawyer's Inn, and they'd met while heading to the showers. They'd struck up an easy conversation and discovered they were kindred spirits.

Greer relieved Carole Anne of half of her books, and they discussed lunch as they walked the rest of the way. Being kindred spirits, they both loved a good bacon sandwich and sweet iced tea.

When they reached the Quad, it swarmed with students. Some sat on the curved stone benches inside the rotunda. Others filled the patio chairs on the Inn's front porch or sat on the Inn's stone steps. Despite the brutal heat, everyone congregated outside, enjoying their last days of freedom.

They climbed three flights of stairs, deposited Carole Anne's books in her room, stopped by the ladies' room, and then caught up with Charlie in the stairwell. Greer assured him she and Carole Anne could handle it from here, but he insisted on accompanying them.

She blinked into the noonday sun when they stepped outside and shielded her eyes from the glare. That's when she saw her books stacked on one of the patio tables. She recognized the blue bookmark she'd stuck in her Contracts book.

A tall, athletic-looking guy with light brown hair and green eyes—her ideal type—stood beside them with a protective hand on the stack. The sun's rays from behind him appeared like a halo around his head, which Greer found appropriate, for he appeared heaven-sent.

"Those are my books," she said, suddenly feeling shy.

The angelic-looking being smiled. "Uh, yes, here you go. I was keeping them safe for you," he said with a slight stutter.

Good-looking and shy? Today must be her lucky day.

"I'm Greer," she said.

"Uh, oh, hi, Greer. I'm Jake."

# Chapter Two

G reer overslept and jumped out of bed with a small scream. She took a lightning-quick shower, threw everything in her luggage, and tossed her key card to the concierge on her way out the door to catch her flight. She found a brush in her purse and brushed her hair on the ride to the airport, but she had thrown her makeup bag in her luggage, so she couldn't do anything about her plain face. Tired, irritable, and knowing she didn't look her best, once on board the plane, she sat toward the back, as far away from everyone as possible. She turned her face away from the remaining passengers who filed in looking for a seat and stared out the window at the bag handlers loading luggage into the belly of the plane.

If she hadn't flown instead of driving like she usually did when coming to Dallas, she never would have stopped by the law school and never had that dream. Even in the light of day, she couldn't process it. It had seemed so real, so clear, that she'd cried out, "Jake!" and bolted up in bed, trying to catch her breath. She looked around, confused by the hotel furniture. What happened to the patio furniture and her books? Where did Jake go? *No, no, no!* Tears pooled in her eyes, and she pummeled the pillows in frustration.

Strangely, she couldn't remember *ever* dreaming about Jake, not even when she'd seen him almost every day for three years. She'd forgotten how they met, but never the last time she heard from him. Seventeen years ago, he called to tell her he was getting married.

Out of the corner of her eye, she detected someone pausing by her row, and her body stiffened. *Keep moving, buddy.* He must have received her telepathic message because she heard him settle in the row behind her.

Finally, after an interminable wait, the captain announced to prepare for takeoff. She continued gazing out the window as the plane lifted into the sky. Thankfully, the flight to Austin was only thirty minutes, but she desperately needed coffee. She closed her eyes while waiting for the beverage service and didn't open them until she heard the captain's voice again, asking them to prepare for landing. She wiped the drool from the corner of her mouth and massaged the back of her neck—she must have slept weird—then yawned loudly and stretched her arms over her head, her mind muddled in a fog of sleep.

Once they landed and could move around the cabin, she put on her coat and slipped her purse over her shoulder. She stepped into the aisle, anxious to get moving. A tall, husky man stepped out of the row ahead of her, filling the narrow aisle. He barely missed hitting her in the face as he struggled to put his long arms through the sleeves of his puffy coat. Behind her—presumably, the man from earlier who had tried to invade her space—cleared his throat and zipped what sounded like a canvas bag.

She stifled another yawn, and when the line began to move, she followed Puffy Coat on autopilot while wiping the sleep from her eyes. She failed to notice when he stopped ahead to retrieve his bags from the overhead bin. Nor did she see the tiny black bag that popped out in the direction of her head.

A strong hand clamped her shoulder as she picked up her right foot. "Watch out!" a deep voice said behind her.

The hand startled her, and she stepped back onto the foot of the man behind her, then lunged forward and back again. Losing her balance, she began flailing at the air but could find nothing to hold onto. She shut her eyes, expecting to fall, but instead, her head landed with a thud against the chest of the man behind her.

Two strong arms held her up. Above her head, the same deep voice asked, "Are you okay?"

Uh, she didn't know. What just happened?

"If you think you're okay, I will set you upright."

Not just deep. The voice was honeyed, too. That alone made her swoon. He smelled clean, like soap with the faintest hint of sunscreen, and had a strong, warm body. Although disoriented, she registered that it had been years since a man held her in his arms. It felt good. Comforting. Would he think she was weird if she asked to stay there for a minute or two longer? Would he fear for his safety and call the Sky Marshal?

She didn't get a chance to discover the answers to those questions—which was probably good regarding the second one — because, to her disappointment, he helped her stand upright too soon. She sighed. It had been nice while it lasted. She straightened her coat and smoothed the back of her hair, then turned around and looked up at the most handsome Asian man she'd ever seen. Correction. The most handsome *man* she had ever seen—Asian or non-Asian. The sight of him took her breath away, and she stumbled backward, landing on her behind. Would the humiliation never end?

Her handsome rescuer gently grabbed her hands with his

strong ones and helped her to her feet again. "Careful now. Are you sure you're okay?"

No, she wasn't sure. Suddenly, she wasn't sure about anything. Was the champagne she drank last night a magical elixir? Or, like the Bangles song, "Manic Monday," was she in the middle of a dream? What else could explain this gorgeous man? Outside the K-dramas, the Republic of Korea, and possibly the greater Los Angeles area, she didn't think such a man existed. She'd never seen anyone like him before, certainly not in Texas.

She slapped her cheek twice. "Am I dreaming?"

His dark, perfectly shaped eyebrows furrowed, and he repeated his question for the third time. "Miss, are you okay?"

He called her *miss*! Still reeling between fantasy and reality, she answered him in Korean. "*Ye.*"

Now those gorgeous eyebrows shot up. "Pardon me?"

Their eyes locked, and she realized her mistake.

"I mean, yes! Yes, I'm fine," she practically shouted and began rambling. "I'm so sorry. I don't know what I'm thinking. I should be thanking you, but I'm wasting your time thinking about Korean dramas. And I don't even know if you're Korean. I mean, you could be, but I don't know." She took a deep breath. "Thank you for helping me. I'm sorry, I can be clumsy."

He looked momentarily taken aback by her rambling confession but then brushed it aside. "Hey, no problem, and besides, it's partly my fault for scaring you."

"Thank you," she said again and gave a deep bow because she still wasn't convinced this wasn't a K-drama fantasy.

He laughed, one of those rich, deep, masculine laughs, and her face flushed with embarrassment. Without another word, she turned and rushed away. Thank goodness all the other passengers had already deplaned, giving her a quick escape.

"Hey, wait up!" he called out, but she kept walking.

Running away from him had been a waste of time. Handsome Hero, as she now thought of him, caught up to her when she reached the gatehouse. He tapped her shoulder to get her attention, and she spun around wide-eyed.

"Yes?" She focused on his Adam's apple because she couldn't bring herself to look him in the eyes.

"I'm sorry. I don't mean to keep scaring you, but I don't know your name."

Now she looked up. "You want to know my name?"

"Uh, well, yes, to let you know you forgot your purse," he said, holding it out to her. "You dropped it when you fell back, and I figured you might need it."

So much for not embarrassing herself any further. "Thank you," she said, and their fingers brushed during the exchange.

"You're welcome." He smiled with the same compassion one might give someone with an intellectual disability.

He slung his backpack over his shoulder and tilted his head toward the baggage claim. "This way," he said, waiting while she got her bearings before leading the way.

To Greer's surprise, he kept an even pace with her. With his long legs, he could have left her in the dust. Being hyper-aware of his presence, she detected him giving her the occasional side-eye, but he didn't say anything more. Not that she could blame him. He must think her a nutcase. She couldn't believe she'd answered him in Korean. What had she been thinking? She needed to cut back on the K-dramas.

They reached the down escalator, and to her relief, Handsome Hero stepped on it first. Even though her coat covered her butt, she preferred being behind him. She stayed three steps back and took the opportunity to appraise him on the ride down. The personification of tall, dark, and handsome, he was over six feet tall. And unlike many of her contemporaries, he still had a head full of hair with only a few sprinklings of gray. She appreciated his short, neat haircut and how it exposed his long, muscular neck. She also liked his casual, rugged style. He looked as if he'd stepped off the cover of an LL Bean catalog. With his dark cargo coat accentuating his broad shoulders and his jeans encasing his long, muscular legs, he oozed masculinity. She guessed him to be at least forty, possibly even closer to her age.

The escalator deposited them on the first floor. Without a backward glance, Handsome Hero turned left toward the baggage carousels. He reached into his coat pocket and pulled out his phone. Like everyone else, he began texting while waiting for his luggage. Greer studied him while pretending to be engrossed in her text messages. But no one had texted her. All she had to look at were work emails.

As the first piece of luggage popped out, Puffy Coat reappeared and blocked her view. He owned the errant black bag that had almost hit her on the noggin and launched into a long explanation of how he had recently taken up photography, so she missed her luggage passing around the carousel. She finally excused herself and glanced where Handsome Hero had been standing. No surprise, he was gone. Common sense told her he had no reason to stick around, but she still felt disappointed.

Her luggage made its way around again, and as she reached to retrieve it, a large hand beat her to it.

"I've got it," Handsome Hero said, lifting the heavy bag without effort and setting it on the ground.

Greer smiled, forgetting to hide her delight. "Oh, I thought you'd gone. Thank you. You didn't have to do that. You've already done more than enough for me."

"Glad I can be of help. Do you have only one bag?"

"Yes." She bit her lip. Now what? Her mind drew a blank. She'd never developed the witty banter skill set and couldn't think of anything to say. More to the point, she couldn't think of anything to make him *want to stay.*

He also had nothing to say, but his eyes searched her face with an intensity that made her self-conscious. She wished she knew what he was thinking. *Ask me for my name or my business card,* she pleaded.

"Well, uh—" they both said, then stopped and laughed.

Handsome Hero scratched the back of his head. "You go first."

She wished he would go first so she'd know which direction this was heading. Aww, who was she kidding? She already knew how the story ended, so she held out her hand. "Thank you again for your help."

"No need to keep thanking me." He appeared to want to say something else but then shook his head. Finally, he engulfed her small hand with his, his grip comforting.

She dropped her gaze and studied his hand. He had long fingers and neat, trimmed nails. Due to their similar coloring, the two hands blended as one. "Goodbye," she said, forcing a smile. She knew she would regret this missed opportunity for the rest of her life.

He nodded and smiled so gloriously that her left hand flew to her chest. Did her heart flutter? It'd been so long that the sensation felt strange.

"Take care of yourself," he said, releasing her hand and turning toward the exit.

Greer watched him walk through the sliding glass doors, hoping against hope that he would turn back one final time.

He kept walking.

"Stop daydreaming, Greer."

She didn't realize she'd spoken aloud until a small, older

woman asked if she was talking to her. Shaking her head, she headed for the restroom.

Her reflection in the mirror made her gasp. She'd forgotten she wasn't wearing makeup, and those dark leftover mascara circles under her eyes didn't help. No wonder Handsome Hero didn't bother to ask for her name. She rolled her luggage outside, paused outside the sliding glass doors to button her coat, and wrapped the scarf from her purse around her neck. Then, she continued toward the crosswalk leading to the parking garage.

As she reached the curb, a shiny red BMW pulled up behind the other vehicles in the passenger pickup lane. A tall, young Asian woman popped out from behind the driver's side. Her short red coat matched her car, and skinny jeans and knee-high boots showed off her slender legs. A white beanie sat atop her long black hair.

Talk about a knockout. Greer had always believed she looked good for her age, but now she felt like a frumpy middle-aged woman. There was no competing against the beauty of youth.

The young woman waved to someone behind Greer and called out in Korean. Greer had watched enough dramas to recognize the language. She turned around as Handsome Hero again appeared out of nowhere like a black ops spy emerging from the shadows. He nodded in her direction and made a beeline for the young woman, responding in Korean and laughing, clearly delighted to see his young friend. And *young* was an understatement. The girl had to be in her early twenties.

He threw his backpack into the car and folded himself into the passenger seat. Cars were coming and going all around them, but the young woman held up her phone for a selfie, laughing and rather pleased with herself. Handsome Hero shook his head and covered his eyes with his hand in embarrassment but didn't seem annoyed. The young woman finally got in, put her car in gear, and eased it into traffic to exit the airport.

Greer watched them drive off. She hoped he might wave goodbye, but his young companion had captured his attention.

And just like that, Handsome Hero drove out of her life forever.

*Chapter Three*

Greer left the airport and headed west on Highway 71 toward Austin. She found it challenging to stay within the ever-changing construction lanes of her hometown's rapid transformation from a laid-back college town to a sprawling tech metropolis. Unlike the Park Cities in Dallas, Austin had become a city she hardly recognized.

On her way home, she stopped at Dan's Hamburgers, a local Austin favorite on the corner of Ben White and Menchaca, for breakfast tacos. She'd never been able to think straight on an empty stomach, and Dan's served the perfect hangover tacos. Many people ate menudo to treat a hangover, but she preferred a good bacon, egg, and potato taco on a flour tortilla. Not the healthy, flavorless kind, but the ones made the old-fashioned way with some grease.

Once she left Dan's, it was a short drive north on South Lamar Boulevard to her home in the highly desired neighborhood of Barton Hills. Two years ago, her parents decided they no longer wanted the burden of homeownership and moved to a fancy downtown condo. When they offered her their home, she jumped at the chance to live in the house she'd grown up in. But the house had been built the same year she was born and needed tons of work. The irony wasn't lost on her. Besides all the necessary upgrades to bring it to code, she had it remodeled into her dream home with the help of her cousin, an architect. It had been a long, arduous, and expensive process, but it was worth every penny. She and her cats had moved in two months ago, right before Thanksgiving.

From Barton Hills Drive, she turned right onto her street and smiled as her house welcomed her home. She'd redesigned her parents' traditional ranch into a charming, French-style house with two dormer windows on the steep roof. Brown and tan brick steps led to a long, covered porch with four slim white columns, and an espresso-colored front door and matching shutters gave the white stucco a pop of color.

She parked in the driveway—her garage still held several unpacked boxes—and opened the front door. "Mommy's home!" she announced as she entered the foyer.

Kevin and Sophie, her two rescue cats who had come with their names, meowed as they weaved in and out of her ankles, impeding her attempt to hang her coat. She took turns picking them up and kissing their little faces. Kevin, a large black cat everyone said resembled a baby panther, was warm and friendly. He greeted everyone at the door like a dog. The petite black female with a delicate face, Sophie, although cautious of strangers, became a loving lap kitty once you gained her trust.

Several minutes later, Greer took her first sip of morning coffee. Ahh. It felt good to be home. She sat on the banquette in the breakfast nook of her kitchen with her coffee and tacos and kept an eye on Kevin and Sophie, who were eating breakfast just a few feet away.

She took a big, satisfying bite of the taco and looked out the bay window to the backyard, where her new pool awaited its inaugural swim. She'd always dreamed of having a pool, but her father had been against it and warned her that it would bring nothing but problems. "I wouldn't have a pool if somebody paid me," he'd said as the final word.

Even at this age, whenever she did something that didn't meet her parents' approval, it created a problem. Her parents loved her and meant well, but they were from a different generation with different ways of seeing things. Before moving into their condo, they'd held on to an avocado green refrigerator they had purchased in the 1970s because "Why spend the money on a fancy new refrigerator when our old one still works?"

She considered her father's arguments but ultimately gave in to her dream in a rare act of opposition. After all, it was her money, and what else did she have to spend it on? Her life consisted of work, home, and family—lather, rinse, and repeat. Why not indulge in an occasional splurge?

Of course, now that she'd built it, would anyone come and enjoy it with her? Kevin Costner's famous *Field of Dreams* answered that question, but her life lacked that same movie magic. She would love to throw a housewarming party, and she had plenty of friends and enough aunts, uncles, and cousins to populate a small town whom she could invite, but everyone was busy with their own lives. Even her best friend since high school, Maggie Davis, was so preoccupied with chauffeuring her fifteen-year-old twins from one activity to another that they rarely had a chance to talk.

After she and her kids finished eating, she cleaned up and rolled her luggage to her dressing room. The room adjacent to her bedroom contained enough closet space to please a clothes horse like herself and plenty of shelves for her purses and shoes. An island in the center with several drawers held everything else. Two ornate, sparkling chandeliers added to the glamour, and a Turkish ottoman gave her a place to sit and put on her shoes while also providing a good napping spot for Kevin and Sophie.

She changed into flannel pajama pants, a cozy, oversized sweatshirt, and warm slippers, then walked to the living room with Kevin and Sophie leading the way. Her decorator had carefully curated the decor of every room with neutral but elegant furnishings and carpets. The walls were a cool gray, and the floors white ceramic tile because she found the maintenance of wall-to-wall carpets too burdensome with cats. A stone fireplace and built-in bookshelves lined an entire wall in the open living room, and a cream sectional, floral accent chairs and glass tables completed the look. Her decorator described the style as "transitional glam."

Shortly after moving in November, she had given her parents a tour of the finished house and was eager to hear their reactions. Strangely, her mother had remained silent, and when Greer pressed her for an opinion, she said, "Well, everyone's taste is different."

"What do you mean?" Greer asked. "Don't you like it?"

Her mother shrugged. "It's nice, but it lacks color."

Greer was disappointed but not surprised by her lukewarm reception. Her mother's taste was more suited to the bright color schemes of a Taco Cabana restaurant.

Greer sat on the sectional, covering her legs with a sherpa throw blanket. When Kevin and Sophie joined her and began kneading the throw in preparation for their nap, she petted their heads, grateful for their company. There were days when she felt weary and alone. Despite not wanting to be in a relationship, she wanted someone to hug her on those difficult days and reassure her that everything would be okay. Someone who would stand in her corner and catch her fall.

Like Handsome Hero had done.

Except she'd gotten ahead of herself when she knew nothing

about him. He'd merely been kind, and she mistook his kindness for a sign of something there. How pathetic to be so attention-starved. In her defense, men no longer rushed to her aid or bothered to open a door for her. She had passed her expiration date and been put out to pasture. What a shame so many men valued a woman only for her youthful sex appeal. Once a woman passed what men considered her prime, they found no value in her and tossed her aside.

Having someone like Handsome Hero, the physical incarnation of her ideal man, coming to her aid had been surreal. For a nanosecond, she'd felt special—until the appearance of the young girlfriend quashed her silly daydreams. She'd been disappointed to discover her newly crowned hero had a chink in his armor. Why were men only interested in women half their age?

*Not so fast*, a little voice reminded her. *What about Jampa?*

She smiled. She'd forgotten about Jampa. Okay, yes, she could understand the physical attraction to a younger man or woman. Besides not having any gray hair, wrinkles, or body fat, they didn't carry the emotional baggage of a middle-aged person. Yet despite the handsomeness of the young barista in the café in her office building, she'd never considered *dating* him. He was young enough to be her son, and despite his friendliness that sometimes bordered on flirtatious, she doubted he saw her as a potential romantic interest. He probably treated all his customers that way.

She let out a sigh. There was no point in feeling disappointed over something that would never happen anyway. Even if the young girlfriend wasn't in the picture, it's not like Greer would ever see Handsome Hero again.

She picked up the television remote, then fumbled and dropped it at realizing something. Apart from his backpack, he hadn't carried any luggage.

~

The Law Office of Hudson and Hamilton, PLLC, occupied two floors of a building in downtown Austin. Considered modest by law firm standards, it had twelve partners, seven associates, and numerous paralegals, assistants, and administrators.

Greer, part of the firm's real estate and construction practices, had been a partner for fifteen years. Due to the number of clients she brought to the firm, her hard work, and countless overtime hours, she'd earned a coveted corner office with large windows that offered a magnificent view up Congress Avenue to the Texas State Capitol. She'd decorated it like an open living area more than an office, furnishing it with a desk, credenza, bookshelves, a leather sofa, club chairs, and a conference table. Several framed prints, her law school diploma, and her State Bar of Texas license hung on the walls.

The weekend in Dallas had left her feeling disquieted. Already a workaholic, she went into overdrive upon returning to the office on Monday. She called Megan Sullivan, her bright, five-year associate, and Molly Graham, a sharp-as-nails legal assistant, into her office. Having an all-female team, and a competent one at that, made her proud. The Good Ol' Boys' Club in the construction sector had dominated the field too long and needed a run for their money. Today, however, she wasn't feeling proud.

"How was the wedding?" Molly asked.

"Fine. Seeing my friends was nice," Greer answered, scrolling through a client list on her computer screen. "How many lien affidavits and first notices are we sending out this month?"

"I believe it's eleven," Megan answered.

"You believe?" Greer looked up at her.

"Well, I can double-check."

Greer shook her head. "Let's review every client file to be sure we're not missing anything. I remember Joe Taylor saying something about expecting payment on the highway construction project. Please check with him and see if he got paid. Do the same for all our files."

Molly's eyes widened. "*All* of our files? That'll take days, and we're already busy because of the lien deadline."

"I know, and I'm going to be working too." Greer looked from one to the other. "Isn't that what we get paid for, ladies?"

Molly opened her mouth, but Megan shot her a warning look and tilted her head toward the door. They each picked up a stack of files on their way out of Greer's office.

At the end of the week, a bleary-eyed Greer was on her way to the office kitchen for tea when she noticed Rita leaning against the doorjamb of Megan's office. She approached to see what was happening but stopped short when she heard her name.

"I think something happened to Greer in Dallas." She recognized the voice as Molly's. "Notice how she didn't say much about the wedding even though she's usually so happy to see her old friends?"

Greer tilted her head to look past Rita and saw Megan sitting behind her desk, chewing her bottom lip in thought. "She does seem different, doesn't she? She's normally chill, even when we have a big project, but now she's strictly business, almost like a machine."

"I agree." Molly's voice had filled with concern. "I don't know how many other legal assistants have told me I'm lucky to work for Greer because although she's tough, she's fair. But I'm not feeling lucky this week. All I feel is exhausted."

Megan looked up at Rita, and Greer moved to the other side

of the door frame so they wouldn't see her. "What do you think, Rita? Should we say something to her?"

"No, you two should keep a low profile and let it go. If something's bothering her, she'll work it out. Besides, she's working long hours too. She's already here in the mornings when I arrive, and she leaves after everyone else."

Greer stepped back slowly and continued to the kitchen. She needed to pull herself together and work it out for her team's sake.

Two weeks after the incident on the plane, Greer still hadn't pulled herself together, although she tried. While at work, she could relegate Handsome Hero to a corner of her mind, but when the workday ended, he came to her mind unbidden. She didn't want to think about him. She wanted to forget she'd ever met him. Her life had been content before. Now, life was taunting her by showing her that the man of her dreams *did* exist but was out of her reach. It was like she was a kid again— when people said she wasn't smart enough or pretty enough to have good things happen to her.

When warm temperatures replaced the arctic blast of early January, Greer began taking daily afternoon walks to work out her frustration. She wanted to tire herself so she could sleep at night and not dwell on the things that could never be.

On one such balmy, seventy-degree afternoon, Greer handed Molly her credit card and sent her to the café to buy iced coffee and snacks for the team, her way of assuaging the guilt she felt for working them so hard. Then she slipped on her New Balance running shoes, rode down the elevator to the first floor, and paused to look inside the café on her way out. Jampa worked the register. Tall and lean, with deep olive skin, he stood out from the crowd. Molly waited in line with her curly head down, looking at her phone, probably playing Candy Crush.

Once outside, Greer pulled her sunglasses from her head and lifted her face to the sun's warmth. She needed to get out more often. Spending twelve hours a day in a one-hundred-fifty-square-foot box was taking its toll on her health and mental well-being. She headed north, in the direction of the Capitol, sidestepping the other pedestrians.

Music caught her attention as she reached the corner of 10th Street and Congress, gradually getting louder. Waylon Jennings's "I've Been a Long Time Leaving" came from a motorcycle stopped at the light, heading southbound on Congress. She had grown immune to motor vehicles blaring their music, but this one made her do a double-take. The black-clad rider looked smoking hot—and familiar. Thick black hair, a perfectly chiseled face, and long legs. Aviator glasses covered his eyes, so she couldn't be sure, but her heart began to race. This Bad Boy looked an awful lot like Handsome Hero. Or his doppelgänger.

He turned his head and looked in her direction, and heat crept from her neck to her face. She checked behind her, but no one stood there.

The light turned green, and he roared past without taking his eyes off her. She watched him go, open-mouthed.

She saw Handsome Hero's face everywhere. When she closed her eyes at night, he was there. As she went about her day, she thought she saw him or someone who looked like him. She even thought she saw him at the grocery store. And now here? Of all places, what would Handsome Hero be doing riding a motorcycle on Congress Avenue, listening to Waylon Jennings?

She walked faster toward the Capitol. Apparently, she

wasn't exerting herself enough, and this was simply another figment of her imagination. She was determined to forget him if it was the last thing she did.

# Chapter Four

Greer collapsed in her desk chair after a morning full of client meetings. Working through lunch was commonplace, but today, she was famished. Her feet danced to the left, turning the chair toward the window. She wanted to get lunch, but the steel gray sky and frigid temperature made her reluctant to leave the building. Late January's mild days had disappeared with the turn of the calendar page, and February was once again proving to be one of Austin's coldest months.

It had been ten days since she'd seen Handsome Hero's doppelgänger on the motorcycle. She had searched for him daily since then as she took her afternoon walks without any luck. Maybe the cold spell was a sign that it was time to give up the search.

Greer was debating whether to order out when Dianne, the head receptionist, buzzed her. Swiveling to the right, she picked up her phone.

"Ms. Garza," Dianne said in a low, professional tone, "I didn't know if you were in your office."

So much for lunch. "I'm here, Dianne." Greer tried to sound cheerful. "What's up? Do you need me?"

"Well, no, ma'am, but Mrs. Donovan is here and would like a moment of your time?"

Greer caught something different in Dianne's voice. "Dianne, is everything okay?"

She chuckled softly. "Yes, ma'am. Everything is just fine."

"Okay then. Sure, send her back."

Greer always made time for Mrs. Donovan, whom she called Mrs. D. She was one of her Korean clients and, admittedly, one of her favorite clients. An older woman with grown children around Greer's age, she had an interesting backstory. Like many women of her generation, she'd been a wife and homemaker until divorcing her husband after nearly twenty years of marriage. She then used her settlement money to invest in commercial real estate and discovered she had a knack for it.

As a result, she'd acquired a sizable real estate portfolio over the last three decades. Five years ago, she found Greer after firing her previous counsel for belittling her as an inexperienced foreign woman with no sense of the Texas real estate market. His loss became Greer's gain. She astutely recognized Mrs. D as an intelligent and savvy businesswoman, and they'd hit it off professionally and personally.

Between their scheduled appointments, Mrs. D habitually stopped by unannounced. She always brought Greer gifts, usually Korean food or trinkets. "I turn you into Korean woman, so you find good Korean man," she would tease.

Mrs. D introduced her to kimbap, a sushi-looking, savory, sweet Korean snack. Greer loved it, but its strong smell had alienated everyone else at the firm. Not that anyone would dare say anything to Mrs. D. The partners held her in high esteem because she never batted an eye about her legal fees. Therefore, no one tried to stop her from dropping by unannounced with controversial snack food, especially Greer. Her mouth watered as she anticipated what today's treat might be.

Mrs. D was so loud that Greer could hear her as she greeted the people she passed in the hallway, and she sounded quite animated today. She rapped on Greer's door, then opened it with a flourish without waiting for an answer. "He-lloooo. How. Are. You?" she said in her sing-song style, emphasizing each syllable. She grinned from ear to ear.

Greer usually responded to this salutation with, "Hey there, woman!" but today, she couldn't find her voice. Frozen like a deer in headlights, she couldn't comprehend the scene before her. She must be hallucinating or having a nervous breakdown. It wasn't out of the question with the way she'd been pushing her body to its limits. What else could explain Handsome Hero standing behind Mrs. D and staring, speechless, over her head?

"It's you," they said in unison.

Mrs. D ignored their stunned reactions and commenced with the introductions. "Lawyer Garza, this my son Gun. I bring him here for you to meet. I tell you before about my handsome son, right? He fifty-one, one year older than you, perfect age for you."

As usual, Mrs. D didn't pull any punches and got straight to the point. She'd come to play matchmaker. Greer put that aside for the moment as she reeled. Handsome Hero was her *son*? Of course, she'd heard Mrs. D talk about him before, but Greer would never have put two and two together in a million years.

"*Eomma*," Handsome Hero said, using the Korean word for *mom*. "What's going on? How do you know this woman?"

"Lawyer Garza is my lawyer. Why you look so surprised? You see her before? Maybe meet before on airplane?" Mrs. D giggled and covered her mouth with her hand like a mischievous schoolgirl.

Handsome Hero—no, what did his mother call him? *Gun*? Yes, now Greer remembered hearing his name. She knew it was a Korean name.

41

Gun gave his mother a sharp look. "*Eomma*, how do you . . . how do you know we met on a plane?"

"Okay, I tell you, but first we all sit. Come, sit down."

It might be Greer's office, but Mrs. D was in charge. She sat in her customary spot on the leather sofa, but Gun waited for Greer to sit.

Greer said a silent prayer of thanks that she'd worn a slimming dress. The black sweater material hugged her curves in all the right places, and the knee-high black suede boots she'd paired it with added a couple of inches to her short stature. Still, she sucked in her stomach as she emerged from behind her desk and sat in one of the club chairs. She crossed, uncrossed, then crossed her legs again. She couldn't remember which position was more flattering.

Gun perched on the rolled sofa arm next to his mother. The outdoorish attire he'd worn on the plane was now replaced with a black pea coat, a sweater, and trousers. The sophisticated city look accentuated his features, and he looked even more handsome than she remembered. "Okay, *Eomma*, out with it. Let's hear what you have to say."

Mrs. D delighted in the spotlight. "Let me start from beginning. For many years, I see my son and Lawyer Garza always alone, both so sad, with no one to share loneliness. This not a good thing—not good to be alone. I want to help, but how? Then one day, I think, *What better woman for my son than Lawyer Garza? What better man for Lawyer Garza than my son? But how I introduce them? My son always traveling and never settle down. What woman want man with no roots, blown back and forth by wind?* Then one day it come to me: people meet who they supposed to meet. It is *unmyeong*."

Greer shifted in her chair. Did Mrs. D have to make her sound so pathetic? Sad and alone? It might be true, but hearing it out loud, especially in front of uber-handsome Gun, was embarrassing. She doubted a man with Gun's stunning visuals had ever been lonely. "It's what? What was that word you used?"

"*Unmyeong*. It's the Korean word for fate or destiny, whatever you want to call it," Gun said with a hint of frustration accompanied by an eye-roll.

"Lawyer Garza, you like Korean drama, so you know about *unmyeong*. Two people meet and fall in love. Even if separate, they meet again. Why? Because they meant to be together, and nothing can keep them apart. It is *unmyeong*."

Yes, Greer knew about *unmyeong* in Korean dramas. That's what she loved most about them. However, the destined drama couples usually met in childhood, so she didn't see how it applied to them.

Gun agreed. "*Eomma*, nice try, but you're getting ahead of yourself in your haste to play matchmaker. Lawyer Garza and I *just* met. We have no history. Don't put her in an uncomfortable position." He glanced at Greer, and a mischievous grin played on his lips. "She may not even like me."

Before Greer could stop herself, she let out a sound that sounded like *pfft*. He must be teasing. What woman wouldn't like *him*?

"No matter if not meet before, you meet now," Mrs. D insisted. "You not think it strange that out of *allll* people in this big city Austin, my son and my lawyer meet without my help? How you explain that, huh?"

Gun shrugged. "I don't know. Coincidence? A strange occurrence of events with no rhyme or reason. It's called life, *Eomma*, and you can't change the facts to suit your circumstances."

Greer interrupted before things escalated. "You still haven't told us how you found out we met on the plane."

A triumphant smile spread across Mrs. D's face. "One hand

cannot clap alone. My granddaughter take picture at airport and show me. She say, '*Halmoeni,* my uncle meet beautiful woman on plane,' and she show me picture. I cannot believe my eyes when I see it is Lawyer Garza. How this possible? How my son meet Lawyer Garza? This why I say it must be *unmyeong.*"

Wait, what? "Your granddaughter took a picture of me at the airport? When? I don't remember seeing her."

"Darcy showed you the picture she took at the airport," Gun said. "Really?"

"Yes, Darcy laugh and say, '*Halmeoni,* Uncle Gun try to act cool in front of her, but I know he like her, so I take picture and show you.'"

Gun let out a short, nervous laugh and scratched the back of his head. "That little stinker."

Greer tried to think back. How had Mrs. D's granddaughter escaped her notice? "Excuse me, but I don't remember seeing your granddaughter at the airport. I only saw a young woman in a red BMW."

"Yes! That's Darcy!"

Gun nodded. "She picked me up, and I treated her to break-fast because she complained that she had to wake up early. You saw us."

So the girl in the red BMW was his *niece?* Not his girl-friend? Greer took a moment to process this news as a warm glow spread over her body. She'd misjudged both Gun and his niece entirely. Darcy hadn't been taking a selfie but a picture of her for Gun's benefit. Now, *she* smiled triumphantly. "She's your *niece?* Wow, she's very pretty."

Gun beamed like a proud uncle. "She's my brother Luke's daughter."

"I like her name. And her car, too," Greer admitted, feeling much more generous in spirit toward her.

"Grandpa Jack buy her car. He spoil Darcy because she only granddaughter."

"Grandpa Jack? As in your ex-husband?" Greer had heard of him. He'd founded a well-known Dallas law firm.

"Yeah," Mrs. D said. "Luke is lawyer too. He work at firm with his father. My daughter go to law school too, but does not work as lawyer."

Greer linked her fingers over her knee and looked at Gun. "The legal field appears to be in your family's blood. But from what your mom has told me, you're not a lawyer, right?"

He waved his hands in vigorous denial. "No. I'm the only one in the family with any sense to avoid that profession." His eyes widened. "I beg your pardon. That was too harsh. Let's say I march to the beat of a different drummer. But speaking of lawyers, my brother, sister, and I appreciate how well you look after our mother. Luke is a business litigator. He doesn't practice real estate law and is disadvantaged because he's not in Austin. We're glad she found you and know she trusts you."

Greer typically received feedback only when people were angry or complained. His compliment embarrassed her a bit. "The truth is, I admire litigators like Luke. My practice is transactional because Civil Procedure was my worst nightmare in law school. But that's another story. Since we've established that *you* are not a lawyer, what do you do?"

"Gun-ah successful engineer and consultant," Mrs. D said before he could respond. "Everybody want him to work for them. Work all over and work for my brother in Seoul."

Gun just shrugged.

"That's impressive." Greer meant it. "I work with engineers as consultants on several of my client matters. I'm surprised our paths have never crossed. How often do you go to Seoul?"

"Usually about once a quarter. It all depends on the status

of each project and how often I'm needed. I'd just returned from Korea the day before we met."

Mrs. D said something to Gun, and they began conversing in Korean. Greer liked listening to his deep, honeyed voice, even if she couldn't understand what he said. He appeared to be a good-natured, filial son and teased his mom the way sons do.

He said something that made Mrs. D laugh, then turned to look at Greer. "You speak Korean, right?"

Greer inhaled. "Who, me? No."

He paused. "Huh. But on the plane, I could have sworn I heard you—"

"Oh, yes, that's right." So he had heard her after all. She flipped her hair back, a telltale sign of nervousness. "I did answer you in Korean. Well, about that. I wasn't quite myself that day. As your mother said, I love Korean dramas and have picked up a few words and phrases."

Gun tilted his head and narrowed his eyes, the way one studies a painting, looking for a different perspective. She halfway expected him to use his hands as a finger frame. "Do the dramas contain subtitles? If you don't speak Korean, how can you understand what they say?"

Greer eyed him skeptically. She was reasonably adept at reading people—most of the time—and the look in his eyes didn't match up to his words. "The ones I watch have subtitles. Otherwise, I'd be lost." The continued intensity of his gaze unnerved her, so she changed the subject. "Your mother tells me you grew up in Dallas?"

"Yes, but I haven't lived there since my high school graduation."

"Oh? Where did you go to college?"

"I received my undergraduate degree from Georgia Tech and my MBA here at UT."

Greer nodded. "I understand the need to get away. I also went to an out-of-state college but returned to Texas and went to law school in Dallas." She chuckled and flipped her hair again. "So we traded places. You came to Austin, and I went to Dallas."

Gun's eyebrows shot up. "You went to law school at SMU? My father and brother are alumni."

She opened her mouth to confirm that, but the phone beeped. Giles Hudson, the Hudson of Hudson and Hamilton, asked to see her in his office.

Talk about terrible timing. Anxious that her guests might mistake this as their cue to leave, she apologized and asked them to stay until her return.

Gun smiled, putting her at ease. "No problem, we're in no hurry. We'll wait for you."

Greer hurried down the hall to Mr. Hudson's office, wondering what he might need. Although in his early eighties, he still had a sharp legal mind, but twenty-first-century technology befuddled him. He left that job to his paralegal and anyone willing to lend him a hand, and *anyone* usually meant Greer.

His office door was open, and as she entered, he apologized for taking up her time. He needed help finding the documents for his afternoon meeting. A distinguished-looking man, he was still tall but slightly stooped and had a head full of white hair and bright blue eyes. He'd always been kind to her and taught her everything she knew about real estate law, so she held him in high esteem as her employer and mentor.

She found the documents on the server and printed them out, then excused herself, anxious to return to her guests. She could scarcely believe that just a few yards away, her Handsome Hero sat in her office waiting for her, just when she'd given up hope of ever seeing him again. Mrs. D was right. It must be more than a coincidence. These things didn't happen randomly. She felt so happy that she wanted to skip down the hallway.

But when she opened her door, she sensed something wrong. Gun stood in the middle of the office, staring at the wall.

She stepped inside. "Is everything okay?"

He turned and flinched slightly at seeing her, then a range of emotions crossed his face as a vein throbbed in his neck. Had he received bad news, or did he feel ill?

He shook his head, and when he looked at her again, his face was blank, as if he had slipped on a mask. "I'm fine, but we need to go. *Eomma*, we've imposed on Lawyer Garza's hospitality too long," he said in a cold voice, then rushed out of the office without saying goodbye. Mrs. D hastily stood from her spot on the sofa. Judging by her bewildered expression, the abrupt change in her son's behavior surprised her, too.

"Mrs. D, is everything all right?"

"Uh, yes, everything is fine," she said unconvincingly. "We go now, but we talk later, okay?"

Greer watched them leave, then dropped onto her chair, her mind spinning. What just happened? Her exhilarating afternoon came crashing down in an instant. Mrs. D would've known if they had received bad news. So, was it something Greer said? Nothing came to mind, and Gun wouldn't have agreed to wait for her to return if that were the case, right?

She forced herself to put the issue aside to focus on work, but at home that night, she replayed the events of the afternoon continuously while lying on her bed with her arm across her forehead. She had taken ibuprofen for her head, but there was nothing she could take for her heart. When would she ever learn not to get her hopes up? The only thing worse than thinking you had missed meeting the man of your dreams was to have him kick you to the curb. She was sure she had felt a spark this time, so what could have happened in the brief time she was gone? No matter how many ways she looked at it, she couldn't figure out what had gone wrong. But she also couldn't shake off the uneasy feeling that there'd been a subtle shift in the earth's tectonic plates.

# Chapter Five

Mrs. D finally returned right after Valentine's Day, walking into Greer's office unannounced as she and Megan worked on a demand letter. As always, she didn't come empty-handed but brought homemade bulgogi, rice, and a Korean toothpaste she proclaimed could whiten the dullest teeth. Greer considered these gifts safer than her previous offering—her unknowing son.

To her relief, Mrs. D carried on as usual, albeit subdued. Whatever had transpired on that strange afternoon had Greer concerned that it would damage their professional relationship.

"Hey, woman, what brings you here today?" she greeted her.

"I think you might like some bulgogi. Rita say you working very hard. You getting too skinny."

Yet another reason why Greer loved Mrs. D. The woman genuinely cared about her well-being, and no one, apart from Mrs. D, would ever call her skinny. "Aww, you don't have to bring me things. You're welcome to stop by my office anytime."

Greer stood and took the bag, then handed it to Megan. "Here, Meg. Take this to the kitchen and help yourself. Share it with the others, but save me some, please."

Megan looked inside, and her face lit up. "Wow. Thank you, Mrs. D. We love your bulgogi and are always hungry around here."

Mrs. D feigned humility. "I not cook as good as I used to, but I hope you enjoy."

Greer waited for Megan to leave, then directed Mrs. D to her usual spot on the sofa. She took the club chair.

"Megan is a cute girl," Mrs. D said, obviously buying time.

Greer smiled. "She is cute. And smart, too. She graduated with honors from college and law school. I was fortunate to recruit her."

Mrs. D smiled awkwardly, then drew a breath. "Greer-ssi, I'm sorry I not come before, but I am too ashamed to face you. I must apologize. I should not have brought my son here. My son not a bad son, but"—she choked up—"he suffer because of me. It is my fault my son lacking in manners and not act properly. I not teach my son proper respect."

Greer doubted Gun's behavior resulted from a lack of training or poor parenting—there was more to the story—but she let it slide. She had no choice. "Mrs. D, there's no need to apologize. Gun is a grown man, and I don't hold you accountable for his actions. Besides, he didn't actually *do* anything. Although I will admit, I was slightly confused by how he left."

She shook her head. "No, I must apologize on behalf of my son. I not good mother to my children, and not raise them properly. Please forgive me." A few tears escaped her eyes, and she reached for the box of Kleenex that Greer kept on the coffee table in front of the couch.

"Mrs. D, I doubt that's true." She hated seeing the poor woman upset but was unsure how to comfort her since she was still in the dark about Gun's behavior.

"Another time, another time, I tell you story, okay? But not today." She wiped her eyes. "Today, I invite you to my church-y this Sunday for birthday lunch-y."

The abrupt change in the conversation didn't come as a surprise. Mrs. D typically bounced from one topic to the next or cut a conversation short. Greer wished she could press her and ask what had caused the change in Gun's behavior, but Mrs. D clearly didn't want to discuss it further. "Your church is having a birthday lunch?" She hoped she sounded enthusiastic.

Mrs. D grinned. "Uh-huh, yes. Every month at church-y, we celebrate birthdays for the month. You come, okay?"

"Sure, I'd love to come. But isn't your birthday still a couple of weeks away?"

"Yes, yes, my birthday in a couple of weeks. My kids visit me then, but first, you come to church-y."

Mrs. D gave her the name and address of the church before declaring she must go. To Greer's disappointment, she didn't mention Gun again—and Greer couldn't ask. Mrs. D had an iron will, and since she was Greer's client, certain lines couldn't be crossed.

Greer would probably never know why Gun had changed and never see him again, and the thought depressed her. After their last meeting, she'd cyberstalked him, hoping to find a clue to what had happened. But he didn't have a social media presence or professional link, so she was still in the dark.

She sighed. Once again, he'd come and gone out of her life, this time probably for good, leaving her to mourn a relationship that died before it had a chance to start.

Anxious to make a good first impression on Mrs. D's church friends and whoever else might be there, Greer dressed in a red jersey dress with a high neck and blouson sleeves that tapered at the wrists. Red complimented her dark hair, or so the sales-woman had convinced her. She chose simple pearl drop earrings, a matching pendant necklace, and black patent pumps for accessories. After grabbing her dress coat and kissing Kevin and Sophie goodbye, she drove to the church on the other side of town.

Greer hadn't known what to expect, but as she drove through the iron gates and past the grassy expanse, she admitted she hadn't assumed the church would be so lovely. Built of Texas stone, it sat far from the busy street and had a traditional white steeple. Majestic oak trees stood sentry all around, casting protective shade.

She parked in a space marked *Visitors* and walked to the entrance under the portico. The wind fought her as she struggled to pry open one of the double doors, and she stumbled into the brightly lit vestibule with her hair windblown. An over-whelming smell of garlic and something else she couldn't identify greeted her.

"Wow!" she exclaimed, covering her nose with her hand. She looked around, unsure where to go, and came face-to-face with an elderly gentleman in a navy suit standing beside a large flower arrangement on a round marble table.

"*Annyeonghaseyo,*" she greeted him and bowed in respect for his senior status.

He didn't reply but merely pointed to the sanctuary door.

"*Khamsahamnida.*" She bowed again with a weak smile, unsure of her welcome.

Greer entered the sanctuary and sat on the last pew in case she needed to make a quick getaway. Stained-glass windows depicting the life of Christ lined the outer wall, and a large wooden cross hung at the back of the baptistry. She scanned the congregants seated up front. They were mostly elderly, and their once raven locks were now white, so Mrs. D would be hard to miss. Vanity prevented her from succumbing to the cruel tricks of time, and she kept her hair color in what she called Elizabeth Taylor black, or sometimes Natalie Wood brown, but *never* white. Greer understood this sense of pride. She, too, had a standing monthly appointment with her colorist.

The pianist and organist began playing, signaling the start of the service. A man who appeared to be the song director approached the podium from a side door. He addressed the congregation in Korean, and everyone stood to sing.

The song's words were displayed in Korean and English on the screen up front, although it sounded like everyone was singing in Korean. Mrs. D slipped into the pew beside her as they sang the second hymn.

"Hello. Sorry, I am late," she said loudly as if they were greeting each other at the food court in the mall instead of in church. "I bring food for the lunch-y, and I run late."

Greer smiled and nodded, not wanting to encourage her to keep talking. Mrs. D couldn't distinguish between an inside and an outside voice. Greer need not have worried, however. No one cared, or they were used to Mrs. D. Greer relaxed, finally took off her coat, and listened to Mrs. D's enthusiastic singing. She chuckled inwardly. The woman was so comfortable in her skin that Greer admired and envied her confidence. She hoped she would be the same way when she grew up. A woman sang the offertory hymn as the offering plates were passed. The song's lyrics weren't on the screen this time, but whatever they were must have touched Mrs. D because unchecked tears flowed down her cheeks.

The woman's solo received applause and amens. Then, the pastor began his sermon. Greer couldn't understand him, but surprisingly, she knew he was preaching about King David. She tried to follow along but could only understand one word in twenty, and her mind began wandering.

The service ended punctually at noon, and Mrs. D said, "Okay, we go eat now."

Greer followed her out the sanctuary doors and down a long corridor. The garlic and the other indiscernible smell grew stronger, and she heard shouting and laughter. Passing through another set of doors, they entered the fellowship hall, where young adults, teenagers, and children were seated at round tables, ready for lunch. Where had they been during the service?

The crowd grew quiet when an elderly gentleman blessed the food. Then the pastor called Mrs. D and two other people to the front, where they stood behind a square, three-layered chocolate cake decorated with several colorful flowers. Everyone sang "Happy Birthday" in Korean, using the English tune.

Mrs. D smiled and clapped, pleased to be the center of attention. When she returned to the table where Greer waited, she said, "*Pali, pali,*" and dragged her to the food line.

Aluminum pans containing Korean dishes prepared by the church ladies sat side-by-side, buffet style, on three long folding tables near the kitchen. Greer helped herself to a serving of *japchae,* a savory dish of clear sweet potato noodles and vegetables in a flavorful broth; *dak dori tang,* a spicy, sweet chicken stew with potatoes; and a spoonful of rice from a rice cooker. Then she moved on to the vegetable side dishes called *banchan,* which included kimchi. She lifted the lid off a stainless-steel pot containing the traditional birthday dish of seaweed soup but decided to pass.

As Greer set her tray on the table, Mrs. D glanced over it like a mother hen. "Oh, why you not get soup? I make, so you must try."

She hurried off before Greer could think of an excuse, not that it would have mattered. The woman wouldn't take no for an answer. She returned shortly, not with the soup, but holding two dessert-size paper plates with thick slices of birthday cake. A woman followed, carrying a tray holding enough soup bowls for the table.

Mrs. D set a slice of cake in front of her. "I love this cake-y. It is my favorite."

Mrs. D picked up chopsticks to eat her cake, but Greer had never been adept at using them. She reached for a fork in the utensil caddy, ready to partake. Being fifty had its privileges, including eating dessert first. She forked a generous bite, popped it in her mouth, and instantly regretted it. Because it was beautiful, she assumed the cake would be delicious, but it wasn't sweet and had no taste. She wanted to spit it out but didn't want to disappoint Mrs. D. Instead, she plastered on a smile while trying her best to swallow.

"I see you're eating dessert first," a deep voice said above her head. "Talk about a woman after my own heart."

Greer looked up and around as an extraordinarily handsome man about her age set a tray on their table. Looking like he'd breached the fourth wall and stepped out of a K-drama and into the church fellowship hall, he flashed an electrifying smile.

Her heart beat double time. Two men in two months. She was on a roll.

Mrs. D greeted Handsome Church Guy in Korean, and he addressed her as *imo*, or "aunt," one of the handful of Korean words Greer understood. She noted his nice gray wool suit and scent when he sat on the chair beside hers.

An elderly couple joined them at the table, and Mrs. D introduced them as her lifelong friends, Dr. and Mrs. Lee.

Greer smiled and bowed her head. "*Annyeonghaseyo.*"

"Ah, and she speaks Korean too," Handsome Church Guy remarked.

Dr. and Mrs. Lee also expressed their surprise and delight.

"Not many people know Korean," Dr. Lee said. "How did you learn?"

She gave a sheepish smile. "*Hangul* drama."

The entire table erupted in laughter.

Mrs. Lee beamed, and her youthful face lit up. "You like Korean drama? Me too!"

Handsome Church Guy extended his hand toward her. "I'm Jason Lee, and as you've probably guessed, these are my parents."

Greer grinned, though still feeling shy. "I'm Greer Garza. A guest of Mrs. Donovan."

Mrs. D introduced Greer as her lawyer or *byeonhosa*, and the Lees exclaimed how wonderful it was to have lunch with someone both beautiful and intelligent. Greer glowed inwardly from the compliment, especially from someone as accomplished as Dr. Lee. He had a PhD in chemical engineering and had recently retired as a professor at the University of Texas.

"My husband and I married fifty-five years in May," Mrs. Lee explained. "We come to United States after we marry, and my husband go to University of Texas to study. We here ever since. Our two sons born here."

"You were born here in Austin?" Greer asked Jason, overcoming her shyness. "Me too."

"Both my brother Justin and I were born here," he said.

"Is your brother younger or older?"

"Younger by two years. Unlike Gun, I'm the older brother. Justin, his wife, and their kids attend church here, too, but they're away this weekend. I'm sorry they're not here to meet you."

No offense to the absentee Justin, but Greer stopped listening after he dropped Gun's name. "How, uh, how do you . . ." She stopped and then started again. "You know Gun?"

"I know Lees for many years," Mrs. D said. "Our kids grow up together."

"When our children were young, I take my boys and Luke-y and Gun-ah camping every summer," Mr. Lee added.

Jason laughed. "Yeah, until we were in high school and preferred to spend our summers at Barton Springs chasing around girls in bikinis. Gun and I often competed for the same girls, but I always won."

Mrs. Lee playfully hit her son on the arm several times while chastising him in Korean.

"All right, all right," Jason said, laughing and holding his hands up in mock surrender.

Greer's eyes widened. Korean mothers were always portrayed as hitting their children in the dramas, regardless of whether they were young or full-grown adults. So, it wasn't portrayed for dramatic effect. It really was a thing. "So, how did your families meet? Did y'all know each other in Korea?" she asked.

"No, our families not from same province," Mrs. D said. "We meet when Mr. Donovan and Dr. Lee go to UT. Mrs. Lee and I meet at gathering of foreign wives at student union. I happy to meet another girl from my country, and we have babies same age."

Mrs. Lee nodded and said something in Korean, and the elders conversed back and forth, utilizing many hand gestures. Greer had witnessed the same type of conversation several times with her parents and among the elders in her family. However, those conversations were usually in English, Spanish, or both.

"We meet when Luke this high," Mrs. Lee said, holding her hand a few feet from the ground. "Jason and Gun crawling, and Justin and Sarah not here yet." She smiled, and her face softened with the memory.

While the elders reminisced, Greer turned to Jason. "I used to spend my summers at Barton Springs."

"Oh, yeah?" he said, raising an eyebrow. "How old are you? You look younger than me, but maybe I saw you there."

Greer laughed. "Maybe, but you wouldn't have noticed me. I never wore a bikini."

"I didn't just chase girls in bikinis," he said with a wink. "Still don't."

She blushed and searched for a snappy comeback but came up empty. Her most recent interactions with a man had left her —no pun intended—gun shy.

Pastor Park chose that moment to join their table and welcome her to their church, so she didn't have the opportunity to angle for more information. The pastor was a well-learned man, and after a few minutes, the entire table was engrossed in an invigorating discussion of eschatology. She enjoyed it so much that she lost track of time until her phone vibrated in her purse. Her mother's number was on the screen when she clandestinely checked it.

She put her hand on Mrs. D's arm and whispered, "Mrs. D, I've got to go. Thank you for inviting me. I've had a great time."

Mrs. D patted her hand absentmindedly, still listening to the pastor. "Okay, Greer-ssi. We talk later."

Jason stood and helped her with her coat, then offered to see her out. He whistled as they walked toward the front of the church.

"I just assumed because you're not wearing a ring, but I should have asked this before," Jason said suddenly, turning toward her. "You're not married, right?"

Greer chuckled and shook her head. "No. I'm happily divorced."

He gave a short laugh. "Same. Any kids?"

"No. How about you?"

"Yes, I have a daughter and a son, both attending college at Texas A&M."

"That's nice. Do you have a picture?"

He pulled out his phone and squinted at the screen as he scrolled through his pictures. "Here they are," he said, turning the phone toward her. They were tall and slender and favored him.

"What nice-looking kids. You must be proud."

"Thanks," he said with a sheepish grin. "So, how well do you know Gun?"

*Wow.* Where did that come from? Had she revealed too much during lunch? Not knowing where he was going with this or how much to reveal, she played it safe. "Uh, not very well. We only met a couple of times, but it didn't go well. I think I offended him."

He looked down at her. "What makes you think that?"

"To be honest, I don't know. It's a long story."

Jason considered that. "I wouldn't worry about it. I doubt you offended him. Gun's a good guy but can be a little weird sometimes."

Greer gave him the side-eye, unsure how to respond. Coming to Gun's defense might seem strange, considering she hardly knew him. On the other hand, if she agreed with Jason, she was sure it would get back to Gun. *She called you a weirdo, bro.* Men could be notorious gossips. And embellishers. She thought it prudent to remain silent.

"I'm glad you came to visit today," he said when they reached her car. "I love these old folks, but speaking to someone my age is nice."

"Thank you. I enjoyed my visit."

"Do you have a business card? My aunt said you're her attorney."

Greer grabbed a card from her purse and, mindful of the Korean custom, handed it to him with both hands.

He studied her card and flashed that charming smile again. "Thank you, Greer. I hope to see you again soon."

He sounded sincere, so she nodded. "That would be nice."

She knew this violated the rules or lessons or whatever all the self-help books said a woman should never say to a man, but she found it difficult not to like him. In addition to his outstanding good looks, he had charisma.

He opened her car door, closed it after her, and watched her drive away.

Even though she told herself not to do it, she looked in her rearview mirror. He waved goodbye before turning back toward the church.

# Chapter Six

Shortly after lunch on Wednesday, Dianne buzzed Greer. "You have a phone call from a Mr. Jason Lee," she said. "Would you like to take it?"

Handsome Church Guy Jason Lee? Why would he be calling her? She cleared her throat. "Put him through, Dianne. Thank you." When the call connected, she answered in her professional voice, "Hello, this is Greer Garza."

"Hi, Greer, it's Jason Lee. We met at church on Sunday."

So it *was* him! She tried to remain calm. "Oh, yes. How are you, Jason?"

He didn't waste time with pleasantries. "I'm good, thanks. Hey, if you don't have any plans on Friday night, how about joining my friends and me for karaoke night?"

Greer took a couple of moments to process this. "Karaoke? Uh, well . . . I don't know. I'm not a good singer, so I don't like singing in front of strangers."

He laughed. "Don't worry. You won't be singing in front of strangers. It's *Korean* karaoke, and it's called *noraebang*. Are you familiar with it?"

That made sense. "Well, from what I've seen in the dramas,

people sing in private karaoke rooms with their friends or coworkers. Not in front of a restaurant or bar full of people, right?"

"Right. It'll just be a few friends and me, and no pressure to sing. I thought you might enjoy seeing some real Koreans in action."

Oh, he was good. He had her at "real Koreans." Besides, what else did she have to do on a Friday night except sit on her couch, surrounded by her cats, *watching* Koreans on her TV? This was her chance to experience the world of drama land first-hand. "Okay. If I don't have to sing, I'm game."

She hoped she wouldn't live to regret this, but she had no valid reason not to go. And even if they pressured her to sing and she made a fool of herself, it wasn't like she'd ever have to face Jason or his friends again.

Predictably, Greer regretted her hasty decision to accept Jason's invitation when Friday rolled around. She was exhausted from the work week and didn't feel like getting dressed to go out again. Wearing her comfy sweatpants and scarfing a pizza in front of the TV was much more appealing than mingling with strangers. Why hadn't she asked more questions, such as who Jason's friends were and what they were like? What if they were uppity and didn't like her? What if she didn't like them? She tried devising a plausible excuse to back out but came up empty.

All Night Karaoke sat in the corner of a strip center at North Lamar and Airport Boulevard. Greer knew the area and found the place easily enough, but the changes in the neighborhood demographics were astounding. Once a predominately white neighborhood, Korean-owned businesses now occupied every store in the strip center.

She parked her car, checked her appearance in the visor mirror, and popped a mint into her mouth. Showtime.

*I'm here,* she texted Jason.

*Coming out now,* he texted back within moments.

She'd scarcely placed one foot out of the car when Jason started across the parking lot. Had he been waiting at the door, keeping an eye out for her?

Whatever the case, he smiled, looking pleased to see her. She'd forgotten how good-looking he was, and her breath caught. She almost stopped breathing when he took her cold hands in his warm ones.

"Hello. Did you have any trouble finding the place?"

Conscious of his hands, she stammered, "No, no trouble."

"Good. Let's go in. Everyone is here." He dropped her hands, and although slightly disappointed, she breathed normally again.

"Oh, am I late?"

"Not at all. We got here a few minutes ago."

The mention of "we" gave her a nervous feeling in the pit of her stomach. She hoped she wasn't walking into a lion's den.

As she walked alongside him, a stunning black and chrome motorcycle parked near the entrance caught her eye. Although not usually a motorcycle enthusiast, this striking machine, with its black leather and silver stud trim, oozed "bad boy" in spades.

"That's so cool," she murmured as she admired it.

Jason glanced over. "That's an Indian Chieftain. Do you like Indians or just motorcycles?"

"Neither. I mean, I'm not a fan of motorcycles, but occasionally I see one I like." She ran her hand along the bike's leather seat. "Like this one. Do you think the owner would mind my touching it?"

He burst out laughing, and she blushed. She had walked into that one.

"I doubt the owner would mind. Come on, let's go inside."

The foyer of All Night Karaoke left much to be desired and didn't portend a good night. The white walls were bare, and the faux leather loveseat had seen better days. A plastic Ficus tree that somehow looked withered sat alone in a corner. A young man and woman engaged in a lively discussion in Korean sat behind a reception desk. They didn't acknowledge them as they walked past.

"This way," Jason said, pointing down a long hall.

Muted music and laughter came from the individual rooms in the hallway. Despite the plain surroundings, the people inside were having fun. He stopped, opened the fourth door on the left, and indicated she should enter first. She wished he wasn't such a gentleman so she could hide behind him.

The people in the room were loud, with spirited voices. They stopped talking when she entered and stood up to greet her. She lowered her eyes and smiled at no one in particular.

A tall, attractive woman standing closest to the door hugged her. "Greer!" she squealed. "I can't tell you how wonderful it is to meet you!"

She had not expected such an enthusiastic greeting. Who was this woman, and why was she hugging her? Greer's confusion must have shown on her face. Jason placed a comforting hand on her shoulder and addressed the woman.

"Take it easy. You've overwhelmed her."

"Oh, bless your heart! I'm sorry. I didn't mean to scare you," the woman apologized after releasing her. "We didn't know you were coming until just a few minutes ago, and I'm *so* excited to meet you. I'm Sarah Lancaster. Mrs. Donovan is my mom, and she's talked about you for years, so I feel like I already know you."

Sarah paused for a short breath and ran her fingers through the top of her silky, honey-brown hair. The kind of hair Greer had always envied. "I can't call you Garza *byeonhosa* like my mom does. That's too formal. I'll call you *Unni* because she thinks of you as another daughter, and I always wanted a big sister, especially since I was outnumbered by these two." She jerked her thumb over her shoulder to where a man wearing a Dallas Cowboys hat stood.

Greer did some quick deductive reasoning. If Sarah was Mrs. D's daughter, the two she spoke of had to be her brothers. The man standing behind her must be one of them, so that had to mean . . .

Oh. That explained the Indian Chieftain outside. No wonder Jason laughed.

Greer shifted her gaze to the man behind Sarah. He had a good-looking, friendly face, like a male lead in a Hallmark movie. But except for his eyes, he didn't look Korean, and when he spoke, his voice held a distinct North Texas twang.

"Oh, for heaven's sake," he said. "Why do you have to call her Lawyer Garza or big sister? Are you filmin' a drama in Korea? Just call her by her name." He reached around Sarah and extended a large hand. As expected, he had a firm, manly handshake. "Hi, Greer," he said, although due to his twang, it sounded more like *Haa, Gre-eer*. "I'm Luke Donovan. It's a pleasure to meet you, and yes, my sister, the drama queen, is correct. We have heard a lot about you. Glad you could join us tonight."

Jason placed a hand under her elbow and steered her to the left. A handsome couple waited for her on the other side of the room. The man bore a strong resemblance to Jason, and sure enough, Jason introduced the couple as his brother, Justin, and his wife, Hannah. They greeted her with warm smiles and exuded a calming aura that was a nice counterbalance to their boisterous friends.

Greer breathed a sigh of relief. She had survived the introductions. As the knot in her stomach began to unclench, Sarah's cry caused it to clench again.

"*Ya!* Aren't you going to greet our guest? Stand up and say hello to Greer."

Gun sat on the banquette hidden behind his brother, who was still standing. He gave Sarah a withering look, then threw back his head, downing the clear liquid inside his shot glass. Sarah didn't flinch. She said something to him again in Korean and threw a fake karate chop.

Greer had been so nervous she hadn't noticed him. Her heart raced, and her cheeks felt warm. It had never occurred to her that he could be here tonight. She gave a hesitant smile. "Hi, Gun. It's nice to see you again."

He slammed his shot glass on the coffee table, making her jump. Then he stood and gave an exaggerated bow. "Greer," he said in a tone that told her he could barely stand to speak her name.

That answered the question plaguing her for weeks—well, sort of. *She* had caused his abrupt behavior change that day. But it still didn't explain *what* she had done to cause the warm, friendly man from the plane to turn into this cold, rude one.

After an awkward silence, everyone took their seats, and Jason invited her to sit between him and Hannah on the banquette. She complied because her legs felt wobbly, and she needed time to regain composure, but she would have preferred to run out of the room and have a good cry. She wouldn't give Gun the satisfaction, though. No wonder she'd felt uneasy.

She glanced around the room and sighed. Like the foyer, it was a disappointment. Apart from the U-shaped banquette wrapped around the sides and one end of the room, it looked nothing like the karaoke rooms in the dramas. Those rooms were bigger and elegant, and people drank from crystal barware. This room looked like a Korean redneck version, especially when

Jason opened the lid of an enormous ice chest filled with beer bottles and Cokes and offered her something to drink.

She almost laughed out loud but asked him for a Coke.

The Donovan siblings sat on one side of the "U," with her and Jason across from them and Justin and Hannah rounding the bottom. They took turns looking through a black binder holding the song lists, and Jason explained that the binder was divided into two parts. The first half listed Korean songs, and the second half listed American songs.

"Do you sing both?" Greer asked.

"Yes."

"Are the words of the Korean songs written in *Hangul*? Can you read *Hangul*?"

"They are, but we know many of the songs by heart. The only one of us who can read and write in *Hangul* is Gun."

Jason encouraged her to pick a song or two, but she smiled and shook her head. She'd briefly entertained the idea of singing tonight, but nothing would make her sing now. While everyone picked out their songs, she took the opportunity to assess the group while sipping her soda.

She'd been right about Jason and Justin—they could be twins. Both had black hair combed back from a broad forehead, wide dark eyes, and a low-bridged nose. But their personalities set them apart. Older Jason wore a designer-label polo-style shirt, jeans, and leather driving shoes, and she'd bet money he drove a sports car. On the other hand, Justin, with his untucked plaid shirt, jeans, and sneakers, looked like the type of guy to drive a minivan—with a "Proud Dad of an Honor Student" bumper sticker.

Short and slightly plump, Hannah had a pretty face and a girl-next-door quality. Like her husband, she laughed easily and appeared good-natured, yet despite that, Greer felt certain Hannah was no pushover. Few Korean women were.

Greer poured more Coke into her cup and discreetly turned her study to the Donovan siblings. Mrs. D spoke in superlatives but hadn't exaggerated her children's good looks. However, she would've never guessed they were siblings if she didn't know them.

Unlike Jason and Justin, Luke and Gun looked nothing alike. Luke's hair sticking out from underneath his hat was much lighter than Gun's. He had a rounder face and a husky build, so no doubt he favored the Donovan side. His polo-style shirt, jeans, and well-worn cowboy boots proved he was not one of the label-conscious Dallas elite. Luke might have a Korean mama, but he was a country boy.

On the other hand, Sarah looked like the perfect mix of her Anglo and Korean parents. Her features were exquisite, and she had a flawless, porcelain complexion. Tall and lean, she didn't look like the mother of four boys. Her clothes were simple but good quality, and she wore a giant diamond on her slender fourth finger. She possessed an effortless style and exuded Dallas chic, yet appeared unaffected or unaware that she had won the genetic lottery.

Then there was Gun. Of the three siblings, he looked the most Korean. He had darker coloring, high cheekbones, and perfect cupid lips. She'd had no idea Koreans had such beautiful lips until she began watching the dramas.

She continued to study him over the rim of the glass, though carefully since he would call her out if he caught her watching him. He turned his head to listen to Justin, and she noted that he had a firm chin and jaw, unlike many men his age who'd developed turkey necks. He took good care of himself, evidenced by the white T-shirt accentuating his toned pecs and biceps.

"Whuut? Are you kiddin' me?" Luke's wail interrupted her musings and broke through the chatter. He flipped through the pages of the songbook with a pair of readers on his nose. "No Johnny Cash? No Hank? Not even George Strait? Oh, come on! This is Texas, for Pete's sake!"

Sarah, who sat with her left ankle on top of her right knee, drinking beer from the bottle, rolled her eyes. She wiped her mouth with the back of her hand and let out a belch that would make any trucker proud. Being raised with two brothers had rubbed off on her. "*Oppa*, this is *noraebang*. Koreans don't do country."

"Well, I know that, but this is ridiculous. What about Kenny Rogers? He crossed over into the pop charts."

"Yeah, back in the eighties," Sarah countered.

The others joined in the teasing, but Luke shook his head.

"Go ahead and laugh, but I know every one of you listens to country. Sarah, how many times did you watch *Coal Miner's Daughter,* huh? You listened to the soundtrack so many times that you wore out the tape and begged Dad to buy you a new one. And I know that Gun loves him some George Jones and Waylon."

Gun shrugged and grinned sheepishly but didn't deny his brother's allegations.

Sarah laughed. "I love that movie! And it wasn't Dad who bought me a new tape. It was Gun *Oppa*. He took me to Sound Warehouse on Upper Greenville and bought it for me."

Greer sat up straight. Back in law school, long before the days of streaming music, she'd shopped at that Sound Warehouse.

"*Hyung*, give the book to me," Justin said. "I'll find you a country song." He flipped to the back of the book and used his finger to scroll down the page. "C5309!" he called out in excitement.

"Whad ya' find?" Luke asked.

"'Love the World Away,'" Justin and Hannah answered in unison.

The others groaned, but Luke grinned from ear to ear. He looked happier than a pig in mud.

Greer turned to Jason and whispered, "What's the deal with the song?"

She'd either spoken too loudly, or Sarah had the hearing of a cat.

"That's Luke and his wife Janet's song from high school. Luke loves to sing that song when he's drinking. It makes him feel like he's back in the eighties when he was in his prime."

"Weren't we all in our prime in the eighties?" Greer observed. "I can identify."

"Excellent point, Greer," Luke said. "And don't pay any attention to them. They're jealous because I had the prettiest girlfriend back in high school. We would slow dance to this song with our hands in each other's back pockets."

This elicited a laugh from everyone, but they suddenly stopped when they heard the opening guitar strum of an old favorite.

"'Luckenbach'!" Hannah exclaimed.

"Did you pick this?" Luke asked Justin.

Justin shook his head.

"Then I know who picked this song." Luke pointed to Gun. "It was this guy right here. What did I tell y'all? He sure does love Waylon. Must be that whole outlaw thing." He laughed and punched his brother on the arm.

Luke had been right about them listening to country. Everyone sang along with smiles or faraway looks on their faces, and no one looked up at the screen because they knew the lyrics by heart. Sarah closed her eyes and swayed with her hand over her heart.

Watching them, Greer felt contrite. She'd stereotyped them

to fit her fantasy, but they were not characters in a K-drama. They were real people and Texans like her. Texans who wore boots, drank beer, and liked country music.

The song ended, and they clapped and raised their beer bottles in salute. Gun was commended for his selection, and then the party started rolling. Sarah and Hannah kicked them off with a couple of peppy K-pop songs made famous by Korean girl groups. Greer hadn't joined in the K-pop craze, but she tapped her feet and enjoyed their performance.

After that, Jason sang Robert Palmer's "Bad Case of Loving You." He incorporated the right amount of swagger into his performance and had a surprisingly good voice. Next, all the men sang Aerosmith's "Walk This Way"—although the way they sang sounded more like the Run DMC version of the song. They then sang Thin Lizzy's "The Boys Are Back in Town" and the Everyman anthem, "Here I Go Again," by Whitesnake.

Jason rejoined her on the banquette and asked if she wanted to switch to a real drink, but she shook her head. "I don't drink beer. I'm more of a Mexican martini kind of girl."

"Then how about a shot of Soju? You can't come to karaoke without drinking Soju, and it will help you relax."

She hesitated, still unsure.

"We won't let you get drunk unless you want to. And if you do, I can drive you home." He winked as he said it, and she laughed. He loved teasing her.

Greer had seen Soju featured in every single K-drama she'd watched. She'd always been curious about its taste, so what better time to try it than now? "All right then. I'm game."

Jason handed her a shot glass, and she held it with both hands as he poured the clear liquid from the green bottle. Since he was a year older and thus her senior, she placed her left hand on her right bicep, turned to the side, and downed the shot. It tasted like . . . well, she couldn't decide if it tasted like licorice or kerosene. Not that she'd ever tasted kerosene.

"Look at her! She knows how to drink!" Justin exclaimed. "Where did you learn Korean drinking customs?"

"She watches Korean dramas," Gun volunteered from across the room.

All eyes turned to him.

"What did you say?" Sarah asked.

"She loves dramas, and she thinks she's Korean. Ask her yourself," Gun urged as he downed a shot of Soju. He sounded bored, as if everyone knew about Greer's love of K-dramas, and this was old news.

Sarah and Hannah squealed and began pummeling her with questions. What dramas did she watch? Which ones were her favorites? Who were her favorite actors? Greer was thrilled to discuss a subject near and dear to her heart, and she became engrossed in the discussion and accepted another shot of Soju from Jason.

"Are we going to talk about dramas all night or sing?" Gun asked, interrupting their conversation. "*Pali, pali,* let's go."

Justin and Hannah jumped up and sang a couple's duet in Korean. They looked like cute newlyweds. Next in the queue came Luke's ode to his high school years, and he marched up and took the mic. Jason had been right about the Soju helping her relax, and she leaned back against the banquette as the melancholy mezzo-piano began to play. Had she drank too much Soju, or did Luke sound remarkably like Kenny Rogers? He even closed his eyes when he sang. She forgot about the others and began singing harmony.

Luke waved her up to join him, and she leaped over Jason's long legs to reach him. He draped his arm around her shoulder and shared his microphone. Their voices harmonized well, almost as if they'd rehearsed. When they finished, everyone whooped and hollered. That is, everyone except Gun. His face remained impassive.

Luke's eyes twinkled, and he raised his hand for a high-five.

"That was awesome!" Jason complimented her as she rejoined him. "But you said you couldn't sing."

"*Unni*, that was great! Now you *must* sing something!" Hannah chimed in.

Greer giggled. "Maybe after I have another shot of Soju."

Justin handed her the songbook. "Here, *Noona*, pick a song, and I'll load it up for you."

She wrinkled her nose in thought. Should she do it? She flipped through the book until she found a familiar song and pointed her selection to Justin.

She took a deep breath, her heart pounding, and picked up the microphone. Standing up front, she felt the weight of all eyes on her. On second thought, maybe this wasn't a good idea. The Soju and the duet must have given her false courage. She focused on the screen at the back of the room while waiting for the music to start because she didn't know where else to look.

Finally, the music began to play. From years of habit, she raised her arms and played air drums to the driving drum groove of Pat Benatar's "Heartbreaker." Her voice cracked on the first note, but she kept going, and her voice and confidence grew stronger. The song debuted when she was a high school freshman still trying to find her place in the world. She'd felt empowered whenever she heard Pat Benatar's confident vocals, even though she didn't know the word *empowered* back then.

Suddenly, she felt as if she was fourteen again, in her childhood bedroom using a brush as her microphone, singing to the posters on her wall and the dolls tucked away on her closet shelf. She lost all self-consciousness and became immersed in her performance. Then she took it up a notch, shook, shimmied, and threw in an occasional headbang and fist pump. She couldn't have done any better if she wore big eighties hair, over-sized hoop earrings, and tight leather pants. She danced around like a boss during the final guitar solo and raised her fist triumphantly as the song ended. "Thank you, Austin!" she shouted.

They clapped, and someone whistled as she tried to catch her breath. But what did Gun think? Had he bothered to watch her performance? She looked in his direction, and their eyes met. His lips curved in a crooked smile, and he looked like the man she had first met on the plane, only sexier. She sighed and smiled with relief until Jason embraced her in a bear hug, blocking her view of Gun.

Sarah announced that Greer inspired her to sing a solo, but Gun snatched the remote from her hand.

"*Ya!*" she exclaimed in protest.

He ignored her, pressing the buttons on the remote with great force, then tied an American flag scarf around his head. The opening riffs of Guns N' Roses's "Paradise City" began to play, and Greer stared at him wide-eyed. Did he intend to channel Axl Rose and sing this song? Apparently, he did. He walked to the front and picked up the microphone from the table.

He flubbed the opening line, and she closed her eyes, not wishing to see him embarrass himself. He said something in Korean, and Sarah reached for the remote. The song started over, and he tapped his foot to keep time with the opening riffs. As the tempo picked up, he waited for the next riff and began a gentle headbang.

Greer waited uneasily, then couldn't believe her ears when he began to sing. He had a strong voice, and she marveled at his ability to keep up with the song's fast-paced lyrics. The others watched without surprise, so she sat back to enjoy the performance. Jason moved his head to the beat of the rhythm, Justin played air guitar, and Luke tapped his thigh. As the song went into double time, they stood and joined in the head-banging frenzy, and Sarah danced around like a G&R groupie.

Like her, Gun struggled to catch his breath when the song ended, and sweat ran down his face. He glanced at her, and she gave him a discreet thumbs-up.

The guys slapped him on the back and gave him a hard time. "Gun-ah, you show off! You about gave yourself a heart attack!" Luke teased.

"You're still doing that same old, tired routine?" Jason chimed in. "That might have impressed the girls back in the day, but no one wants to see a geriatric singing this song."

"Don't listen to them, Gun *Oppa*! You were awesome!" Sarah looked at Greer and Hannah for confirmation. "What did you think, Greer? Gun's been doing that song since the nineties, but it's been a while since he last sang it. Didn't he do a good job?"

"He did a *great* job!" Greer said. "I love that song. It holds great memories for me."

Gun's face darkened, and she bit her lip. What had she said now?

They took a short break, and Jason excused himself to go to the men's room. Gun picked up his black leather jacket and addressed the room in Korean as he walked to the door. The others said goodbye to him, and Greer sat up straight. So he was leaving? Just like that?

Before she had time to think, she bolted from the room. She reached the front door as he tossed a long leg over the motorcycle. It had crossed her mind that he might own the stunning machine.

"Gun!" she yelled.

He looked up in surprise but didn't acknowledge her.

"It was you I saw that day, wasn't it?" She stood directly in front of him, slightly out of breath. "You were riding your motor-cycle on Congress Avenue. Tonight, when Luke said you like Waylon Jennings, I knew it had to be you."

"So what if it was?"

Greer shrugged. "I don't know. I guess . . . well, I didn't think I'd ever see you again after the plane, so . . ." He remained stony-eyed, so she searched for something to say. "By the way, I like your bike, but are you sure you're okay to ride?"

As soon as the words came out of her mouth, she knew she'd made a mistake.

"You think the title of *Counselor* on your fancy law license gives you the right to meddle in my life?" he said. "Is that what you came out here to tell me?"

"No, of course not, and that's not what I wanted to say. What I'm trying to say, what I want to *ask* is, well, I don't know what I've done, but it's clear you feel I've done something to offend you. So if you could please tell me—"

"Why do you care about my feelings?" he barked. "Do you and I have that kind of relationship? You're my mom's lawyer, and that's it. Got it? *You* and *I* are not friends."

Wow, talk about mean. She wrapped her arms around her body to shield herself from the cold and his verbal assault. "You're right. We don't have any relationship. It's just that when we first met—"

"Then what are you doing out here? Didn't you come here with Jason? Get back inside to your date." He started the Indian's powerful engine, thereby silencing any further conversation.

Greer turned to go inside, then stopped as a fire stoked within her. She turned around and gave him her best stink eye. It gratified her to see him look taken aback.

"What are you doing? I said to go back inside!" he yelled.

*Oh, no, he didn't.* "I'll go back inside when I'm good and

ready! And who do you think you are to talk to me like that? You're not the boss of me, you jerk!"

"Woman, are you crazy?"

"Yes, as a matter of fact, I am! So unless you want to see me unleash the crazy, you better not push me around! *Got it?* And as far as you and I being friends, don't flatter yourself. Do you think I'd stoop so low to be friends with someone like you?" She clapped her hands and pointed to the street. "Now go on, get out of here! Git! *Pali, ka!*" Since he had insisted on speaking Korean all night, she would show him she knew how to say, "Hurry, go!"

Full of outrage, Gun muttered something in Korean and roared off in a huff.

She didn't flinch but stayed put until he drove away, then turned to rejoin the others.

Jason waited for her right inside the door with a pensive look.

# Chapter Seven

The fairway on the par 4, 425-yard ninth hole at Waterloo Municipal Golf Course doglegged to the left, and Gun's tee shot had been short. Instead of flying over the bunker at the joint of the fairway, his ball landed right in the middle. It had been a stupid rookie mistake, typical of his mistakes all morning. He'd lost his ability to focus, but unlike those who yelled, cursed, and threw their clubs in the air, he remained sullenly silent.

As he prepared to take his next shot in the middle of the sand, two of his companions stood on the ledge of the bunker, shaking their heads, probably curious about what had caused this poor performance. The third, however, smiled and relished his misfortune.

"Looks like your day keeps getting worse," Jason observed with a smirk, turning the knife in the wound. "Are you so hungover from last night that you forgot how to play?"

Gun growled. "Jason, I've listened to your smack all morning. If you're done, why don't you shut it?"

"Whoa," his three companions said in mock fear.

Jason kept pushing his buttons. "I'm not done by a long shot, not that you'd know anything about that. I'm only getting started. What are you going to do about it?"

Gun glared at him from behind his sunglasses even though Jason couldn't see it. "Why don't you come here and find out what I'm gonna do about it."

Ever the peacemaker, Justin tried to intercede. "*Hyung*, let's just play, okay?"

Like most older brothers, Jason ignored him and kept goading Gun. "What's got you so upset today? I don't think it's because you're hungover. You've played with a hangover before. It wouldn't have anything to do with Greer, would it?"

Gun gripped his golf club so tight that his knuckles turned white. "Didn't I tell you to shut it? And no, this has nothing to do with that woman. She's of no concern to me."

"That woman is of no concern to you. Is that right? You were fine last night until I announced that I had invited Greer to join us. Then you started hitting the beer and Soju and acting like you were Axl Rose. What made you pull that sorry old party trick from your back pocket? It looked like you were showing off a little, trying to impress Greer."

"I was not showing off!" he yelled, frustrated that they could always see right through him.

The others laughed.

"Okay, I was irritated that you invited her. But it's only because I didn't want company."

"But if she's of no concern to you, why did it matter that I invited her? Why didn't you ignore her?" Jason asked. "I've never seen you act so rude. Could it be that you were . . . jealous?"

Gun snorted. "Jealous? Over her? Yeah, right, that's a good one. I don't even see her as a woman!"

"*Hyung*, you sure are getting worked up for someone who doesn't care," Justin said.

"Justin's got you there, bro," Luke agreed. "But why don't you see Greer as a woman? She's nice, pretty, and can sing too!"

"And she has a cute little figure," Justin added. "I like a woman with curves."

Gun stared open-mouthed at them. "Have y'all lost your ever-loving minds? Yeah, she's pretty, but so what? Pretty women are a dime a dozen! And *Hyung*, you think she's *nice*? I see she managed to fool you, too!" He removed his hat, ran his fingers through his hair, and put the hat back on. "Not only do I not care about that woman, but I hope she never shows her face to me again! Satisfied? Can we get on with our game, or do y'all want to stand around and talk about women all day?"

"So you won't care if I ask her out, right?" Jason's voice held a challenge.

"What did I say, huh?" Gun sputtered and spit in frustration, trying to get his words out. "Besides, didn't you already ask her out? What do you call last night?"

Jason opened his mouth, but Luke swung his arm out, indicating that everyone should stop. Being the oldest had its privileges. They all knew better than to defy Luke.

"That's enough," Luke ordered in a voice that meant business. "Let's play before we hold up the other group. Gun, Jason, drop this little spat. Otherwise, you two girls can pull each other's hair out in the parking lot while Justin and I finish."

Jason smirked but refrained from saying more, and Gun played the remaining holes in brooding silence.

They finished their game, and Gun couldn't remember the last time he'd played so poorly. Afterward, he drove Luke back to their mother's house. As he pulled into the driveway, Luke asked him to wait in the truck while he went into the house to grab something.

"What is it?" Gun asked.

"Janet was looking for something up in the attic, and she

came across a box that belongs to you. It contains a few belongings you left in your apartment when you moved to Korea. After all these years and moving three times, we thought we'd already given you everything."

Gun shook his head. "I don't want it. Dump it in the trash."

Luke turned to him. "Hey, man, what's going on with you? You can deny it all you want, but I know that—"

"Fine, give me the box. I don't want to talk about it anymore."

Luke studied him. "Gun-ah, I don't know what's going on in that head of yours. I don't know if you're suffering from a bad hangover, or if you're going through a midlife crisis, or if it's . . ." He took a deep breath before continuing. "Bro, you know I'm on your side. I've always supported you, right or wrong, and pleaded your case with Dad. But you better get your head on straight, do you hear me? Now, hold up while I go inside and get that box."

Luke got out, grabbed his golf clubs from the truck bed, and went inside. He returned almost immediately, carrying a brown moving box. Someone, probably Janet, had written *GUN* on the sides of the box with a black permanent marker.

Gun rushed out of the truck to intercept him. He grabbed the box and headed toward his mom's trash bin.

"Mom said don't even think about it!" Luke ordered. "Take it home with you and dump it in your trash."

Gun did an about-face and placed the box in the back of his truck.

"Mom also said not to be late for dinner tonight." Luke slapped his brother on the back. "Go home and sleep it off, man. It'll be all right."

Gun got back in his truck and drove south. At home, he parked in his garage, unloaded his golf clubs and the ominous box from the back, and lifted the trash can lid to dump it. Then he stopped. While the box represented a time in his life he preferred to forget, there was the possibility that it contained something of value. He was in no mood to deal with it now, though. He placed it on the top of a utility shelf in the garage where it would be out of sight and out of the way until he was ready to deal with it.

He entered the house through the kitchen door from the garage, carrying his golf clubs with him. Buddy, his golden retriever rescue, greeted him at the door. The dog had the perfect name since he was as fine a wingman as Gun had ever known. His long, fluffy tail did double time.

"Hey, Bud, what's goin' on?" Gun grabbed Buddy's face and kissed him on his forehead before rubbing Buddy's flanks. "How are you doin'? Are you hungry? Where's Bullet?"

His house had an open floor plan, so he could easily see Bullet, his silver-gray cat, and the third resident bachelor lying on his comfy cat perch. During Gun's absence, he typically slept in front of the living room window, soaking up the warmth of the late winter sun.

Bullet opened one eye and flicked his tail at the mention of his name, then yawned and stood on all fours. With his back arched, he began stretching his limbs slowly and deliberately. Gun and Buddy watched Bullet with practiced patience. They had grown accustomed to waiting on him. Finally, Gun scooped him up, scratched his chin, and set him on the floor. "All right! Time to eat!"

Bullet stared at him with wide green eyes, and Buddy danced around in anticipation of lunch.

Gun devoured a sandwich and drank honey water for his hangover while his housemates ate. Then he soaked in the hot steam of the custom shower he'd designed for days like this. He'd woken up that morning with a killer headache and a stiff neck. He twisted his head from side to side to stretch his tight neck and shoulder muscles, chuckling when he thought of how Bullett could teach him a thing or two about stretching.

As the hot water ran down his back, he finally began to loosen up. Luke and Jason had been right about him being hungover, but he could sum up the reason for his foul mood with one word: Greer. Just thinking about her made his neck muscles tighten again.

It was strange how one insignificant decision could change your life. He would have never met Greer if not for his last-minute decision to change his afternoon flight to the early morning. When he'd first spotted her on the plane, he could tell she was good-looking from her profile alone. He congratulated himself for changing his flight, or he might have missed seeing her. He stopped by her seat, hoping for an invitation, but she determinedly turned her face toward the window. He took the hint and found a seat behind her. During the flight, he stood and stretched his legs, hoping for an opportunity to talk. But when he looked down, her head drooped alarmingly to the right as she slept.

Once they landed, he'd been delighted to catch her fall because it finally allowed them an opportunity to meet without pretext. He fantasized about a different time and place when her silky, dark hair spread across his chest. Then she turned around, and something stirred within him. Talk about beautiful. He had to restrain himself from touching the curve of her face. He wouldn't make a move when she was in a vulnerable state. He didn't want her to think that's why he helped her, although he'd kicked himself several times for not asking for her name or number.

So he couldn't believe it when he spotted her standing at the corner of Congress Avenue. He wasn't usually so lucky. She wore professional clothes, indicating she worked downtown. As he drove through the light, he tried to pull over but couldn't find a parking place. By the time he circled the block and returned, she was gone.

Then his mother dragged him to Greer's office, and he thought maybe his mom was onto something about fate. Three times had to be more than a mere coincidence. He poked around her office when she left to help her boss, and that's when he saw it. How had he not realized it before? Any fantasies he entertained about her crashed and burned. Disaster averted, or so he'd thought.

He was dumbfounded, then furious, when Jason announced he'd invited Greer to karaoke. What the heck was that all about? Jason had met the woman at church a week ago and had already asked her out? The guy didn't waste any time. He was still chasing any woman that moved. Not that he cared if Jason asked Greer out, but he didn't want to be a chaperone on their dates.

Sarah, Hannah, and Justin hadn't helped either, calling Greer *unni* and *noona*. They acted like they were filming a drama, and he found their behavior ridiculous. But Greer had even won over his *hyung* and had him eating out of her hands after their duet. "'Weren't we all in our prime in the eighties,'" he mimicked Greer with a falsetto voice.

Gun let out a deep breath. They'd just been having fun, and he couldn't entirely blame them. He, too, almost succumbed to Greer's feminine wiles. Almost. He observed her all evening and caught her looking at him, too—and he couldn't take his eyes off her when she sang that Pat Benatar song. She'd put confident energy into her performance. The woman could move, and she looked very sexy.

But then she closed her eyes when he flubbed the opening line of "Paradise City." Strike One. He didn't need her pity.

*"I love that song. It holds great memories for me,"* she'd said.

He scoffed. *That's right, Greer. Make it about you.* Strike two.

Strike three was when she followed him outside to apologize when she had no idea what she was apologizing for. *When we first met.* Talk about clueless. He hadn't been in the mood to hear her lame excuses and had a sense of satisfaction from the hurt and confusion in her eyes when he cut her off. But he'd gone too far and acted like a bully. Yet, despite the hurt she felt, she'd shown a lot of grit when she stood up to him and began throwing it back in his face.

He let out a laugh. She was something.

His mother had been badgering him for weeks to apologize for the incident in Greer's office. Now, he would have to add his behavior last night to the list of his transgressions. Greer brought out the worst in him, but he should have enough control over his emotions to treat her with civility.

He rubbed his eyes and sighed. He'd like to place Greer on the utility shelf next to the box and deal with her later. But mindful of Luke's warning, he had to shake it off and get his head on straight.

~

*September 1989*
*Dallas, Texas*

At two o'clock on Friday afternoon, Greer and the Section One students walked out of their classroom under the law library and into the bright sunshine. Having finished their last class of the week—Civil Procedure—they talked excitedly about their weekend plans, including the Lawyer's Inn happy hour that night. However, three of them found joining the frivolity difficult. Their last hour had been one of the most terrifying of their lives.

Professor Banks, their professor, began every class the same way. He entered through a side door, effectively bringing all chatter to a halt, and walked to the podium. After setting his textbook and notes down, he ran his finger across the seating chart like an ominous roulette wheel. Everyone held their breath. He called the name of his first victim and asked them to stand, then did the same to call his second and third victims. Those not chosen uttered a collective sigh of relief. They were spared for today but would have to watch their classmates suffer for the next hour.

Banks then began questioning the assigned reading. This method of questions and answers—like cross-examination in a courtroom—was known as the Socratic Method.

"Mr. Cooper," Professor Banks began in his commanding voice. "What were the four categories of minimum contacts established by the Supreme Court to determine personal jurisdiction over a corporation in *International Shoe Company v. Washington?*"

The first question was a giveaway, provided Mark Cooper had read the assignment. The question was easy for a reason. It was meant to lull him into a false sense of security. But it was a downhill slide from there. All the professors utilized the Socratic Method, but Banks was especially ruthless. It didn't matter how often they'd read the assignment in preparation for class or how many sentences they had highlighted in the passage. The professor crafted his questions from the least anticipated minutiae. His victims were left dazed and stupefied, wondering how they could have missed the issue in the case.

The three classmates who endured this torture only moments ago walked with their heads hung while the others assured them it was nothing that a few beers wouldn't cure. Charlie entertained them with his impersonation of the professor, eliciting laughs, but there was a strain in their laughter.

They all knew their day was coming. It was just a matter of time.

They walked across the Quad, where their friend Darrell Stewart sat on the rotunda steps, wearing his usual Hawaiian shirt, shorts, and flip-flops and drinking a beer. Greer envied his carefree spirit. No one looking at him would guess he was at the top of his second-year class and had received the highest score on last year's Civil Procedure exam. Moreover, unlike many top-ranked students, Darrell was a good guy, always willing to dispense helpful advice to his juniors and share his study outlines.

"How'd it go, man?" Darrell asked Charlie. "Did Professor Banks call on your butt, or did you get another reprieve?"

"Haha, no. I managed to escape, but I know my time's coming," Charlie answered.

"If you're lucky, ol' Banks may miss you. He's supposed to call on everyone at least once each semester but prefers to call on the girls. If they're pretty, he'll call on them twice."

"Uh-oh, Greer," a guy's voice said from within their crowd. "That means you're in trouble."

"Ha! He's right! You're in trouble!" Charlie howled, pointing at Greer.

The crowd joined in his laughter, and, encouraged by their support, he kept going. "I'm going to be hiding behind Greer from now on! Professor Banks will be calling my name, 'Mr. Bell, Mr. Bell.' But I'll be sitting behind Greer like this." He threw his head back like he was sleeping and began to snore. "He won't be able to see me, and the only thing he'll hear is the sound of my snore, hahaha!"

"You might as well sacrifice yourself now, Greer!" the male voice said. "Raise your hand in class and spare us all!"

She whipped around, intent on discovering the traitor in her midst. Who'd volunteered her to be their virgin sacrifice?

Well, maybe not a *virgin* sacrifice, but a sacrifice all the same. She was too short to see above her tall companions, though, and she forgot about rooting out the traitor when she caught sight of Jake. He was walking on the other side of the Rotunda, heading toward the law library, and she ran after him. "Jake! Wait up!"

He stopped, turned, and looked surprised to see her, "Oh, hi, Greer."

"Are you on your way to class?" she asked while trying to catch her breath.

"Yeah. How about you?"

"I'm done for the day and ready for the weekend!" She pumped her fists.

Jake didn't appear as excited about that as she was. He pushed up the bridge of his glasses with his index finger and cleared his throat. "I was wondering—"

"Hey, Gigi, are you coming?" Charlie's booming baritone interrupted them. He and a couple of their friends were walking toward the Inn.

"Uh, yeah, I'm coming. Just give me a few minutes, okay?"

Charlie gave her a disapproving look. "Okay, but don't be too long." He didn't like Jake, and she suspected the feeling was mutual.

"Are you coming to our dorm happy hour tonight?" she asked, getting back to Jake.

"I don't know. I want to grab something to eat off campus or go to a movie. I was going to ask you to join me, but if you'd rather hang out with your friends—"

"No, no! I'd rather go with you. Where do you want to go? What time should I be ready?"

"I don't know yet. Can I call you later?"

"Sure, I'll be around." She smiled. No way she would miss an opportunity to spend an evening with him.

"Okay. Well, I better get to class. See you." He waved and walked on toward the law library.

She felt like shrieking. Jake had finally asked her out! She hadn't been this excited since she sat in the front row at the Duran Duran concert. Wait until she told Carole Anne.

And speaking of her friend, Carole Anne emerged from the Inn's front door on her way to class. She looked ready to burst. "Gigi, I'm glad I ran into you. In the newspaper's entertainment section, I saw that a new mobster movie is playing at the Multiplex. Do you want to see it tomorrow?"

Carole Anne was a conundrum. For such a genteel young woman, she was enamored with the mob culture portrayed in the movies and owned both *Godfather* movies on VHS tape. Greer was convinced Carole Anne had been born in the wrong era. She would've made an excellent gangster's moll.

Greer placed her hands on her hips. "A mobster movie, huh? Imagine that. Sure, I'd love to go."

"Awesome! I can already smell the popcorn," Carole Anne said in a sing-song voice and turned toward the law library.

"Carole Anne, wait! You'll never believe it. Jake asked me out!"

Carole Anne screamed and grabbed Greer's hands, and they jumped up and down on the sidewalk. "I wish I didn't have to get to class," she said as she walked backward. "I'll come by your room afterward. I can't wait to hear all about it."

Greer nodded excitedly. She felt lucky to have someone like Carole Anne to share her feelings and support her. She listened sympathetically when Greer expressed her frustration with Jake and never judged or made that face people make when they disagree with you but are just trying to humor you. She'd even volunteered to act as Greer's spy since Carole Anne and Jake were members of Section Three.

Charlie, on the other hand, never minced words. "It's not

gonna happen, Gigi," he had told her, "so don't waste your time on that bonehead. There's plenty of other fish in the sea."

Greer wasn't ready to give up on Jake yet, but admittedly, his behavior confused her. After he had chivalrously collected her books, she felt sure it would lead to a natural connection. But he appeared bewildered by her gratitude and, at times, acted standoffish. Then, when she had begun to believe his chivalry a singular event, he became friendly again. She'd since learned he came from a small town in West Texas where his family was one of five prominent families, and his dad was the county judge. He'd had a sheltered, traditional upbringing, perhaps explaining his reticence.

While the jury was still out on Jake, Charlie was right about him not being the only fish in the sea. Mitch McBride and Will Schneider, two second-year students, had caught her eye. Mitch, a former college football player from Texas Tech, lived on the Inn's second floor. Loud, brash, and wild as the West Texas wind Marty Robbins sang about, he walked around with a swagger and a mischievous gleam in his eyes. Yet despite the bravado, he was a charmer, and girls liked him.

At the other end of the spectrum was Will Schneider, a former frat boy from an Ivy League college who ranked fifth in his class. Considered ideal boyfriend material and a prize catch, many girls vied for his attention. He had been sitting at a table in the law library when Greer passed, looking for a torts study guide. When he looked up, his bright blue eyes and Rob Lowe good looks mesmerized her, and she forgot to look where she was going and tripped over a couch. She wanted to die from embarrassment, but Will had rushed to her aid, fussed over her, and didn't make her feel like she was stupid.

She could hardly believe it when he asked her to a movie when he had so many girls to choose from. They went to see *When Harry Met Sally* at the movie theater in Highland Park

Village, and Will bought her ice cream. The date had gone well until he walked her back to the dorm. He kissed her, but it wasn't a gentle first-date kiss. Instead, it felt like he was trying to rip her lips off. That had been too much, and she pulled away.

She sighed. Like Goldilocks, she wished she could find a guy who was just right. Her dream date would take her to the state fair next month. She would buy a cute top and wear it with her denim mini skirt, and he would try to impress her by winning her a stuffed animal. Then they would hold hands as they walked through Fair Park, and he would buy her a corn dog and a funnel cake. She'd shared her dream with Charlie and the guys in her study group when they were taking a break, and they'd howled with laughter and teased her about being old-fashioned and naive. Only David Jones had whispered out of earshot from the other guys, "Greer, if a guy likes you, he'll do those things."

Jake was an old-fashioned kind of guy. Now that he'd asked her out, her dream might come true.

"Hey, Gigi, where've you been?" Charlie called, sticking his head out through his third-story window. "We're waiting for you." He placed a speaker on the sill, and soon, "Paradise City" blared across the Quad. He treated everyone to a concert every Friday.

Greer raised her fists in the air. "Woohoo! Way to go, Charlie!" she shouted.

This was going to be an awesome weekend.

# Chapter Eight

Greer took off her readers and rubbed her eyes. She'd been editing a construction contract for the past—she glanced at the clock—three hours. Molly had put the file on her desk and given her a not-so-subtle hint that she needed to get it done *today*. Greer had taken the hint.

Four days after karaoke, she still had a hangover, and reading through sixty-five pages of fine print didn't help her aching head. Even the lights in her office felt too bright. What had possessed her to drink so many shots of Soju? She scoffed. She knew the answer to that question.

Gun.

After their horrendous goodbye, to control the rage she felt, she'd stormed back inside and slammed back two more shots of Soju. It was a foolish and reckless move. She was older, supposedly wiser, and should have known better, but she couldn't understand Gun's hostility toward her. It went beyond a mere lack of romantic interest. What did he find so offensive about her, and why wouldn't he share his alleged grievance with her? He should have at least allowed her to defend herself. Instead, he'd roared off on his motorcycle like a bat out of hell. She found it difficult to reconcile the kind man on the plane with this side of him, but it wouldn't be the first time she'd misjudged a man's character.

On the other hand, Jason was kind, respectful, and consistent. He and Gun were the most unlikely friends she'd ever met. Jason texted Friday night to ensure she arrived home safely, then again on Sunday afternoon while she visited her parents. His text said he had enjoyed their evening and hoped to see her again, but he was leaving town and would contact her once he returned. She appreciated his consideration but was no spring chick and held no false expectations of him calling.

Adding to her troubles was that she'd dreamt about Jake again. She must've heard "Paradise City" dozens—no, *hundreds* —of times since law school. What was it about Gun's rendition of the song that broke through her subconscious? She couldn't put her finger on it, but there was a connection. She shuddered. What did it matter? With any luck, she would never see him again. She didn't need the drama.

Greer emailed the redlined contract to Molly and let out a loud yawn. She felt exhausted just from thinking about it. An iced mocha would hit the spot right about now. Plus, it would be nice to see Jampa. He always lightened her otherwise burdensome workdays. Not only did he make her laugh, but he displayed remarkable wisdom for his age.

She grabbed cash from her wallet, left her cell phone on her desk, and walked outside her office to the paralegals' station. "Hey, Rita, I'm going for a coffee break. Can I bring you anything?"

"No, I'm good, thanks." Rita's eyes stayed glued to her computer screen as her fingers flew across the keyboard.

Greer snuck out through the back exit to avoid anyone who might stop her and ask for help, then took the elevator to the first floor and entered the busy café. She hadn't expected it to be this crowded.

Jampa stood behind the counter, making drinks and filling pastry orders, but he noticed her waiting in line at the other end. "Hey, how's it going? Do you want your usual? I'll start on your order."

Greer grinned. It paid to be friends with the local barista. "Yes, I do, and I want whipped cream too!"

"Whipped cream!" Jampa teased in mock alarm. "You're living on the edge."

He was too cute. Coming down here had been a good idea, and she was already feeling better. She handed her money to Cheyenne, a friendly girl with purple hair, and dropped the change into the tip jar. "You're busy today." She stated the obvious as she walked to where Jampa worked.

"Yes, ma'am, but I like it that way. It makes the workday go by faster."

"I'm with you on that one," she agreed, and they shared a smile.

Jampa handed her the drink, and his fingers overlapped hers. He held onto the cup for a beat longer than necessary, and she blushed. "Sorry I'm too busy to talk. But I'll see you next time, right?"

"Of course you will. Take care." She waved goodbye while walking backward, reluctant to leave. She wanted to bask in Jampa's hunkiness a little longer.

Unfortunately, this meant she did not see the devil behind her lying in wait.

"Well, look who we have here. If it ain't Greer Garza."

Her body tensed. She knew that voice without having to turn around. It was a voice she hoped to never hear again and it belonged to her ex-husband, Beau Broussard. He spoke loud enough for the entire café to hear, and her first instinct was to run as fast as she could in the opposite direction. Even though it had been more than nine years since their bitter divorce, she knew nothing good would come from this encounter.

Greer took a deep breath and turned around, and her eyes widened at his changed appearance. Besides his significant weight gain, his hairline had receded farther back, and his forehead and nose had deep lines. Gun and Jason looked younger than their age, but Beau looked every day of his fifty-four years, if not older. "Hi, Beau," she said through clenched teeth. "What are you doing here?"

He scoffed. "You mean you don't know? I'm here to see that shyster. What's his name? I thought you'd know, but I guess the people in your firm don't think you're important enough."

He laughed in that mocking way she remembered all too well. She'd always found it as irritating as fingernails dragging across a chalkboard.

"Well, you're right. I don't know, and since it doesn't concern me, I'll be going now." She'd said hello, and that was more acknowledgment than he deserved. She didn't have to stick around and listen to his foolishness.

"Honey, what's that lawyer's name?" Beau said, ignoring her, just like he did when they were married.

A slim, dishwater blonde stepped from behind him. A little on the plain side, she wasn't unattractive, but she wouldn't win any beauty contests. But what she lacked in looks, she made up for in attitude. She slipped a proprietary arm through his and looked at Greer contemptuously.

"Greer, this is my wife, Felicia. As you can see, I finally married up." He looked down at Felicia. "Honey, what's the name of that lawyer we're meeting?"

"Nick. Nick Taylor," Felicia answered with a dour expression.

Greer ignored the dig but remembered what he was

babbling about. Beau had retained Nick Taylor, another partner in the firm, to advise him regarding his family's East Texas oil and gas leases. He had never forgiven her for the divorce, so he'd chosen hers out of all the firms in Texas. He'd always adhered to the notion that "revenge is a dish best-served cold," and this was the proof. Of course, she objected to the representation, but Nick and the other partners had salivated over the fees a client like Beau would generate.

"Aren't you a partner at that firm?" Beau taunted. "But guess it doesn't matter what a little ol' Mescan gal like you thinks. Everyone knows the only thing that matters to you lawyers is money, and I got plenty of it."

"It's more like the issue didn't merit any discussion," she replied calmly, although she seethed with rage. How dare he come to her workplace and spew such hateful insults? It felt like a violation.

She gave the couple a smug smile, turned to leave, and nearly tripped over Gun's boots. He put his arm around her middle to keep her from tumbling forward, and she squealed. She was grateful she didn't fall or spill her drink everywhere, but what was he doing here? Next to Beau, he was the last person on earth she wanted to see. She didn't need two men ganging up on her.

"Baby, are you okay?" Gun said in a saccharine tone she'd never heard him use before, and she shot him a look.

*Baby?* Who was he talking to? Was she in the middle of another dream? If so, this one qualified as a nightmare.

Gun released her, turned her around, and placed his arm around her, so apparently, he was talking to her. The last time she'd seen him, he had effectively told her to kiss his well-toned, tanned derriere. Or something along those lines. She rolled her shoulders to shake off his arm, but he tightened his hold. Either he was poor at interpreting nonverbal clues or choosing to ignore her. Then, to add to her confusion, he took the drink from her hand and sipped its precious contents.

"Thanks for getting my drink, baby."

*His* drink? That did it! She was about to give him an elbow shot to the ribs, but Beau cut in.

"And who are *you?*" He puffed out his chest, posturing for Gun's benefit.

"Who, me?" Gun asked, feigning innocence. "I'm Gun Donovan, Gigi's boyfriend. Sorry, I'd shake your hand, but—" He held up the drink and jiggled the ice.

"Huh! So you speak English. I wasn't sure. I thought maybe you spoke Chinese or somethin'. Well, *I'm* her ex-husband, Beau Broussard. I'm sure you've heard all about me."

Greer rolled her eyes. How ironic that an ignorant bigot like Beau would accuse Gun of being unable to speak English. The man had no shame.

Gun squeezed her shoulder, signaling her not to retaliate. "No, I've never heard of you. I knew Gigi was married before, but she's never mentioned your name or said a word about you."

Beau's hazel eyes flashed. The man hated to be deemed irrelevant. He fixed Gun with an alpha-male stare, and she worried he would start a fistfight in the café. It wasn't beneath him.

She peeked at Gun from the corner of her eye. He smiled as if unaware that he'd thrown the proverbial first punch. However, his fingers told a different story as they beat a slow rhythm on her arm. Like Beau, he'd also assumed the "go ahead if you dare" stance.

She sighed and rolled her eyes again. Men.

Beau blinked first. Like all bullies, he knew whom he could pick on and whom to leave alone. Although he was a big guy, Gun was taller, in much better shape, and had backed Beau into a corner. Beau weaseled his way out the way he did everything else. He blamed his wife. "Felicia, why didn't you tell me we're about to be late for our appointment?"

Felicia looked disgusted but didn't argue with him.

Since Beau couldn't push Gun around, he fired a parting shot at Greer. "Looks like your life's gone downhill since our divorce, but I'm not surprised. I never thought you'd amount to much." He shot one last look in Gun's direction and tromped out of the café with Felicia.

Greer couldn't hold back any longer. She lunged in Beau's direction, but Gun held her back. He pulled her close and whispered, "Don't say or do anything. Let them leave."

His breath tickled her ear, further enraging her. On the plane, she hadn't wanted him to let her go. Now, she couldn't wait to break free from him.

He loosened his hold when Beau and Felicia were out of sight.

"What the heck was that all about?" she asked.

"Yeah, that's exactly what I'd like to know," said a voice behind her.

She turned around, and Jampa stood only a couple of feet away, his mouth in a straight line and his fists clenched. He glared at Gun. She'd forgotten about Jampa! She should've known he would feel compelled to come to her rescue.

"Is this guy bothering you?" Jampa asked.

"No," she assured him. "In his weird way, he was trying to help."

"Hey, kid, you make a good drink," Gun told him. "I normally don't like these fancy coffee drinks, but this is good."

Greer glared at him. Really? Was he taunting Jampa? The kerfuffle with Beau must have brought on a rush of testosterone. "Jampa, I'm fine. I'll explain it all to you later, okay?"

Jampa hesitated, but then his body relaxed. "Well, if you're sure, then all right. Because you know I'm here for you if you need me." He shot another defiant look at Gun.

She mouthed, "Thank you," and then turned back to Gun. "And you come with me." She had to get him out of the café and away from other potential trouble. Grabbing him by the wrist, she succeeded in yanking him forward only because she'd caught him off guard but couldn't pull him any farther. Unlike the wrist grabs in the dramas, dragging someone by the wrists was not as easy as it looked, especially when they were twice your size.

"Hey, I almost spilled my drink!" he cried.

Her temper snapped, and she whipped around. "It's not even yours! It's *mine*, remember? You took it from me during your little stunt back there!"

He stared at her as he sipped the few remaining precious ounces. The straw hit the bottom of the cup, and he sucked in the air before finishing with an exaggerated "Ahhh." Then, to add insult to injury, he handed the empty cup to her. "Can you please throw this away?"

He was infuriating. For the second time that day, Greer wanted to slug him. She pointed her index finger at him, then jerked her thumb over her shoulder, causing him to follow her. She led the way to the building maintenance office on the other side of the elevators. Few people knew of its existence, and they could talk there without interruption.

Gun whistled and walked with his hands in his pockets as if taking a casual stroll in the park. She stood with her hands on her hips and tapped her foot impatiently, waiting for him to catch up and then let him have it.

"What the heck was that all about?"

He made a face. "What was what all about?"

Greer scoffed. "Give me a break. Am I a joke to you?"

"What?"

"I can't figure out what kind of game you're playing. You were kind to me when I was a stranger, but that changed after your mom introduced us. That tells me it's personal, yet we hardly know each other. What could I have done to you? And then today you do this . . . " She trailed off and chewed on her thumbnail while reflecting on his strange behavior over the last few months. It didn't make sense. She looked up. "Like right now. Why are you looking at me like that?"

His expression turned uneasy. "Uh, looking at you how? I just—"

"And how did you know my nickname is Gigi?"

Gun shrugged. "Your initials are G.G., so I took a shot."

"And why did you tell Beau you're my boyfriend?"

He clicked his tongue, and his eyes shifted to the right, avoiding hers. "I don't know. I guess I thought it would be fun to mess with him."

Greer took a deep, steadying breath and crossed her arms. "You thought it would be *fun*? I see. So, is that what you've been doing with *me*? Just 'messing with me'? You must've gotten a real kick out of discovering the klutz from the plane is your mother's lawyer."

"No, no, no. Don't put words in my mouth. My mom asked me to drop off some documents for you. That's the only reason I'm here. While I was upstairs, I overheard the women in your office talking. They were worried about you running into your ex-husband, so I thought I'd come down and—"

"You thought you'd come down and do what? Save me from my ex-husband?"

"Well, was I wrong? I heard what he said to you. That guy's a jerk—"

"Well, he isn't the only one," she sneered.

He scowled. "What's that supposed to mean?"

"Okay, yes, there's no doubt he's a jerk, and he's a racist too.

But that's my business, not yours. Besides, you're one to talk. You haven't exactly treated me much better."

Gun gawked. "Are you seriously comparing me to that moron?"

She lowered her voice to mimic him. "'You're my mom's lawyer, and that's it. Got it? You and I are not friends.' Does that ring a bell?"

Gun held up his hand. "All right, all right. Point taken. I was too harsh that night. I admit it. But today, I was trying to help."

"I don't need your help," she threw back. "Besides, when you act nice and helpful, it sends the wrong signals. It makes me think you're a good guy. But then, the next time I see you, your walls are back up, and you act like a condescending jerk. I can't take the Jekyll-and-Hyde act. Look, I know you don't like me. So what do you say we reach an agreement? If we ever run into each other again, let's pretend we don't know each other and walk on by, okay?"

He scoffed. "You are unbelievable! But I guess it shouldn't surprise me. You can't see what's right in front of your face. You stand here accusing me of being hot and cold, but what about you?"

She shook her head and let out an exasperated breath. "What about me? Please tell me because that's what I've been trying to figure out, and it's driving me crazy."

Gun shrugged. "I'm just saying, before you start throwing stones, why don't you examine your life?"

She studied him, baffled. "Do you have me confused with someone else? Many people tell me I have a doppelgänger."

He leaned in so close that she arched her back to look at him. It was unnerving. "Greer, I could never confuse you for anyone else. Never. Let's forget about today, all right? Better yet, let's forget we ever met."

She watched him storm off toward the revolving doors, then

hurried back to her office, where her team and everyone else were looking for her. How could a simple coffee break have turned into such a mess? She'd wanted to clear the air between her and Gun but now felt more puzzled than ever.

Gun bulldozed through the revolving doors for a quick getaway. He looked up and down the street for his truck before remembering he'd parked in the parking garage. Great. He was batting zero for two today. Instead of risking running into Greer, he walked around the corner to enter the garage from the street level. He had no desire to face that crazy woman again. Whoever coined the phrase "No good deed goes unpunished" had been on to something.

He should never have come here today. While he'd known he had to apologize at some point for his behavior on karaoke night, he hadn't been in any hurry. He had better things to do with his time. But his mom had grown impatient, and yesterday, she'd given him a manila envelope of documents to deliver to Greer. "Here, take this. Apologize to Lawyer Garza. *Pali, pali,*" she ordered.

It annoyed him that *he* would be the one apologizing to *Greer*. Talk about irony. But whatever. He could never win a fight with his mother, so he had to follow through, or he'd never hear the end of it.

He'd stepped out of the elevators, rehearsing the apology. It would be short and to the point, and he would accept responsibility for his recent behavior. That was it. He wasn't about to grovel. When he walked through the glass doors of Greer's fancy law firm—how fitting that she worked for a firm as pretentious as she—the office buzzed with activity. People came and went out of the individual offices, and the phones rang nonstop.

A young blond woman who wore too much makeup with a nameplate that said *Brittany* sat at the reception desk.

Her bright pink lips curved in a seductive smile. "Hello, how may I help you?"

Gun held up the manilla envelope. "I'm here to see Ms. Garza."

Brittany batted her false eyelashes. "I can take that from you and deliver it to her."

Gun shook his head. "Thank you, but I'd prefer to deliver it to her in person if that's okay."

Her smile faded. "In that case, you can take this hall to her office. Rita and the older women in that section can help you." Her voice had turned haughty.

Gun thanked her, concealing his amusement at her immaturity, then walked down the long hall he'd walked with his mother only a month ago. The lawyers who occupied the offices spoke louder than necessary, and he overheard bits and pieces of conversations. Why did lawyers think everyone was entitled to their opinion? He made it a point to avoid law firms as much as possible, but sometimes, it was unavoidable, like when he was forced to visit his father's firm.

He reached the circular station outside Greer's office, where a woman with short red hair, who introduced herself as Rita on his last visit, huddled in discussion with two other women.

"I tried to call and warn her about her ex-husband coming to the office this afternoon, but she left her phone in her office. Should I go down to the café and find her?"

Gun cleared his throat, and three pairs of startled eyes turned to look at him.

Rita quickly regained her composure. "Oh, hello. Aren't you Mrs. Donovan's son? How may I help you?"

"That's correct. How are you ladies doing?" He flashed his most charming smile. He could be the perfect Southern gentleman when the occasion called for it. "I'm acting as my mother's runner today and brought some documents for Ms. Garza. I couldn't help but overhear the last part of your conversation. Is Ms. Garza not in her office?"

Rita looked uneasy. "No, sir, she's not in now. She popped down to the café on the first floor a short time ago. She'll be sorry she missed you, but I'll give her the documents."

That wouldn't do. "Tell you what. I'm heading downstairs, so why don't I stop by the café and tell her you're looking for her?"

"That would be wonderful if it's not too much trouble."

"No trouble at all. I could use a cup of coffee right about now."

"Can you also tell her time is of the essence and she should use the back entrance?"

He handed Rita the documents and assured them he would find Greer.

As Gun stepped into the elevator, he wondered what kind of man Greer's ex was that had the women up in arms. Wasn't he also a lawyer? They were probably making a mountain out of a molehill. His mother excelled at that.

He shook his head, not believing he'd volunteered for this fool's errand. When would he ever learn? He'd seen the café on his way in today, but it was strange that he hadn't seen Greer. Their paths must have crossed in the elevators, like two ships in the night. He smirked. Of course, they were.

When he reached the crowded café, his height allowed him to look over everyone's head. He spotted Greer immediately. She stood by the counter, accepting a drink from a young Asian barista. Was she flirting with him? She began walking backward, not paying attention to her surroundings, and narrowly missed running into a guy engrossed with his cell phone.

Gun didn't see anyone who fit the ex's profile or looked like a potential threat. His job here was done, and he could walk away with a clear conscience. But as he turned to leave, a man called out Greer's name in a voice that rang throughout the café. His eyes flew back to Greer as she turned around, and her eyes looked . . . the first word that came to mind was *sorrowful*.

He should've turned and walked away. This was none of his business, but he couldn't ignore her struggling to put on a brave face. *Aish!* Seriously, that woman! Why did she always try to act so tough? His gut told him to get out of there before he did something he would regret. He told his gut to shove it and entered the game.

He knew he had to be a party of interest to intervene. He'd learned that much from years of listening to his father yammer on at the dinner table. So he hugged her, called an audible, and pretended to be her boyfriend. It was a risky move, but the look on Greer's face when he called her *baby* had been priceless.

Everything would've been fine—the loud-mouthed ex and the barista kid were no problem—but Greer's resentment surprised him. No wonder his instincts had warned him to run. So she didn't appreciate or need his help, did she? Fine. Ever since that meeting in her office, he'd known he should avoid her at all costs. He never apologized, but he didn't see the need now. She made it clear that she wanted him to butt out of her life, and that was fine by him. As far as he was concerned, they'd evened the score.

# Chapter Nine

On Friday at noon, Greer ordered her team to shut it down and go home to avoid the madness invading downtown. It was the start of spring break for the local schools and universities, not to mention the start of Austin's annual South by Southwest Film and Music Festival. The downtown area was already inundated with visitors from around the world, and many streets around their office would close for the various events.

Greer stayed behind to catch up on emails, and every few minutes, someone popped their head in the door to wish her a good weekend. The office grew quiet, and she gave up on the emails and leaned back in her chair. She turned toward the window and watched the venue tents set up along Congress Avenue. She wasn't in the mood to respond diplomatically to emails from opposing counsel. She wasn't in the mood to work. She wasn't in the mood to do *anything*.

Over the last few weeks, she felt her life had slipped out of her control, and she didn't like the feeling. She had worked hard to ensure that there were no surprises and no missteps. Running into Beau—the biggest, most embarrassing misstep in her life—

was a cruel reminder of a time she preferred to forget. A time when she had been in a free fall of despair. She had just learned of Jake's impending marriage—he had sent her a wedding invitation!—so she was on the rebound and would have dated anyone.

Initially, Beau was charming, not to mention handsome, and she could forget about Jake for a little while when she was with him. There were warning signs, of course, but everyone told her she expected too much, and that's why her relationships never lasted. Perhaps they were right. Beau was the only man who wanted her, whatever his reasons, and she wasn't getting any younger, so she ignored the storm warnings and pressed on. She had never been in love with him, but there had been plenty of heat between them. Besides, she knew plenty of people who married with stars in their eyes and ended up miserable and divorced.

Of course, things only got worse after they married, and she knew within the first six months that she'd made a grave mistake. Beau took pleasure in belittling her, and his verbal abuse was like a slow-drip torture. She attempted to get him to attend counseling with her, but he refused, just as he refused to acknowledge there was a problem. Finally, she knew she had to leave the marriage to keep her sanity. It shocked him when she moved out of their house and filed for divorce. No one divorced a Broussard.

After their divorce, she'd hoped never to see him again. Running into him at the café had been a shock. Running into him in front of Gun had been humiliating. She rubbed her forehead. Ugh. The café. She had put it off as long as she could. As much as she dreaded it, she had unfinished business with Jampa.

Jampa was sweeping the nearly empty café with his back to her when she entered. "Jampa," she called, for once not sure if he would be glad to see her.

He turned around, and she detected a moment's hesitation in his eyes before he smiled. "Hey, how's it going?" He rested the broom against a table and took his earbuds out so she might have surprised him.

"I'm good. How about you?"

"Good. Just cleaning up after the lunch rush." Again, another pause. Something had changed between them.

"I want to apologize for the other day, and I also want to thank you."

He looked puzzled. "What do you have to apologize or thank me for?"

Greer shrugged. "I want to apologize because of the incident between my ex-husband and the other guy. I'm sorry we caused a scene that escalated to the point you got involved."

His usually friendly face was stiff. "I still don't understand how that's your fault."

"I know I'm not responsible for my ex-husband's behavior or the other guy's. But it's my fault because I should have walked away. If I'd walked away, things wouldn't have gotten so heated. When the consequences of my actions result in potential harm to others, I'm liable for those actions." She paused and searched for the right words. "Jampa, if things had escalated further, you could have lost your job. I appreciate your coming to my defense, but I don't want you to jeopardize your livelihood or something worse."

He shook his head and folded his arms. "First, please don't talk to me like my lawyer. Second, just like you're not responsible for those two guys, you're not for me. So, there's no need to apologize. But I'd like to know something since you've brought it up. Are you worried about me only because you think you'll be liable if I lose my job?"

He took a step closer. "You come to the café once or twice a week? I've been working here for a year now, so how many times have we seen each other and, in that time, gotten to know one another? The other day, I wasn't acting like a random bystander or a Good Samaritan coming to a stranger's defense. But maybe it's just been one-sided."

His words surprised her and frightened her a little, too.

"What? Do you have no response to that? Has this all been in my imagination?"

The men her age might play games, but Jampa didn't mess around. This wasn't what she expected, and finding nowhere to hide, she said the first thing on her mind. "Jampa, I'm twenty years older than you!"

"Yeah, I know. How can I forget? You remind me of it at least once a week."

"But it's the truth! You're young and have your whole life ahead of you!"

"What does age have to do with anything? Who cares if you're twenty years older than me? I don't care, but obviously you do."

He took a deep breath when she didn't respond, and his tone softened. "Look, Greer, I'm not trying to be like your ex and that other jerk. By the way, who was that guy? But I'm not letting you apologize when you didn't do anything wrong. And please don't thank me for whatever you think I did. What good is a man if he can't come to a woman's defense, especially a woman he cares about?"

Jampa had called her out for not wearing any clothes. At least, that's what it felt like. She wanted to crawl under a rock.

"I don't want apologies or thanks. I like knowing you. Why is that so hard to accept?"

"What?" She heard his words, but they didn't make sense.

"Greer, people come in and out of here every day. They're in a hurry or have their noses buried in their phones, and that's fine. But you're not like that. You're different. You were nice to me even before you knew anything about me. You smile. You ask how I'm doing. You ask about my family. I'm surprised that a woman like you, a smart and successful lawyer, would take an interest in me. It makes me feel good that you notice me. So, whatever you think I did the other day, I was proud to do it. Don't diminish it or take it away from me."

Greer had a lump in her throat and considered running out of the café. While she was a fierce advocate for her clients—her burly construction clients told her she was scary—personal confrontation had never been her strong suit. But Jampa had been brave enough to put his feelings on the line so she could not take the coward's way out. She owed him a response.

*Don't think, Greer. Just tell him what's in your heart.* That was the problem, though. She had told her heart to hush and quiet down for so long that it had lost its voice and become mute. She took a deep breath and shuttered on the exhale.

"Jampa, I don't have the right words, and whatever I have to say will sound inadequate. You aren't wrong. What you feel is not one-sided. I, too, have been flattered that someone bright and handsome like you would notice me. Truthfully, it's been an enormous boost to my ego—something I've sorely needed. You might be in my shoes one day and know what I mean. Although I hope not. I hope that the light in your eyes never goes out.

"When people say life is hard, it's because it's true. And it doesn't always turn out the way you hoped or planned. Disappointment after disappointment leads to resignation until you think the safest thing to do—the *only* thing you can do—is keep your head down, mind your own business, and stay out of the line of fire. You trudge along day after day, convincing yourself that you're okay. And in a way, you are because you're not getting hurt or disappointed anymore.

"Then, one day, a kind young man notices you hiding in the shadows, and you can hardly believe it. That's not supposed to happen. After all, society has told us women of a certain age to get out of the way. Our days in the sun are over. But each time you see his smile, you can't help yourself. You start remembering glimpses of your former life when you felt appreciated just for being you, and little by little, you slowly lift your head again. You take a cautious step out of the shadows while telling yourself, 'Be careful, don't get your hopes up. It doesn't mean anything. He's probably like that with everyone.'"

She paused and smiled. "I've enjoyed getting to know you too. Seeing you is a bright spot in my day. I won't say I'm sorry—I say that a lot, don't I?—but I do regret if I led you on."

Jampa took a step closer, and she noticed there were tears in his eyes.

"How do you like me now? I don't seem so cool anymore, do I?" she said with a chuckle, wiping her tears.

He drew her into a comforting embrace. "No, I think you're cooler than ever."

Greer spent Saturday morning doing chores around the house and reflecting on her conversation with Jampa while she cleaned. She had never intended to reveal so much, but once she started speaking, she couldn't stop. She was surprised by the words coming out of her mouth, and she expected Jampa to feel uncomfortable with such a raw and honest confession. Instead, his gracious acceptance had been like a balm to her soul, and his hug was as comforting as her favorite sherpa throw.

Feeling optimistic for the first time in—well, forever—she shopped online for patio furniture. She picked out a dining table and chairs for six, three chaise lounges, four accent tables, and a bench. There was no sense in ordering patio furniture without cushions, so she bought those, too, in a turquoise and white stripe. It was enough furniture to host a party, and she might have been hoping for too much. Her finger lingered on the mouse, but she closed her eyes and clicked *Place Order Now*.

She accepted a last-minute dinner invitation from her friend Paula Robinson that evening. Paula was at loose ends while her husband played poker. Greer recounted to her the incident in the café with Beau but left out the part about Gun. She didn't know how to explain him and had trouble figuring him out herself. Paula's antennae would have sensed something "there" even though there wasn't.

"You're kidding me! That man has some nerve!" she said, letting out a few choice expletives. "I'm glad you divorced him when you did." Then she listened suspiciously as Greer told her about Jampa, conveniently leaving out her part in the conversation. Paula would be horrified.

She was right because Paula almost spit out her Fireball cocktail when Greer relayed Jampa's confession. "Wow, that guy is so full of it! I hope you told him you have no desire to be his Sugar Mama. That's the only reason these young guys hit on women our age. They think we'll support them."

Greer smiled half-heartedly but remained silent. Even friends with the best intentions had a way of bursting your bubble. She realized she was no longer twenty-five or a size six, but was it impossible that a younger man could be attracted to her? Paula was four years her senior and happily married for over thirty years. She had two grown daughters and was expecting her first grandchild. Although she didn't mean to be cruel, it was easy to be cavalier when your life was idyllic.

Greer's friends in long marriages had never experienced singleness in midlife. They didn't understand how a kind word was like a cold drink of water to a weary wanderer at this age.

$\sim$

As the week passed, the seeds of doubt Paula had planted began to germinate. Her small victory now felt hollow, and Greer wondered if Jampa had said what he did simply as his way of applying for the job of Cabana Boy. The last thing she wanted was to be manipulated. She was at the point of retreating to her safe, comfortable shell when Jason called.

He'd returned from a spring break ski trip with his kids and asked her to dinner on Friday. She was on the verge of declining, but he'd been kind and kept his word about calling. Besides, it was only dinner. He wasn't asking for a commitment, and she doubted he was the type to want more.

That night, Kevin and Sophie watched from their spot on the ottoman as Greer went back and forth from her closet to stand in front of her tri-fold mirror. She'd been thirty-two the last time she had a first date, and things had shifted since then. Wait, was it a date or just dinner? Whatever the case, it had been years since she'd been to a non-work dinner with a man.

She narrowed her selection to black slacks paired with a sweater or an understated black turtleneck dress. The sweater, although fashionable, had a sweetheart neckline that revealed some cleavage. Too much cleavage, and she didn't want Jason to misunderstand her intentions. She decided to play it safe and went with the dress. It wasn't very exciting, but black was slimming.

Kevin meowed to let her know someone was at the door right before Jason rang the doorbell. She hurried to let him in and had to pick up her jaw from the floor. Jason looked *a-may-zing*. Like her, he'd dressed in black with a V-neck sweater over a white pinstripe shirt and black slacks, but he wore it best. ZZ Top had been right about a sharp-dressed man. She should have worn the cleavage-baring sweater.

"Hello," he said, flashing his million-dollar grin. "Nice place you got here."

"Hi," she said breathlessly, hoping he couldn't hear her racing heart.

The grin spread. He knew he looked hot.

"Please, come in. I'd like you to meet my cats." That was one way to calm her heart and weed out a date.

He looked down at Kevin, who stared at him with his large yellow eyes. Sophie had scampered off to hide from this stranger.

"Hey there, big kitty," he said stiffly.

"Not a cat person?"

He gave a short laugh. "I have a dog but am not opposed to cats."

She considered his answer a nonresponsive admission that he didn't like cats. Good to know. Not everyone was perfect.

They didn't linger, and he escorted her outside to his white Porsche Cayenne. He opened and closed the passenger door for her, and once they were buckled in, the car roared down the hill on Barton Hills Drive toward downtown.

He took her to an Italian restaurant that opened two months ago but had already generated positive buzz on social media. It was modern and noisy. Most diners were young and hip, and the women were half-dressed. Greer looked down at her conservative little black dress. She didn't fit in with this chic crowd. Her dress was more suited for a guest appearance on *Little House on the Prairie*. She could play the role of Laura Ingalls Wilder's grandmother at her age.

Despite all the fashionable young women, Jason focused on her. Whenever she'd been out with Beau, his head swirled around at every woman in the room like an owl eyeing prey. Jason told her his backstory as they sipped on their wine. He'd lived and worked in Houston for twenty-five years as a petroleum engineer. Now that his kids were in college, he'd moved back to Austin a year ago to be closer to his parents. He continued working remotely for the Houston engineering firm and taught as an adjunct professor at UT.

They perused the menu, and there were so many delicious options that Greer wanted to try them all. Jason solved the problem by suggesting they order several dishes to share. What a relief that he was neither a fussy eater nor concerned about watching his weight. Going out to eat with someone with a bazillion dietary restrictions was never fun. She suspected he worked out, as he was in good shape for a man over fifty.

They exchanged abbreviated war stories about their divorces. He didn't have much to say about his ex-wife but talked plenty about his first love, a girl he met in college. He'd wanted to marry her, but the girl had left him to move to New York to further her career.

Greer buttered a piece of hot, fresh bread. "Now that you're divorced, have you ever considered looking her up?"

He shook his head. "That was another lifetime ago. I don't believe in lightning striking twice."

She wasn't so sure about that. That he brought her up in the first place counted for something, but Greer didn't press the matter. She had good instincts for reading people and sensed he preferred not to discuss it further. Whoever she was, Greer felt envious. It had always saddened her that no man carried *her* in his heart.

They worked their way through the appetizers, including some of the most delicious bruschetta and roasted meatballs she'd ever eaten. They then shared a savory pork chop and a mouth-watering homemade ravioli. While they ate, they swapped stories of growing up in Austin and found they had gone to many of the same places, such as the old Highland Mall and skating rinks. By the time they ordered dessert, Greer felt entirely at ease.

Their amicable conversation continued as they drove back

to her house, but she became uneasy when Jason walked her to the front door. She'd always found this part of the date awkward.

"Thank you, Jason. I had a great time tonight," she said, averting her eyes, hoping he didn't expect to come inside. Thanks to her young cousins and coworkers, she knew that courtship had become a relic from a bygone era, but she wasn't ready, nor was she willing, to skip that phase, even if it cost her another date.

But Jason didn't ask, lean against her door, or exhibit any other signs indicating he was waiting for her to ask him in. He smiled and sounded sincere when he said, "It was my pleasure, and we'll have to do it again soon." Then he placed his hands on her shoulders and leaned in for a kiss, and she squeezed her eyes shut. But they flew open in surprise when he kissed her on the forehead, not on her lips.

"That . . . that'd be great," she mumbled while fumbling for her keys.

He waited while she opened the door. "Good night, Greer."

Once inside, she leaned against the door and breathed a sigh of relief. She did it. She'd survived her first date without any embarrassing mishaps or unwelcome advances. But in addition to relief, she felt something else, a strange sensation she couldn't identify. She touched her forehead at the spot Jason had kissed her and realized it was warm. She touched her cheeks. Her entire face was warm. She'd been so worried that she hadn't thought about the possibility that she might enjoy the kiss.

# *Chapter Ten*

G reer woke up early on Saturday morning. She'd thought she wouldn't be able to sleep after her date with Jason, but she slept like a rock.

*My date with Jason.* She smiled as she waited for her coffee to brew in the kitchen. She felt proud of herself for wading into the dating pool again. Granted, she was standing on the first step in the kiddie pool with her hand gripping the rail, but at least she had gotten her feet wet. It was a start, and there was nothing to worry about. Jason was as kind and funny as the day they met and didn't exhibit any strange Jekyll-and-Hyde behavior like others she knew.

Feeling rejuvenated, she decided to unpack the boxes in her garage. She finished her coffee, munched on a slice of toast, and then got to work.

By four o'clock, she'd unpacked everything and made separate piles labeled *Keep* and *Give away*, but she was tired and hungry. She searched the refrigerator and pantry, but the meager provisions were uninspiring. She hadn't been to the grocery store in weeks. She hated cooking for one.

After jotting down a short grocery list, she grabbed her

purse and keys, scratched the kids' heads, and reassured them she'd return soon. The afternoon had become warm, but it would be cool again when she finished shopping, so she grabbed the funnel neck pullover she'd worn in the morning. It had a large floral print and wasn't the height of fashion, but she'd never seen anyone at the grocery store she cared to impress. She slipped the sweater over her white T-shirt and black leggings and headed out.

As expected on a beautiful spring afternoon, her local HEB was full of shoppers. She grabbed a cart, placed her purse in the child's seat, and pulled out her list. Then she shoved her sunglasses on top of her head and put on her readers. First stop, produce. She bagged fresh fruit, vegetables, and aromatics and hurried away. The aroma of fresh bread from the bakery next to produce caused her stomach to rumble. Once she moved safely away from the intoxicating scent, she took her time wandering through the aisles while still learning her way around the store. Before her move, she hadn't shopped at this store and missed the HEB in her old neighborhood.

An Easter display between the meat and dairy sections caught her eye, offering a collection of cake mixes, cupcake liners, and other decorative supplies. She pushed her cart closer to take a better look. It would be nice to bake an Easter cake for her parents and cupcakes for her work team. She reached for a package of yellow cupcake liners decorated with pastel Easter eggs and studied it while contemplating the odds she would take the time to bake. She sighed. The odds favored the cake mix and liners sitting in her pantry until she threw them out next Easter.

She attempted to return the liners to the shelf, but they were packed too tightly and didn't fit. Good grief, she'd pulled the package less than sixty seconds ago. She tried rearranging them, but they tumbled in an endless cascade to the ground.

Why did these things always happen to her?

She squatted to retrieve the packages on the floor while shoppers walked all around her. Several gave her strange looks, but no one stopped to help. She was gathering the packages in the crook of her arm when she heard distinct footsteps. A pair of worn cowboy boots and faded jeans appeared in her line of vision near the floor.

Before she could look up, a deep, familiar voice said, "Hey there, Gidget. Need a hand? Or would you prefer I walk on by?"

*Gidget!* Only *he* would think of calling her that. And, of course, he would be the one to appear in the middle of yet another embarrassing moment. He was like a bad penny.

Without waiting for her answer, Gun began picking up the wayward packages, some of which had rolled over by the eggs. Holding several of them, he returned and nodded at the display stand. "Is this where they go?"

She nodded, and he arranged them back on the display. Considering his quick temper, he performed the task with patient deliberation. She wouldn't have been so patient. As she studied his hands while he worked, her recollection of them holding her in the airport rushed back. He seemed so different then. The warmth of the memory cooled her anger, and she said the first thing on her mind. "Were you able to solve the Rubik's Cube?"

Gun cast her a look. "Yeah, as a matter of fact, I could. What made you think of that?"

"You appear to be mechanically inclined."

"Well, I am an engineer." He finished his work, faced her, and stuffed his hands in his pockets. An awkward silence ensued. Absent a shared task or something to argue about, they had nothing to say to each other.

"Well, thanks for your help, *Moondoggie*," she said to break the silence.

"Moondoggie?"

"Didn't you call me Gidget? I thought perhaps you were into using aliases now."

He looked disconcerted, which she found curious. Even more curious was that he didn't respond with the expected gibe. Instead, he scratched the back of his head and avoided her gaze.

"What are you doing here?" she blurted out, then winced. Even to her ears, she sounded rude.

Gun glanced at his grocery cart, then back at her. "Buy-ing gro-cer-ies." He enunciated each syllable as if speaking to someone with poor cognitive skills.

"Duh. I can see that. What I meant was, why are you at this store? Do you live around here?"

"Yes."

Okay, so much for sharing. She should leave. This was going nowhere. She'd just set her hand on her cart's handle when he gave her the once-over.

"What's with the outfit? Is this what all the fashionable *ahjummas* are wearing this spring?"

What? "What are you talking about? And who are you calling an *ahjumma*?"

In two long strides, Gun stood in her personal space. He reached for the sunglasses still on her head. She tried to swat his hand away, but he towered over her, and her small hand was no match for his. She might as well have been trying to swat at a water buffalo.

"*You*, you're the *ahjumma*. What's with wearing sunglasses and readers at the same time? Is this a new look?"

If Greer had been a cat, she would have arched her back and hissed at him. So, he considered her an *ahjumma*? He knew she was acquainted with the word's meaning, used out of respect for a woman of a certain age, like the English equivalent of *ma'am*. But it could also be a derogatory term to describe a frumpy, middle-aged woman. *Ahjummas* had tight perms and dressed in gaudy floral prints paired with plaid.

As if he was one to talk. She curled her lip and gave *him* the once-over. He wore a wrinkled white button-down shirt that he hadn't bothered to tuck in. The shirt sleeves were rolled up and exposed his muscular forearms. His jeans had seen better days but made his long legs look longer. And he had a day-old beard and slightly disheveled hair. Either he could apply hair gel with the expert skill of a hairdresser, or he'd just rolled out of bed. On second thought, the look worked for him. He looked sexy. But she couldn't let him know that.

"And you? Who are you supposed to be? The Kimchi Cowboy?" She lifted her chin in triumph. She loved it when a snarky comeback came to her at the right moment. Usually, she couldn't think of an appropriate insult until it was too late.

His lips twitched ever so slightly, but he didn't retaliate. Before either of them could get in another jab, her stomach rumbled, and she placed her hand over it.

"Hungry?"

"No, I'm fine."

But her treacherous stomach rumbled again.

"Well, I'm hungry, and there's a great little Mexican food place near here. Would you like to join me?"

*Join him?* Had he forgotten about all their disastrous encounters? Their mutual agreement to stay away? Didn't he dislike her?

In addition to his engineering talents, he could read minds. "What do you say we call a truce? Just for today."

She still hesitated.

"Come on, the people of the Korean Peninsula have been living under a truce for over sixty years. If they can do it, you and I can put our differences aside for one hour while we eat.

Wouldn't chips, queso, and a Mexican martini hit the spot right now?"

He had her at chips and queso. The Mexican martini was the cherry on top. She'd always been easy when it came to food.

They agreed to finish their shopping and meet up front in fifteen minutes. Gun loaded her groceries in the back of her Lexus SUV, followed her home, then took her bags to the door and commented that he liked her house.

She asked him to wait outside. Though proud of her home, she hadn't finished putting everything away and didn't want him to see it when it didn't look its best. She fed the kids, turned on the lights and television to keep them company, and rushed outside.

Gun got out of his dark gray Toyota Tacoma and came around to open the door for her. They traveled two minutes south from her house on Barton Hills Drive until he turned left onto Wilke Street and drove up the hill. Though only minutes from her house, this part of the neighborhood belonged to a different subdivision. The homes were older and had abundant trees, giving the area a hidden woodland feel. She'd loved riding her bike through these streets as a kid. It reminded her so much of something out of a fairy tale that she'd even hoped to come across a woodcutter's cottage.

They took a left onto his street, and she knew his house immediately. It was Korean-inspired. Other than in magazines and on the internet, she'd never seen anything like it. "Oh my goodness! What an amazing house! You built it, right?"

He smiled. "Yes. My uncle helped me design it, and I built it with a local contractor."

He parked on the steep driveway, came around, and helped her out of the truck. She grabbed two grocery bags from the back and gazed in awe at the house, a mix of modern and historic Korean architecture. Dark granite steps fanned from the curb to the long porch and double wood doors. Gray slate tiles covered the roof, and deep eves curved at the ends. It looked like a Japanese pagoda, but Gun informed her that its style was *hanok* because the house was Korean. It could've easily been a stop on the parade of homes, but despite its grandeur, it felt serene. She would never have imagined Gun to have created such a peaceful-looking retreat. Every time they met, they were at war.

The sunny afternoon had turned into a cloudy evening and began to sprinkle. Gun gently touched her back and escorted her up the steps to the house. A handsome golden retriever stared at them from a window to the side of the double doors.

"I didn't know you owned a dog!" she exclaimed.

He beamed like a proud father. "That's Buddy. Come in and meet him and Bullet."

Buddy barked as they entered the house, and Gun introduced him to Greer. She presented her fist, and Buddy raised his paw for her handshake. Gun then directed her to another window where a gray cat slept on a cat perch.

"This is Bullet," he said, rubbing the sleeping cat's head.

Bullet lifted his head and opened one eye. He stared at Greer, flicked his tail, and laid his head down to continue his power nap.

She chuckled. At least he hadn't completely ignored her.

Gun invited her to look around while he put away the groceries, and she was happy to oblige. While the outside of the house nodded to tradition, the inside was modern-industrial.

"Did you decorate the house yourself?" she asked.

He shook his head. "No, Sarah did. I'm sure my mom has told you she gave up practicing law and became an interior decorator. She pointed out options and asked me what I liked."

Greer started by inspecting the kitchen, which was equipped with the latest appliances and worthy of a professional chef. A gas stove with six burners and a stainless-steel hood hung above it. The state-of-the-art dishwasher had more controls than a rocket ship, and the glass-paneled refrigerator looked like the kind in restaurants. Espresso-colored cabinets, a brick backsplash, and pendant lighting warmed the area above the island with its double sink and more workspace.

Between the kitchen and living area, a modern geometric chandelier hung above a wood and metal dining table with enough seating for eight. Two leather sofas faced each other in the living room, with accent tables and chairs at the end. Sarah had used an area rug in bold primary colors to anchor the entire space. While decorated to suit a man's taste, the house could easily hold a large party, even a large family.

She finally turned her attention to the one vintage piece in a sea of modernity: an old-fashioned piano with an ornate music holder. She'd seen it when she first walked in but saved it for last. Although aged, it had been well cared for, and its cherry-wood gleamed.

Several pictures of Gun's family adorned the top of the piano. One was a picture of a young couple who had to be Mrs. D and a man Greer presumed to be his father. Mrs. D, with her long, flowing hair, had been movie-star gorgeous, and Gun's father had been quite handsome, like a blond Chris Hemsworth. No wonder they had produced three beautiful children. However, the most conspicuous picture was a colorized photo of a young woman whose blond hair had a deep part in a style reminiscent of old Hollywood. She wore a short string of pearls around her neck and smiled demurely at the photographer.

"She looks like Sarah," she said, pointing at the picture.

Gun came to stand beside her and smiled. "Sarah and Luke favor my dad's family. That's my nanny. This piano belonged to her. She left it to me when she died."

"I can see you loved her very much. Do you mind if I ask why she left the piano to you?"

"She lived in Northeast Texas, near Tyler. That's where my dad is from. I would sit with her at this piano when I wasn't running through the Piney Woods with my cousins when we visited. Nanny had ten grandchildren, and I looked the least like a Donovan, but she never treated me differently than she treated Luke, Sarah, or my cousins." He smiled. "I like to think that I was her favorite."

Without thinking, she touched his arm. "What a blessing to have this special memento of your time with her."

"Yeah, the time we spent at Nanny's are some of my favorite childhood memories. I inherited my love of music from her. She played the piano at her church."

"So you must play, right? Can you play something for me?"

He hesitated but then motioned for her to step back while he pulled out the piano bench. He folded the keyboard lid and invited her to sit beside him. Their bodies were so close that she hung her right leg to the side.

Gun's hands hovered over the keyboard, then played a gentle, ethereal tune. Although pretty, she was unfamiliar with it.

"It's 'Clair de Lune' by Debussy," he said, reading her mind again.

Ah, "Moonlight." No wonder. His nanny had taught him well, for he had good form and captured the magical essence of the piece. She watched his long fingers caress the keys and effortlessly hit the chords, something she'd had difficulty doing with her tiny hands during her years of piano lessons.

She was so immersed in his performance that she gasped when he segued to Elton John's "Your Song." Elton John was one of her favorite artists. She hummed along, careful not to drown out the music. The song always took her back to her childhood when she would lie on the grass with her transistor radio by her side in the summertime, looking up at the sky and daydreaming about her future.

She became lost in her memories, and her body gravitated toward Gun. He hit a wrong note but recovered and kept playing.

She clapped when he finished. "That was wonderful! Is there anything you can't do?"

His face turned red. Hmm. Could it be that this hunky man with an acerbic tongue, who drove a motorcycle and impersonated Axl Rose, was shy? "Thank you," he said, turning and placing his hand behind her on the piano bench. Their faces were only inches apart.

She flexed her fingers, fighting an ache to place her hand on his cheek and feel the warmth of his skin underneath her palm. He inched closer, and she could feel his breath on her skin. Her heart began to beat faster. She couldn't decipher the look in his eyes, but if she were writing a romance novel, she would describe them as dark pools of desire. Despite his previous asinine behavior, she wanted him to kiss her. Any man who loved animals and his grandmother and played Elton John couldn't be half bad. She would think about the repercussions later.

"Greer," he said in a low, husky voice.

"Yes?" She closed her eyes, waiting for his kiss.

Then, right on cue, her stomach rumbled, and her eyes flew open. She hoped Gun hadn't heard it.

But he had. The romantic look in his eyes was gone. "I forgot you're hungry. Should we get something to eat?"

"What?"

Her stomach rumbled again, and she jumped off the piano bench. She waited for Gun's inevitable caustic comment, but he gave her a thoughtful look and didn't appear disappointed that her hunger pangs hijacked their romantic moment.

Gun was right about the restaurant. El Gallito was tucked into a hidden corner of Ben White and Manchaca, a mere ten minutes from their neighborhood. She must've passed it hundreds of times without noticing it. They got the last spot in the minuscule parking lot, and Gun came around to her side and helped her down. "Watch your step," he cautioned.

When they stepped inside, the delicious aromas of onion, garlic, peppers, and cumin greeted them, causing Greer's gastric rumblings to shift to hyperdrive.

A young woman wearing an apron came out from the direction of the kitchen and greeted them. "*Hola, Señor* Gun. *Cómo estás?*"

"*Hola*, Jessica. *Muy bien, muy bien, gracias. Y tu, como estas usted?*"

Greer stared at him in wonder. The man was full of surprises.

"I see you brought your girlfriend," Jessica said, switching to English. She had a warm, pretty smile.

"Yes, I did, and she's starving."

Greer opened her mouth to correct the record but caught his eye and decided to go with it. "I didn't know you spoke Spanish," she said instead.

"Of course. Don't you?"

They slipped into a booth, and Greer confessed she understood more than she spoke. "How did you learn?"

"From Juanita and Pedro."

"Who are they?"

He hesitated. "I don't know how much my mom has told you about our family, but it's a story better told over a drink."

Jessica brought chips and salsa to their table and took their drink order.

Gun ordered a large bowl of queso and said, "Can you bring it out quick? She's vicious when she's hangry." He winked at Greer as he said it, and she rolled her eyes.

The drinks arrived in minutes. Jessica poured the Mexican martini from a shaker into a martini glass, and Greer took a cautious sip. It was iced-cold perfection. "Ahhh," she said and smacked her lips.

Too late, she remembered she was not alone. She peeped at Gun, and sure enough, he was watching her.

"It's that good, huh?"

They laughed, and he clinked his beer bottle with her martini glass. "*Salud*," he said.

Thank goodness the queso arrived soon afterward. She dug in without embarrassment, for once not concerned about Gun. He was hungry, too, judging by how he did his best to keep up with her. Their knuckles bumped as they dipped the warm, crispy tortilla chips into the silky, flavorful cheese filled with onions and jalapeños. Neither one of them spoke again until they had consumed several mouthfuls.

Gun ordered another round of drinks and then began sharing his family history. She knew part of his backstory from his mom but refrained from saying so. She wanted to hear *his* story. He told her that his dad was a founding partner in a successful Dallas firm, and he had grown up in Highland Park, adding, "You went to SMU, so you're familiar with the area."

He then told her about Juanita and Pedro, the couple who had worked for his parents. They taught him and his siblings Spanish and were like a second set of parents. He kept in touch with them, but he still missed Juanita's cooking.

"What was your favorite of all the food she cooked?" Greer asked.

"Let's see." Gun thought for a moment. "It would be a tie between her enchiladas and menudo."

"Menudo?" Greer couldn't believe it. "*I* don't care for menudo, but *you* like it?"

"Hmm. I didn't realize you were into racial profiling," he teased. "Yes, I love menudo. I'm a Texan, so it's part of my birthright, but many Koreans also like it. It's spicy and has tripe and pig's feet, all things Koreans like to eat."

"Huh. I hadn't thought about it before, but you're right. The more I learn about Korean culture, the more similarities I find with Hispanic culture. Including a love of spicy food."

He smiled. "See there, *señorita*, we have more in common than you realize."

Greer grinned, pleased with this turn of events. Earlier, he had called her an *ahjumma*, but now she was a *señorita*. Maybe it was the beer or the queso responsible for the change in his attitude. A good bowl of queso did have the power to bring people together.

"What was it like? Growing up in that neighborhood?" she asked. "During law school, my friends and I would take a break from studying and drive through the neighborhood. It was like another world to us. We loved looking at the enormous, mansion-like houses, especially at Christmas. The decorations were incredible."

"Well, I'm not going to lie. It was great. We had a privileged upbringing and never wanted for anything, but our family was far from perfect. Luke, Sarah, and I used to joke that D doesn't just stand for Donovan. It also stands for dysfunctional."

They had demolished the queso, so they ordered more food. Menudo for Gun, and Caldo de Res, a rustic beef and vegetable soup, for Greer. When their soups arrived, along with a holder full of fresh, hot corn tortillas, they sighed.

"So, the night at karaoke," she ventured. "I was surprised to learn you all speak Korean with such fluency. I even heard Darcy speaking it at the airport. My parents didn't insist I learn Spanish. My mom thought it would put me at a disadvantage in school. Did your mom make the three of you speak Korean?"

Gun bit into a rolled-up corn tortilla and chewed before answering. "Darcy's Korean is terrible. She wants to work overseas, so we're making her practice. As for my siblings, we hardly saw our father when we were young. First, he attended college, then law school, and later, he worked long hours as a young lawyer. I remember seeing him twice each day—early morning and late at night. He would wave goodbye to us at the breakfast table, and at night, he would come into our room to say goodnight. It didn't matter how late or if we were sleeping, he'd wake us up anyway. We had these old bunk beds, and Luke got the top bunk. My dad would step on the lower bunk where I slept to get to Luke, and the wood would creak under his weight."

He imitated the creaking sound of the bunk beds before pausing with a faraway look in his eyes. "Wow, I'd forgotten all about that. In answer to your question, our mother was our primary influence during our formative years. In those days, she'd only been in the States for a few years and had limited knowledge of English. She spoke to us in Korean and raised us according to Korean customs. Boys call their older brothers *hyung*, and girls call their older brothers *oppa*."

She smiled. "I think it's awesome. I like hearing it."

He laughed. "Well, of course *you* like it. You like anything that feeds your K-drama fantasies."

She blushed, embarrassed that he had figured her out, but there was no point denying it.

They spent the rest of the evening talking about whatever

popped into their heads. She liked the way he kept eye contact with her when she spoke. He did not appear bored or fidgety or dominate the conversation. She enjoyed hearing his laugh and how he threw his head back with laughter. At one point, she realized her elbows were on the table, her face in her hands, and she openly mooned over him. That wasn't a good look, so she sat back against the booth and absorbed everything about him, content to be in his orbit. He enthralled her. Yet, unlike when they first met, she didn't feel intimidated. Tonight, he seemed familiar. This setting seemed familiar, too, and she shuddered with a sense of déjà vu.

Jessica came to refill their water glasses, and Greer complimented her on the music selection coming from the jukebox.

Jessica shrugged. "My parents are the same age as you. They like this old music."

They chuckled, as they hadn't realized the music of their youth was now considered "oldies." Gun encouraged Greer to choose a few songs and handed her a five-dollar bill.

They finished eating but lingered long enough to listen to her selections. First, there was Journey's "Lights" and Bryan Adams's "One Night Love Affair." Then the Simple Minds hit "Don't You (Forget About Me)."

"Ironic choice," Gun commented without explanation.

Next, they sang along to Tears For Fears' "Everybody Wants to Rule the World" and moved their heads like two bobblehead dolls. Gun grabbed her hand during the line in the bridge about holding hands, and although it took her by surprise, it felt natural.

When Night Ranger's "Sentimental Street" began to play, he stepped out of the booth. "May I have this dance?" he asked, offering his hand.

She placed her hand in his and practically jumped out of the booth. He took her in his arms, and they began to dance in the almost empty restaurant. Never one for public displays of affection, for once, she wouldn't have cared if it was a packed house. She'd have danced with him on the fifty-yard line at halftime.

He held her with a gentle strength that felt safe yet exhilarating. She buried her nose in his shirt and took a deep breath. She wanted to remember his scent and everything about him. The warmth of his skin was intoxicating. She contemplated tracing his collarbone with her finger when he twirled her around several times, then took her back in his arms. She placed her head on his chest, wanting this night, this moment, to last forever. He dipped her as the song ended, and when she looked up at his face, the dark pools of desire had returned.

They left after their dance, and there was no awkwardness or lack of conversation during the short drive to her house.

She looked at the night sky as he helped her out of the truck. "Did you notice there's a full moon tonight? Isn't that a funny coincidence?"

He didn't look at the moon but stepped closer, blocking her escape. "But not ill met, proud Titania."

"Huh?" He stood so close she had trouble thinking. And breathing. "Oh, right. Shakespeare. Do you see me as a fairy queen?" she asked sincerely, meeting his gaze. The look in his eyes told her he was about to kiss her, and she caught her breath. She suddenly couldn't decide whether she wanted him to.

As he often did, he studied her face without saying anything, but then he took a deep breath and stood back for her to pass. "Enough partying for tonight, fairy queen. Come on, I'll walk you to your door. Please go inside and make sure everything's okay."

She did as he said, then joined him back on the front porch. "Thank you, Gun. I'm glad you called for a truce because I had a wonderful evening."

"No, Greer, I should be the one thanking you."

He insisted she go inside and lock the door before he left. From her front door, she watched him walk to his truck, and as he waved goodbye, she heard him say, "Good night."

After he drove away, she pumped her fists in the air. "Yes! Yes! Yes!" she shouted, scaring Kevin and Sophie, who had slinked into the foyer to welcome her home. "Sorry, my babies," she called to their scampering backsides, then danced to the kitchen, shaking her hips. "I'm bad, I know it. I got the moves to show it."

She couldn't have imagined a more perfect night. Hopefully, it would be the start of many more.

# Chapter Eleven

Kevin patted Greer's cheek with his paw to wake her. She squeezed her eyes, determined to keep them closed, rolled to the other side, and smiled into her pillow. She didn't want to wake up. She dreamed the most wonderful dream—that she met her ideal man—and wished to remain in this blissful state. Kevin jumped over her shoulder and patted her other cheek. Then he meowed loudly.

She opened her eyes and stared into Kevin's face, only inches from hers. She glanced toward her feet, where Sophie glared at her, too. The poor little things were hungry, but she didn't want to get out of bed. She wanted to go back to sleep and keep dreaming. Then, as her mind cleared, she pulled her bangs down to her nose and inhaled. A faint smell of Gun's cologne lingered in her hair. So, it hadn't been a dream after all. It had happened. She'd spent an incredible evening with Gun Donovan.

She stretched within her soft, floral sheets and looked toward the large window. It had rained all night, but the sun shone this morning. What a perfect metaphor to describe her life at this moment.

She'd always romanticized a man based on his looks, but never had he lived up to the fantasy. Last night, however, she learned there was more to Gun than his handsome face. He was funny, charming, intelligent, and, as it turned out, a Renaissance man. She couldn't believe he'd designed and built his house, although being a successful engineer, it made sense. But a musician, too? What other hidden talents did he have? She hoped for the opportunity to find out. And then there was his amazing smile . . .

She closed her eyes and pictured it with an involuntary smile. "And he loves four-legged babies!" she gushed to Kevin and Sophie.

Kevin meowed and licked his chops, unimpressed. He jumped off the bed and headed toward the kitchen, his tail high up in the air. *Tell me over breakfast*, his body language implied.

Greer sat up and cuddled Sophie, then scratched her chin. "Isn't that just like a man? Ordering us women to the kitchen?"

That afternoon, Greer picked up Italian takeout and visited her parents' condo for lunch. As usual, except for the occasional nod and "Oh, really," she remained silent while her mother chattered away.

Her mother did manage to pause for a breath and ask about Kevin and Sophie—her "grandcats," as she called them. But before Greer could answer, she launched into another monologue of excruciating detail about a phone call with one of Greer's aunts. Although Greer was used to not getting a word in, today, she was anxious to tell about her dates with Jason and Gun.

However, she had to get the timing right because her father watched NASCAR in the other room. As a Vietnam veteran, he held strong opinions, and she didn't want him asking questions —not yet. Even though he wasn't at the table, he was listening to their conversation because he kept popping in and out of the room, interjecting his opinions like a Greek chorus. Her mother didn't appreciate his unsolicited comments and cast him a menacing look, not wanting him to interrupt her show.

Greer reached for the cheesecake while her mother prattled on. Before returning to the other room, her dad casually asked about her work and whether she had any issues at her new house. She knew he was really asking about the pool, just waiting for the right moment to say, "I told you so." She took a bite of cheesecake and decided it might not be a good time to talk about her dates.

On her way home, Greer rolled down the driver's window and opened the sunroof. Her hair blew behind her as she drove across the Congress Avenue Bridge, and she stuck her left arm out the window, feeling the warm breeze against her skin. Even her parents' indifference couldn't spoil her good mood today. She found the song she sought on her playlist and cranked up the car stereo. She sang along to Whitney Houston's "I Wanna Dance with Somebody" while tapping the beat on the steering wheel, unconcerned about the strange looks she received from other drivers.

She was bursting at the seams to share her good news but had no one to share it with.

When Gun's mother, his aunt Hee-ja, and Jason and his family sat down to lunch after church, the conversation was typical of their generation. First, they critiqued the pastor's sermon. Then, they discussed Mrs. Han's hip replacement surgery. Finally, they spent several minutes discussing the sale of short ribs at the local Korean market. Aunt Hee-ja announced that the ribs were on sale for such a reasonable price that she had bought more than she needed and would share them with the Lees.

On the other side of the table, Jason had just swallowed a spoonful of Tofu stew when Justin met his gaze. "So, *Hyung*, how'd your date go Friday night?" he asked quietly. "Are you going to see her again?"

All three elders rested their chopsticks on the table and looked at Justin. "What you mean, date? Who you date?" Mrs. Lee asked.

Justin's eyes widened. "Jason went out with Greer on Friday night," he blurted out, the same way he'd done forty years ago when their mom asked whose baseball broke the living room window. He'd never been able to take the heat.

"So, you and Greer go out on a date?" Jason's dad asked.

He nodded. "Yes, we went to dinner Friday night."

He grinned. "Good for you. Greer is a pretty girl and a nice girl, too. You young people should go out and have fun."

Jason smiled back. "Thanks, Dad. I feel the same and hope to see her again."

Despite ratting him out, Justin also wished him well, and Hannah told him she liked Greer and hoped this meant they would see her more often.

Jason glanced at his mother and aunt Hee-ja. His mom smiled, but he knew it wasn't genuine, and his *imo's* impassive face didn't fool him. It concealed seething anger. He found their reactions surprising and unexpected. His mom had always regretted that his first wife was not a Korean girl, but she eventually came around, especially when his daughter, his mom's first grandchild, was born. So, was that why she was upset now? Was she still hoping the next woman in his life would be Korean? That was a possibility. But why had the news angered his *imo*? Other than Greer being her lawyer, their dating didn't affect her.

He sat back in his chair as it suddenly dawned on him. Ohh . . . of course. She wanted Greer for Gun. He chuckled inwardly. Aunt Hee-ja should have known better than to reveal her hand. Things were about to get very interesting . . .

His mother was in the kitchen when Gun let himself into her house Monday afternoon. She'd demanded he come over because she had something for him to give to her brother in Korea, and he wanted to pick it up and get home so he could finish his travel preparations.

"Why you not tell me Jason and Lawyer Garza are dating?" she asked as soon as he walked through the doorway. "They go on a date Friday night."

Blindsided, Gun assumed his best poker face. Greer failed to mention she had gone out with Jason—not that she had a duty to tell him—but he couldn't think about that now. His mom, like a shark that smelled blood in the water, would eat him alive if he showed that this news affected him. His only hope of getting out of there alive was to deploy a countermeasure of indifference. "What does this have to do with me?" he asked. "Why are you telling me this, Mom? Are you just in the mood for a good gossip?"

She exploded and slapped the back of his head. "Wake up, my son! Why you not concerned? If you not do something, Greer will end up with Jason!"

He shrugged. "If what you tell me is true, it sounds like they're already together. I know you were trying to play match-maker the day you took me to her office, but you know how that turned out. Some things aren't meant to be."

"If not meant to be, then why did you and Lawyer Garza meet in first place? Of *all* the people in Austin, you meet Lawyer Garza, *my* lawyer. You cannot tell me this is mere coincidence. It must be fate."

Gun sighed. "Mom, would you listen to yourself? Don't you go to church? Please don't give me any of this Korean mysticism business. There is no such thing as fate or destiny. That's romantic nonsense used in the dramas as a ratings ploy."

"I go to church, and the Bible say finding a wife is a good thing. Gun-ah, don't you want to be happy? Don't you want a happy home?"

"I *am* happy. I don't need a wife to be happy."

"*Aigoo*, listen to you, speaking with such confidence. Even the moon wanes when it is full. Do you think a cat and dog will help you in your old age? Look at your brother and sister. They have families, but who you have, huh? You only think you don't need wife because your first wife was nine-tailed fox. Not every woman is like that wench. Lawyer Garza is good girl with a soft heart. Give her a chance. You'll see."

He stepped back to avoid another head slap. "Mom, it's not going to happen. You know, *fate*, as you call it, is a two-edged sword. Sometimes, people are ill-fated, and our case is a perfect example. Believe me when I tell you, Greer and I will *never* be together."

His mom snorted. "We'll see, my son, we'll see. Never say never."

As he drove home, Gun scolded himself for not seeing through her ruse. Didn't he know her better by now? Questions taunted him. Were Jason and Greer dating? Although his mom was a nosy busybody, she generally had reliable intel, even though her generation's idea of dating often differed from his. Just because Jason and Greer had gone to dinner, it didn't mean they were dating. He should know. *He* had also been to dinner with Greer.

He went over their time together, and Greer had never mentioned Jason to the best of his recollection. Nothing about her behavior indicated that she was seeing someone, and she didn't strike him as the kind of woman who played the field. The kid in the café came to mind, and Gun sucked a breath through his teeth. She had been pretty darn protective of him, and he of her. What was his name? Jumpy? Jumanji? Something weird like that. Nah, whatever his name, Greer was not seeing that kid. But was she seeing *Jason*?

At home, Gun went to his office to prepare for his trip to Korea. He'd purchased an apartment in Seoul years ago, and a complete wardrobe and anything else he might need were waiting for him there, so he didn't have much to pack apart from his laptop and a Dopp kit. Even Buddy and Bullet's care was on cruise control. Luke's son, Dylan, was the boys' caretaker. Darcy had the job before, but Dylan took over when he moved to Austin last August to attend UT.

Buddy's bark shook Gun from his stupor, and the front door opened.

"It's me, Uncle Gun," Dylan called. He greeted Buddy and Bullet, and the three ran upstairs to the game room. Together, they sounded like wild horses galloping up the stairs.

Gun chuckled, glad for the distraction.

He had been rounding the corner of the cereal aisle when he spotted Greer kneeling on the grocery store floor. Mindful of their last disastrous meeting, he knew he should mind his business and keep moving, but he couldn't leave her in that predicament. And for once, it had turned out to be the right call. He couldn't remember when he'd had a better night and couldn't get that picture of Greer bathed in the moonlight out of his head. *Do you see me as a fairy queen?* she had asked innocently, unaware of the implications of her words. At that moment, she was too pretty and irresistible not to kiss, but the hesitation in her eyes made him pull back. That was the second time his kiss had been thwarted that night. It had frustrated him, but in hindsight, it was for the best. He had to man up and tell Greer the truth before he made any romantic advances.

Unable to get her off his mind and hoping for another shot at that kiss, he'd been whistling "Sentimental Street" like a fool over the last two days. He had planned to call Greer before his flight to Korea and make tentative plans after his return. But now he reconsidered. He didn't believe she and Jason were dating, but Jason had never been able to resist a challenge. Now that he had taken Greer out, Gun doubted he would give her up without a fight, especially if Gun were the one challenging him for her affections. He wasn't afraid of Jason, but he was uncertain his heart was up for the battle. Although he'd faced a different opponent, he'd been down this path before, another lifetime ago, and had never forgotten the beating he'd suffered.

Was he prepared to put everything on the line again at this age? Gun couldn't answer that question. If he believed in fate at all, as he had told his mother, he believed people were ill-fated. Star-crossed. Only time would tell.

He found the file he'd been searching for and went upstairs to join Dylan and the boys.

# Chapter Twelve

**B**luebonnets blanketed the highway medians. Cars parked along the shoulder, and families climbed the hill and took pictures of their children among the fields of the state flower. A young couple took a picture of their toddler wearing a yellow bow as big as her head. The little girl laughed, and the mother clapped with delight while the father snapped the picture on his phone.

Jason squeezed Greer's hand, and she turned from her reverie.

"Are you okay?"

She smiled. "Yes, just looking at the young families enjoying spring."

They were on their way to dinner, their fourth date in as many weeks. Though still unconvinced that the dating scene was for her, Greer had decided to give it another go. Her two loves in life had been her high school boyfriend, Jeff, and then, of course, Jake. She had always superstitiously believed the third "J" would be the charm. Maybe that man was Jason. It might not be love, but she liked him. He was a mature grown-up who didn't play passive-aggressive games, and he made her laugh. That counted for something.

They drove north on I-35 through downtown Austin, and Jason's phone rang as he took the 6th–12th Street exit. He said a mild curse word and answered the call in Korean on the car's Bluetooth. The caller's loud voice permeated the cabin, and she sounded upset. Whatever she said made his forehead crease and his brows draw together. He hung up and made another call, and this time, Greer recognized the voice on the other end, even though they spoke in Korean. It belonged to Mrs. D, and Greer began to worry.

"Gun's been in a motorcycle accident," Jason said after hanging up. "I'm sorry, we'll have to postpone dinner. I'm picking up my aunt because she's too upset to drive to the hospital."

He didn't wait for a response, which was good because Greer's heart was suddenly in her throat. He took a right on Neches Street and another onto 7th Street to head back to the highway. Once on I-35, they headed north to the historic Hyde Park neighborhood, just north of the University of Texas.

When they arrived at Mrs. D's charming bungalow, Jason went to the front door while Greer waited in the car. Although Mrs. D had been her client for several years, there'd never been an occasion to visit her home. From what she could discern in the deepening dusk, the house, with its immaculate lawn and tidy flowerbeds, had Mrs. D's stamp all over it.

When they finally emerged from the house, Mrs. D had been crying. Greer's heart went out to the poor woman, so she offered to give up her seat in the front, but Mrs. D insisted on sitting in the back. From there, she and Jason carried on a steady flow of conversation in Korean during the short drive to the hospital.

Jason dropped them off at the emergency room entrance

and went to park the car. Mrs. D grabbed Greer's arm to steady herself while Greer inquired after Gun at the reception desk. They signed in, the receptionist buzzed them back, and they walked down the linoleum-tiled floor to his room. Greer hesitated, not knowing Gun's condition, then slowly opened the door.

Gun lay sleeping in the hospital bed, and Mrs. D burst into tears.

"There, there. He's going to be okay." Greer patted her shoulder and stood back in the hall to give them privacy.

Jason arrived a few minutes later and joined Mrs. D, followed almost immediately by a doctor in scrubs. Greer fidgeted with her pendant necklace while listening to their muted voices as they discussed Gun's condition. After several minutes, they filed out of the room, and Jason informed her they were waiting for the CT scan results to ensure no internal bleeding. According to the witnesses at the scene, a teenager had run out in front of Gun on a dare. He'd slammed on his brakes, and his motorcycle went into a skid. When it finally stopped, he fell in the middle of the road and hit his head. Thank goodness he'd been wearing a helmet, something he usually didn't wear. He hadn't sustained any other injuries or broken bones.

Mrs. D dabbed her eyes with a tissue. "I never like that motorcycle!"

"Greer, would you take her to the cafeteria for tea?" Jason asked. "I want to wait for the doctor to return with the test results."

"Why don't you go?" she suggested. "I think she'd feel more comfortable speaking Korean and you're family. I'll stay here and text you when the doctor arrives."

After they'd gone, Greer stayed in the hall until she couldn't take it anymore. If Gun were sleeping, he wouldn't notice if she snuck into his room to see if he was okay. Ever since Jason told her about the accident, she'd been worried sick but trying not to let it show. She didn't want Jason to misunderstand her intentions. That was also why she hadn't asked about the woman who had called, even though her curiosity was killing her.

She kept her body hidden behind the door as she opened it, then cautiously peered into the room. Gun's eyes were closed. She tiptoed to the chair by his bed, and he didn't stir when she sat. There were scratches on his cheek, but they didn't detract from his looks. If anything, they made him look more ruggedly handsome. She hoped those were the only injuries he'd suffered. She looked at the vital signs monitor. His blood pressure and heart rate were normal.

Since he continued to sleep, she stared at him to her heart's content. She extended her forefinger toward his face and air-traced the outline of his dark eyebrows. Then, his long, dark eyelashes. They were so thick they looked like fringe fanning across his high cheekbones. Next, she air-traced the bridge of his perfect nose and chiseled jaw with its five o'clock shadow. Finally, she moved to his lips, with their perfect cupid's bow. Only one month ago, she believed she would know what those lips would feel like pressed against hers.

She would never forget that incredible night. It had been magical for her, and she'd believed Gun felt the same way. Afterward, she kept checking her phone, sure he would call, and daydreaming about their next encounter. She even began looking for a new outfit.

But three days passed, and she didn't hear from him. Although disappointed, she remained hopeful. After a week passed, her hope began to fade. Then she remembered he said he was leaving for Korea, so maybe he couldn't call. All hope died when she searched online and discovered South Korea is the world's most wired country. A lack of modern technology didn't prevent him from calling. Not unless his work had taken him to a remote mountain Buddhist temple, and even then, she was sure the monks had cellular service. She finally realized that the night that had meant so much to her had meant nothing to him.

Initially, she felt hurt. Then, the hurt gave way to anger. Anger at Gun for leading her on. Hadn't she asked him to stop sending mixed signals? She felt angry with herself too, for disregarding the rules of engagement. Gun hadn't lied to her or promised her anything. On the night of karaoke, he rudely told her that their only connection was his mother. Their dinner had been due to his call for a temporary truce, nothing more. She was the one who'd allowed her heart to go unguarded and get ahead of itself. She had checked her phone one final time, hoping for a text from Gun, and Jason called while her phone was still in her hand. She took it as a sign.

Now, the small wound in her heart that had begun to heal opened again. She couldn't keep doing this to herself. It was time to say goodbye and move on with her life. She placed her hand on the bedcovers and gently touched his left pinky finger with her right one. His eyelids didn't flutter. She whispered a short prayer, and as she wiped away the tears that began to spill, Gun's fingers closed around hers.

She gasped, and her eyes flew open. Gun's eyes were open, too. He didn't speak or look angry, although she could never be sure about him. Did he have side effects from the fall?

She stood and leaned in close, only inches from his face, and searched his eyes for signs of lucidity. "Do you know your name? Do you know who I am? What year is it?"

His dark eyes blazed. "Are we filming *Winter Sonata*? I'm not Bae Yong-joon, and I don't have amnesia if that's what you're thinking."

And he was back. And acting as antagonistic as ever. But

the relief she felt caused an emotional pressure valve to be released within her, and she began to ramble. "Oh, good! Wow, you had me worried there for a minute. I guess you are okay if you can remember *Winter Sonata* off the top of your head. Talk about a classic. I've never asked you this before. Do you watch dramas? You seem to know a lot about them. How else would you have known *Winter Sonata* is about a man who develops amnesia after a car accident?"

Gun released her hand and gave her a suspicious look as if *she* were the one concussed. "What are you doing here?"

"Oh, right. About that—"

The door opened, and an Asian woman she'd never seen before rushed to Gun's bedside and threw herself at him. Following on the woman's heels were Mrs. D and Jason. Mrs. D cried, and they all spoke over one another in Korean. Greer stepped out, as the room could barely fit two people, much less five. After several minutes of not knowing what to do with herself, she walked to the waiting room.

She texted Jason, letting him know she would wait for him there, then sat in one of the hard plastic chairs and looked around at the people in the room. Some texted while others spoke too loudly into their phones. Her heart went out to those who sat silently, their fear and worry written on their faces. Gun would be fine, but sadly, that was not the case for every patient.

She chewed her thumbnail and bounced her leg. Who was the woman in Gun's room? When he didn't call, she'd considered the possibility that he was seeing someone. She remembered thinking he looked like he had rolled out of bed at the grocery store. Had he not been alone in that bed? Now that possibility seemed probable. The woman hadn't acted like a platonic friend. But would Gun have asked Greer to dinner while seeing someone else? She scoffed. What a ridiculous question. As Charlie liked to say, "He's a man, ain't he?"

She heard murmuring and looked up as the mysterious Asian woman entered the waiting room. Speak of the devil. Although no longer young, she was still attractive. Her hair was swept up in an elegant chignon, and she wore a skin-tight red dress and matching red lipstick. Her five-inch stiletto heels looked like they could serve double duty as a weapon. She looked like a femme fatale, or Dragon Lady, who had stepped out of a martial arts movie, although technically, those films were usually Chinese.

The Dragon Lady spotted Greer sitting across the room and strutted to her. She swayed her hips and caught every male eye in the waiting room, both young and old. Greer had to hand it to her. She knew how to work a room.

She sat opposite Greer and crossed her shapely legs, giving her a brazen once-over. "Are you here with Jason?" she asked in accented English, skipping any introductions as if Greer was not worthy of one.

"Hello, we have not been introduced. I'm Greer Garza. And you are?"

The Reptile arched a penciled eyebrow and placed her hand on her silicone-enhanced chest. "Me? You must not be well acquainted with our family, or you would know better than to ask. I'm Gun's wife."

Gun's *wife*? Wow. She hadn't seen that one coming. So that's how she was going to play it? Little did she know that long before Greer met Gun, Mrs. D had filled her in on his situation. "I heard y'all divorced. A long time ago."

Seeing her comment hit its mark—an arrow to the Dragon's heart—was gratifying, but the woman recovered quickly. "Gun and I are no longer married in the eyes of the law, but it makes no difference to us. Our hearts and fates will always be bound together." She leaned forward to emphasize her next point, and Greer noticed the crow's feet around her eyes. "Since you dared to be in Gun's room when you are not family, I want to make sure you know your place."

Was she serious? Was she so insecure that she had to tell Greer to back off—or had Gun sent her to deliver a message? That didn't seem like his style, though. She doubted he needed a woman to fight his battles.

Greer didn't care if Gun and this woman's hearts, hands, and feet were bound together. His personal life was none of her business. "Well, *ahjumma*," she said, satisfied to see her gasp with indignation, "you don't need to feel threatened by me. You and Gun appear well-suited for each other, so good luck to both of you. Now, if you'll excuse me."

She left the incensed Dragon Lady and walked back to Gun's room. Through the partially open door, she could hear Gun and Jason talking.

"Why is she here?" Gun seethed. "What does she want?"

"Hey, man, I know, and I'm sorry. All I could think of was getting your mom here to see you. It didn't occur to me to tell her she shouldn't be here."

"That's okay, brother. I know you were in a tough situation, but please, keep her away from me. I don't want to see her. That woman is a nuisance, and I'm not in the mood for her phony sympathy."

Humiliation washed over Greer from the top of her head to the bottom of her feet. She'd been foolish to think one dinner had changed anything between them. Gun couldn't have been clearer about having no feelings for her.

She coughed and walked into the room. Gun sat up in bed with his arms crossed, and Jason stood by his bedside. They didn't appear sheepish about almost getting caught. "Sorry to interrupt," Greer said to Jason, avoiding eye contact.

"Your timing is perfect. I was going to text and let you know we're ready to leave, " he said. "This guy's too mean and hard-headed to get injured. They're just keeping him overnight for observation."

Greer gently roused Mrs. D, who had dozed off in the chair, and helped her to her feet. She stepped outside while they said goodbye to Gun.

To her relief, her participation in the conversation wasn't required during the drive back to Mrs. D's house. She had a terrible headache. After seeing Mrs. D safely inside, Jason drove her home. The drive from Hyde Park to Barton Hills was a mere twenty minutes at this late hour, yet still not fast enough. Before she got out of Jason's car, she had to ask one question. She no longer cared if he misinterpreted her intentions.

"Who was it that called you? About Gun's accident, I mean."

He looked surprised. "That was Sunny, Gun's ex-wife. She was the woman at the hospital tonight. She called Gun when the paramedics were on the scene, and they answered and told her about the accident."

So that was the Dragon Lady's name. *Sunny.* "Yes, I saw her."

Something in her voice must have betrayed her true feelings because Jason let out a roar of laughter. "Well said," he replied without further comment.

Greer stared at the assortment of hand lotions in her local Walgreens drugstore without seeing them. She'd been unable to focus all week and needed something to rouse her from her stupor. Maybe chocolate would help. She abandoned her study of lotions to search for the candy just as Gun passed her aisle. The conversation she'd overheard at the hospital was still fresh, so she didn't call out to him and stayed rooted to her spot.

He passed by again, and this time, he saw her too. He back-tracked to where she stood, smiling at her like an old friend and looking like he had stepped straight off the golf course. He wore a navy and gold Georgia Tech hat, and his polo-style shirt and khaki shorts showcased his tanned arms and legs. Except for the scratches on his face, he appeared to be the picture of health. No one looking at him now would guess he'd been in the hospital just a week ago. She was glad to see he had not sustained any lasting injuries from his accident, but she wasn't glad to see *him*.

"Hey there, Greer," he said, sounding like Luke. "We gotta stop running into each other like this."

She scoffed. Was he kidding her right now? After the fuss he made at the hospital, calling her a nuisance. *Now*, he was acknowledging her? Was he *Sybil*, the woman with multiple personalities? This was too much, and she couldn't handle him right now. She turned on her heel and walked away.

"Greer? Hey, are you okay?"

She stopped with her back to him, uncertain whether to keep walking or turn around. It went against her nature to ignore him. She wanted to get in his face and confront him, but it wouldn't do any good, and she'd had enough of his mood swings to last a lifetime. She would give him what he wanted and stay away. She was done with him.

Moments later, she walked out of the store without her prescriptions and, worse, without any chocolate.

Gun arrived home in a rage. What in *the world* was wrong with that woman? He couldn't believe she hadn't bothered to acknowledge him and had walked away without a word. They'd been to dinner, danced, almost kissed, and now she *dissed* him?!

Was she some psycho? And why had she come into his hospital room if she didn't like him?

He hadn't heard her when she entered the room, but her soft voice praying had stirred him, and he wondered if he was dreaming. Why would Greer be in his hospital room? His eyelids had felt heavy—from whatever they'd given him—but he'd forced himself to open them, and there was Greer. She wasn't a dream, and she was crying softly at his bedside. She looked small and vulnerable, and he'd wanted to comfort her, but as usual, he was at a loss for words. Then, that silly woman had ruined the moment by questioning his cognitive abilities. He could read Greer like an open book and knew she wondered if he had amnesia. He snorted. The woman watched *way* too many Korean dramas.

So now, after her show of concern at the hospital, she *ignored* him? Oh, man, he sounded like that crazy woman in *Fatal Attraction*. But really, what was up with that? Was it because of Jason? He'd heard through the grapevine, otherwise known as his mother, that she and Jason were still going out. But he doubted that was the reason behind her two-faced act. She'd come with Jason to the hospital, yet that had not stopped her from slipping into his room.

He slammed his palm down on the kitchen counter. *Aish!* He'd wasted too much time thinking about it, and the reason didn't matter. He was done. He should've followed his instincts about her from the very beginning. A leopard didn't change its spots.

He stormed into the garage and pulled the box Luke had given him from the utility shelf. He didn't know why he hesitated to throw it away in the first place, but he would fix that and get rid of it *right now*. He yanked the lid off the box and looked inside.

And froze.

~

*October 1989*
*Dallas, Texas*

Law students lined the hall of the third floor of Lawyer's Inn as Bobby Brown's "My Prerogative" blared through four-foot speakers. A beer keg and a trash can punch sat near Carole Anne's room at the end of the hall, and she emerged to join the party as Greer refilled her cup with the punch.

Greer put down the cup. "Hey, girl. It's about time you joined us. Come dance with me."

"Oh, well, okay," Carole Anne said and began a lady-like sway to the beat.

"Like this. Throw your whole body into it." Greer moved her head and shoulders from side to side and hopped, trying to imitate Bobby Brown's music video.

Carole Anne gave a trill of laughter. "Oh, Gigi. You're so fun."

"You mean crazy, don't you?" She picked up her cup and took a sip, then gasped. "Ooh, before I forget, Paul Russo is here! I saw him down by Charlie's room."

Carole Anne smiled at the name of her crush. "Thanks for letting me know. I'll casually walk that way and pretend I didn't know he was here."

They laughed again, and then Carole Anne asked, "What time is Jake coming?"

Greer looked at her watch. "He said around eight, but it's already eight thirty. Do you think he's still coming?"

"He'll be here, don't worry."

"I hope you're right. I'm going to touch up my makeup in case he shows up. Come to my room later and tell me about Paul."

"Okay, I'll find you."

Greer followed Carole Anne, who worked her way to the opposite end of the crowded hallway. She stopped and said hello to friends she passed along the way and avoided others, like Tracy Summers. A rail-thin, bleached blonde with dark roots, she was one of Jake's Section Three classmates, and according to Carole Anne, they were quite friendly. Greer hoped she would leave before Jake arrived.

Mitch McBride and guys from his second-year class were there arguing about football. Mitch winked and tousled her hair, saying, "Hey there, cutie," as she passed.

Charlie stood outside his room, surrounded by several girls. He had his left arm around a redhead and his right arm around a blonde. He lifted his chin, gave her a "Hey, what's up?" and then turned his attention back to his fan club.

Carole Anne had found Paul Russo. He was using his hands to explain some finer point of law while Carole Anne batted her ridiculously long lashes up at him.

Greer reached her room and opened the door to find several people inside listening to Chicago's "What Kind of Man Would I Be?" on her CD player. Not surprising. The residents of the Inn had an unofficial open-door policy. They never locked their doors, and friends came and went out of each other's rooms. "Hey, what are y'all doing in here? Why aren't y'all at the party?"

Kyle Hebert stood in front of the bookshelf, looking through her CDs. "You have the best CD collection in the dorm, and we need more music for the party. I'm going to borrow Prince and the B-52s."

Also unsurprising, Monty Phillips sat in her desk chair. He was playing the Chicago song, just as he did every afternoon when he came to her room, put the disc in the player, and sang along with an anguished look. At times, Greer noticed tears in his eyes. She'd asked before about the girl, but all he ever said was they'd gone to Duke together, and she'd broken his heart.

"Again, Monty? You were here earlier today listening to this song. Why don't you mingle? There are a lot of girls here tonight."

He shook his head. "One more time, please, Greer. Then I'll leave. This is the best song ever." His hands gripped the armrests as if he feared she'd pull him out of the chair.

"It *is* a great song, but my favorite song on the CD is 'Will You Still Love Me?' I love that line about two people bound by destiny."

"That's a bunch of bull," Kyle said. "There's no such thing as destiny."

"Maybe, but I'd still like to believe it exists. What's wrong with that?"

"Aww, Greer, you're such a romantic," Chase Andersen said in her defense. Tall, blond, and perpetually tanned, Chase looked like Malibu Ken. He and his college-age girlfriend, Vickie, were lounging on her bed.

"And would you two get a room? Like your own! Chase, why do you and Vickie always hang out here when your room is around the corner?"

"Greer, please don't be mad at us," Vickie pleaded. "I don't know why, but your bed is much more comfortable than Chase's. Plus, we like listening to your music."

"Stay here as long as you want, but take your business to your room, okay?" Greer winked.

"You got it, boss." Chase grinned. "Hey, how's the party going? Is anything interesting happening out there?"

"Nothing much, just the usual. I popped in to put on more lipstick." She selected a reddish-brown shade from the top of her dresser and applied it to her lips. She also sprayed Fracas, her favorite scent, on her wrist points.

"Ooh, putting on lipstick and perfume. That must mean Jake is here," Chase teased.

"No, it means my lips are chapped."

"Sure it does," Kyle retorted.

Greer blushed. There was no point in denying it. The whole dorm knew about her crush on Jake.

"Tell me something, Greer," Kyle said. "Have you and Jake ever gone out? Or do you have a one-sided crush that's never going anywhere?"

Greer became defensive. "Well, not exactly. He *has* asked me out, but something always suddenly comes up."

Kyle rolled his eyes.

Chase gave a low whistle. "Wow! Stealing his lines from the *Brady Bunch*. Talk about rude. I didn't know Jake had it in him."

"Speaking of Jake, he just passed by," Monty said, pointing toward the open door.

Greer flew from the room and spotted Jake midway down the hall. "Jake!"

He turned around and blinked several times, surprised to see her, which she found strange. Didn't he come to see her? "Hi, Greer," he said when she caught up to him. "We stopped by to say hello to some people before we head out to grab something to eat."

"You mean you're not going to stay? And who's *we*?"

"I came here with Kie," he said, referring to his buddy, another member of Section Three. The two of them were inseparable.

"Oh, I see. Where are y'all going to eat? Could I go?"

"Uh, we're meeting up with Kie's friends who are in town for the game tomorrow. It's a bunch of guys, and I don't think you'd feel comfortable."

Greer shrugged. "I'm comfortable around guys. I'm the only girl in my study group."

"These are Kie's friends, so it's not up to me. And speaking of Kie, I better go find him."

But while he spoke, Kie walked up behind him with the wretched Tracy. "Hi, Greer. Jake, are you ready to go? I ran into Tracy, and she wants to come with us."

Tracy had a smug look on her face.

Greer folded her arms. "You said you were going out with a bunch of guys."

"Well, I am. I mean, I was. Listen, Greer, it's not up to me, but I guess if you want to tag along—"

"Tag along?" Her voice rose. "Do you see me as a stray dog?"

"No, of course not," Jake stammered. "That's not what I meant."

"Then I don't understand the problem. When we had lunch the other day, you said you would see me tonight. Now that you're here, you seem to have changed your mind. Or do you not want me around your friends?"

He sighed. "Greer, please don't make a big deal out of this!"

"I'm not making a big deal out of it. I want you to be honest with me—"

"Is there a problem here?" Charlie asked. He and Carole Anne now stood beside Greer.

Jake looked from her to them and held his hand up. "No, no problem at all. I explained the situation to Greer, but she misunderstood."

"Then why don't you try explaining it to me," Charlie said.

Kie jumped in to defend Jake as Mitch and his friends approached, seeming to want in on the action.

Greer bit her lip. She hadn't meant to cause a scene or drag her friends into her drama. Everyone talked around her, but all she heard above the din was the Fine Young Cannibals' "She Drives Me Crazy" blaring in the background.

"Hey, Greer! Did you forget about me?" a male voice called behind her. "Are we still going out?"

Everyone turned, and Jake looked at her pointedly. "You have a date? I thought you wanted to go out with us."

"Greer, let's go!"

# Chapter Thirteen

G reer stood on her back porch, coffee mug in hand, when the cold front blew in, promising rain. Its sudden gust whipped through her hair and cotton pajamas, sending her wind chimes dancing to their melodious tune.

She inhaled deeply. She loved the smell of rain, but judging by the dark, ominous clouds, much more was in store. Central Texas experienced its most dangerous weather in May, including hail and tornadoes. She'd seen clouds like this before and knew a storm was brewing.

She'd felt uneasy since waking up this morning, and her instincts warned her it was due to more than a drop in the barometric pressure. Today was the fifty-fifth wedding anniversary celebration of Dr. and Mrs. Lee. Against her better judgment, she'd allowed Jason to pressure her into attending after he told her some cockamamie story about losing face.

"Come on, Greer. I can't be the only guy at the party without a date," he'd said with a fake pout on his handsome face.

Talk about blowing smoke. She doubted he ever lacked female company, but she'd always found it hard to resist a hot guy when he begged her. That weakness had gotten her into trouble more than once.

How could she tell him her real reason for not wanting to attend was she didn't want to face the Donovans? It would be wonderful to see Luke and Sarah, but she had no desire to see their brother. Speaking of that middle-aged lothario, she hadn't seen hide nor hair of him since running into him at the drug store three weeks ago. She'd met with Mrs. D twice, but Gun's name was not mentioned, and she found it frustrating.

As she dressed for the party, she reflected on her latest dream. Jake's scorn in front of his friends had been humiliating. She'd placed him on a pedestal for so many years that she'd forgotten about their rocky start. It was a wonder she ever liked him, much less fell in love with him. Thank goodness she had the support of friends like Kyle and Monty to rescue her and escort her away from the fray, but the voice in her dream didn't sound like either. Why couldn't she remember what happened afterward? So many things from that time were lost to her, and she couldn't help but wonder if she had forgotten something important.

Was that why she kept dreaming about Jake? The first dream was easy to explain, but this was getting ridiculous. Were the dreams trying to tell her something?

When she'd asked her father if he believed in the significance of dreams, he looked at her like she was crazy. "You're not Joseph or Daniel," he scolded. "Do you think you're receiving a special message from God? They're just dreams."

She wished he wasn't so harsh but supposed he was right. Still, she couldn't shake the feeling there was more to it, especially after this latest dream. Like Scarlett O'Hara, she could think about it tomorrow. Right now, she had a party to go to.

An hour later, Greer walked into the Asian Community

Center but could have mistaken it for the set of a historical drama. The women were dressed in hanbok, the traditional Korean dress, everywhere she looked, in as many colors as a rainbow. Watching historical dramas had taught her that a *hanbok* comprised two parts—a long-sleeved wrap jacket called a *jeogori* and an ankle-length skirt called a *chima,* worn above the breasts, not at the waist. The color combination of the jacket and skirt was endless and up to the woman's imagination.

She signed the guest book and stood in line to congratulate the honorees. As she waited, she looked over the many pictures of the anniversary couple on a table. Two images caught her eye. One was a black-and-white photo of the Lees dressed in traditional Korean wedding dress on their wedding day. They were a handsome young couple with smiling, hopeful expressions. The second was a recent portrait taken by a world-renowned Austin photographer. In the photo, Mrs. Lee laughed while her husband kissed her cheek. The photographer's reputation and fees were not unfounded. She'd captured the sweet spirit of this couple.

Greer smiled. It must be wonderful to grow old with someone and see the dreams of your youth come true.

Standing beside the anniversary couple, Justin and Hannah enthusiastically greeted her. Hannah had her hair in an updo and wore a red jacket-and-cream-skirt *hanbok.*

"Hannah! You look gorgeous. Like a leading lady in a drama."

She blushed a deep crimson that matched her *jeogori.* "*Unni,* you look wonderful too! Like a beautiful bride!"

Greer looked down at her dress, white lace over a white chiffon slip with a round neckline and short sleeves. "Should I not have worn white? Do I stand out too much?"

"No, *Unni,* you stand out in a good way."

Justin gave her the once-over and whistled. "*Noona*, you're a knockout!"

She blushed. They were so kind, and she appreciated their much-needed boost to her ego.

Likewise, Jason's parents gave her a warm welcome. "It's no fun being around a bunch of old folks, especially for a girl as pretty as you. So we thank you for coming," Dr. Lee said with a twinkle in his eye.

"*Aigoo*, you're such a smooth talker, Dr. Lee. I can see where Jason gets his charm," Greer teased, causing everyone to laugh.

She gave her congratulations and then walked to the front near the kitchen. Justin suggested she might find Jason there, attending the last-minute dinner details.

Many people milled about greeting one another. She scanned the crowd, but she couldn't find Jason. A makeshift dance floor had been set up, and she spotted a handsome DJ testing the sound equipment. He had a tall, lanky teenage assistant with an adorable face helping him. The young man waved to her as if he recognized her, and she waved back. Did she know his parents?

She continued searching for Jason when a familiar voice called, "Lawyer Garza!"

She turned around, and Mrs. D leaned against a pillar, watching her. She looked fabulous in a pale green skirt and lavender jacket. "Mrs. D! You look beautiful! I've never seen you in *hanbok* before, but it suits you."

Although in her late seventies, Mrs. D wasn't too old for a compliment. She flared her skirt from side to side for Greer's praise and giggled like a young girl. "Look, I get nails done too," she said, holding her hands out for inspection.

"I like the pink color. Look at you, woman. You went all out!"

"Ah, you too." Mrs. D looked her up and down. "You look like young bride. Now you need groom. You come alone? Why you not have date?"

"Uh, well, Jason invited me," Greer murmured.

"I see Jason up front, talking with everybody but not you," Mrs. D pointed out.

She made another lame attempt at an explanation. "Well, I just got here."

"Uh-huh. Well, anyway, you go now. Find Jason. We talk later, okay?" Mrs. D didn't buy her story.

When she finally found Jason, he gave her a halfhearted hug. "Greer, you look fantastic. I'm sorry I don't have time to talk, but please sit with us at the family table when we serve dinner."

She assured him she understood and wandered off, feeling adrift. She didn't know anyone else besides Mrs. D and Jason's family. She wanted to return to the shelter of Mrs. D's table, but it would be awkward if all her children were there.

Jason tapped the microphone to get everyone's attention. He announced in Korean and English that everyone should take a seat. Mindful of his invitation to join them, she went up front again. Dr. and Mrs. Lee and Jason's two children sat at the table. Justin and Hannah were there, too, along with their two children. That made eight and, with Jason, nine. Each table had a seating capacity of ten, but there didn't appear to be any room for her.

To drive home this point, Jason's daughter removed one of the chairs and declared the table too crowded. Greer, hovering on the periphery, couldn't tell if the young woman's actions were intentional and meant to keep her away. She didn't feel like making an issue out of it, whatever the case. Today was special for the Lee family, and she wasn't a part of their family.

She found an empty chair at a table occupied by three

elderly couples. They smiled and bowed in welcome but spoke limited English. She ate her dinner quietly and finished as Jason stepped to the microphone. This time, he invited people to join his parents on the dance floor, and everyone rushed to join them. She turned to watch the cute little grandfathers and grandmothers dancing as the DJ played traditional Korean love songs and Trot songs. Nothing of the K-pop variety for these seasoned folks. He also played American standards by Frank Sinatra, Dean Martin, and Tony Bennett. She found it surprising but guessed they had a universal appeal.

Greer hated to eat and run, but there was no reason to stay. Apart from congratulating Dr. and Mrs. Lee on their special day, her attendance was a waste of time. Before her drive across town, she stopped by the ladies' room as a precaution. Walking out afterward, she spotted Sarah waving her arms to get her attention.

"*Unni!*" Sarah squealed as Greer approached her table and then wrapped her in a hug.

"Sarah! It's *great* to see you!" She hadn't realized how alone she felt until now.

Sarah grinned. "We've known the Lees our whole lives. We couldn't miss their party. Where have you been hiding? Why didn't you eat with us?"

Greer thought it best not to answer.

A woman sitting at the table stood and looked enquiringly at Greer. She was also Asian, and a layered bob framed her heart-shaped face. Like Sarah, she wore a sleeveless sheath dress, so Greer's dress wasn't so out of place.

Sarah turned to introduce the woman. "This is my sister-in-law, Janet. She's Luke's wife."

"Greer, what a pleasure to meet you. I'm sorry I missed your duet with my husband. Thank you for indulging him. I know he's quite a character." Janet spoke in a low voice. Her poise and serene demeanor were a perfect foil for her rowdy husband. No wonder Luke had been smitten with her since high school.

Mrs. D motioned for them all to sit. Over the years, she had regaled Greer with colorful tales involving her friends. Now, she pointed out these people so Greer could associate a name with a face. She indicated a woman in a bright blue *hanbok* and relayed yet another elaborate story. Like most immigrant communities, the Korean community was a tight-knit group.

"Wow, I didn't realize how much y'all are up in each other's business," Greer noted.

"Oh, you have no idea," Sarah chimed in.

Mrs. D shot her daughter a look.

"What?" Sarah retorted in Korean, not intimidated by the glare.

Greer was curious what that was about but refrained from asking. She had more pressing matters on her mind, such as who else sat at the table. The number of empty plates indicated more than the three women. "So, is Luke here?" she asked.

"Yes," Sarah answered. "He and Scott—my husband—went to check on Dylan. They should be back soon. I can't wait for you to meet Scott."

"Dylan?"

"Dylan is our son," Janet answered. "He's a freshman at UT. Since he worked part-time as a DJ in high school, Jason asked him to help with today's party."

So Dylan must've been the young man she'd seen earlier. Come to think of it, he did resemble Luke. No wonder he looked familiar. But how had he known her?

"Hey there, Greer," said a familiar twang.

She stood, and Luke gave her a side hug, or what she called the "church hug." He had traded in his jeans and boots for a nice navy suit. "It's good to see you. You're looking awfully pretty today. I take it you've met my lovely wife, Janet?"

Greer grinned, cheered by the hug. "Yes."

"*Unni, Unni,*" Sarah said, vying for her attention. "This is my husband, Scott, and I've told him all about you. Scott, say hello to Greer."

"Well, hello, Greer. It's great to meet you. I love your name. My mom loved that actress. Our family's got a penchant for unique names."

Greer blinked several times, astounded by Scott's good looks. Tall, with blond hair and crystal blue eyes, he could rival any Hollywood star and made a perfect match for the lovely Sarah. She couldn't remember meeting so many good-looking people in one family.

Like most families, they began talking on top of each other. Janet asked Luke if Dylan had eaten. Sarah informed Scott that she had called his parents to check on the boys. Greer found their silence regarding Gun conspicuous and planned to get Sarah alone. She'd already figured out that Sarah didn't have a filter. If asked, she would spill the beans.

"Sarah, I—"

"It's about time y'all got here!" Sarah exclaimed to someone over Greer's shoulder. "We were beginning to wonder."

Greer broke out in goosebumps. Without turning around, she knew Sarah spoke to Gun. But was he not alone?

"We got here as soon as we could, but it's raining hard, and there's a lot of traffic from the airport to the other side of town," he said from behind her.

Greer whipped around to face Gun. Their eyes met, and she felt her chest tighten. He had gotten a haircut and wore a light gray suit that appeared custom-tailored to fit his body. He looked incredible, but he hadn't cleaned up for her benefit. A tall, elegant Korean woman stood beside him. The sight of her caused Greer's heart to drop into her delicate silver sandals.

Suddenly, Jason came toward her. "Greer, I've been looking

all over for you. Why didn't you—" His voice faltered at the sight of Gun and his date.

"Hi, Jason," the woman said with a smile. "Do you remember me? It's been a long time."

Jason stared at her wide-eyed for a few moments. "S-S-Susie. What . . . what are you doing here? When did you get back into town?"

"Just now. Gun kindly picked me up from the airport."

Jason stammered a reply, but Greer didn't hear what he had to say because Gun took her by the hand and led her toward the dance floor. "Come on, my dear, let's dance."

"I'm not your *dear*, and what do you think you're doing?" She yanked her hand from his. She was not a rag doll to be dragged around at his whim.

"I'm trying to give Jason and Susie some privacy," Gun replied. "It's been over thirty years since they've seen each other."

"What? This is insane." She threw her hands up in frustration. "I feel like I'm in the middle of a *makjang*. Why do I always feel like I've lost my bearings when it comes to you? I don't know what's going on or why you hijacked my date, but whatever the case, I don't want to dance with you."

He tilted his head, and his brows furrowed. "Why not? You didn't mind dancing with me that night at El Gallito. You're not still mad at me, are you?"

She stuck her finger in his chest. "Don't bring up El Gallito! That's off-limits to you. And where have you been? Why haven't I seen you around? Do you expect me to fall into your arms and dance with you when you finally reappear?"

He rolled his eyes. "Is that what's bothering you? Okay, you're right. I should have called, but as you can see, I've been busy looking for a suit and getting my hair cut. But I like the idea of you falling into my arms."

"Stop joking around! I told you not to play hot and cold with me."

Gun sobered. "Yes, you did, and my behavior since then has been consistent. Speaking of hot and cold, why did you come into my hospital room and then ignore me a week later?"

She turned her head to avoid his gaze. "I was checking on you out of concern for your health, one human being for another. Anyone would have done the same."

"Oh, so that's what you were doing. You came into my room for humanitarian reasons. I see."

The conversation was out of control, and Gun enjoyed baiting her.

"Speaking of that night, why do you want to dance with me when you called me a nuisance and told Jason you didn't want to see me?" She crossed her arms and waited for his answer.

Gun scowled. "When did I tell Jason I didn't want to see you? I never said that."

She recounted the conversation she'd overheard that night in the hospital.

Realization dawned on his face. "Yes, I did say that, but I wasn't talking about you. I was talking about Sunny, my ex-wife."

"What?" She felt like she had the wind knocked out of her sails. It had never occurred to her that he was talking about Sunny.

Gun took her hand again, and they walked to the dance floor. He placed his right hand on her back and pulled her close. She knew she should create a scene and make a dramatic exit, but he looked terrific, and she wanted to dance with him. Otherwise, she would have dressed up for nothing. She might as well make the most of it.

They began to dance to an old-fashioned Korean Trot song. Their bodies were close, and although she hadn't forgiven him, she breathed in his intoxicating scent like the last time they danced. She had to find out the name of his cologne and spray it on her pillow at night. The Trot song ended and was followed by the romantic ballad "Is There Any Chance?" She knew the song because her parents were avid Marty Robbins fans.

She focused on Gun's lavender tie and listened to Marty Robbins's smooth baritone asking his woman for a second chance at love. She found the theme suspicious and a strange coincidence that they were dancing to it. Her body stiffened, and she missed a step and tripped over Gun's polished shoes. As usual, he caught her in time.

She looked up and met his eyes. "I know your nephew is helping the DJ. Did you ask him to play this song for us?"

He smiled. "Yes."

At least he didn't deny it. "And are you responsible for bringing Susie here?"

"Partly, yes."

She searched his face. "Why? Why did you ambush Jason like that?"

"I didn't do it to punish him if that's what you're thinking. And you know why, Greer. I let things get out of control, and now it's time to set things right. To how they're meant to be. I want us to find our bearings."

He didn't mock or tease her anymore. She realized she did know the reason why, and it frightened her. This Gun made her uncomfortable. She liked him better when they were cool enemies. It was easier to maintain her distance.

The room began to spin, and Greer briefly held onto his arm to steady herself. Then she left him alone on the dance floor and returned to his family's table for her purse. She kept glancing toward the dance floor while Sarah and Mrs. D pleaded with her to stay, hoping Gun wouldn't follow her.

Luke ended any further discussion by saying firmly, "*Eomma*, let her go."

He gave Greer a comforting pat on the shoulder. "Please be careful going home, Greer. We'll see you next time."

She gave him a grateful smile, hoping for a quick getaway, and rushed outside into the pouring rain.

# Chapter Fourteen

Gun filled his lungs with fresh air as he went for his pre-dawn daily run. He loved this time of day, when the neighborhood was still sleeping, and the only sounds were his breathing and his feet hitting the asphalt. Yesterday's rain had washed everything clean, and it suited his mood. He felt like a new man.

After returning home, he fixed an enormous breakfast of steak, eggs, potatoes, and waffles for himself and his boys. But a late night and a full stomach caught up with him, and the three of them dozed off on the leather couch upstairs while he flipped the channels between a golf tournament and *The Dirty Dozen*.

He woke from his nap feeling energized and restless. He had a lot to think about and a lot to plan. Besides his morning runs, he'd always found the best way to clear his head was to go fishing. He rose from the couch, bounded down the stairs, and gathered his fishing gear. After loading it into his truck, he returned to the house to say goodbye to Bullett. "You take guard duty while we're gone, okay, pal?" he said, patting Bullet on the head.

The cat looked up at him with his large green eyes and

thumped his tail as if to say, *Yes, sir.* Gun looked around for Buddy, but Buddy was already waiting for him by the door leading to the garage, and his tail wagged impatiently.

He took W Ben White Boulevard, then headed east on US 290, glad to have the sun behind him. The day was warm but not uncomfortable. He rolled down the window for Buddy, who stuck his head out while riding shotgun.

Gun tuned the radio to a local country station and sang to the oldies the station played every Sunday. Country Gold, they called it. He belted the familiar tunes with an exaggerated twang and rubbed Buddy's head. "Thanks for being my wingman."

In response, Buddy thumped his tail to the beat.

Gun took the Montopolis Drive exit, turned right onto Chapman Lane, hooked a left onto Burleson Road, and another right onto McKinney Falls Parkway. "We're almost there, pal."

He'd stayed up last night visiting with Luke and Sarah, and their visits always left him wishing he could see them more often. If he lived in Dallas, he could fulfill that wish, but as much as he missed them, he wouldn't return to that life. Listening to old country songs consoled him and made him feel close to his family. It was funny how that worked. His dad loved country music, and they'd listened to it on the two-and-a-half-hour road trips to East Texas to see Nanny. Luke had been in his element, his arms resting on the back of the driver's seat, head leaned forward, singing along with their dad. Gun had not been a country music fan in those days. He'd detested it but preferred listening to it over his parents' arguments.

He always envied Sarah because she tuned everything out by playing with her dolls or burying her nose in a book. Their mother would sit up front in stone silence, looking out the window, not giving a clue as to the thoughts running through her mind, but he could guess. She sat in a station wagon beside a man she could hardly tolerate, with a car full of kids, going to a small East Texas town where everything about her stood out like a sore thumb. It was quite a different life from the one she'd known in Seoul.

Gun could guess what she was thinking because he, too, felt out of place. Ironically, he hadn't felt that way about growing up in a White, privileged, homogeneous Dallas community but had felt out of place in his own family. He and his father were not cut from the same cloth. They shared no similar interests besides golf, and nothing he had done had ever pleased his father. Luke was the golden boy, the chip off the old block, and Sarah was the princess. Gun was the odd man out.

Also, no one would question Luke and Sarah's parentage, but he didn't appear to have received one single chromosome from Jack Donovan, and it had crossed his mind that he might not be his biological father. He knew he favored his mother's family, but could his biological father also be Korean? Finally, when he was fifteen, his doubts about his paternity were so great that he dared to ask his mother about it. "Mom, is Dad my real father?" He'd asked the question in Korean, fearing his dad might overhear him.

"What?" His mother, who had been washing dishes, turned to look at him.

She had heard him, though. There was nothing wrong with her hearing. He'd learned the hard way from all the times she'd caught him and Luke sneaking into the house late at night. He also knew by the dangerous look in her eyes that he skated on very thin ice. But the question was already out there, and his curiosity had gotten the best of him, so he pressed on.

"How come I'm the only one who doesn't look like Dad?" he continued, speaking in Korean. "I'm the only one who doesn't look White. Does Dad hate me because he knows I'm not his real son? Is that why he's always harder on me than Luke?"

His questions were sincere. He wanted to know the source of his father's constant displeasure with him. But the murderous expression on his mother's face told him she didn't see things the same way. She pulled her hands out of the sink, took off one of her gloves, and used it to slap the back of his head. Hard. He'd been taller than her for years, but she still managed to find her mark. Korean mothers were notorious for packing a wallop. His mother, every bit the Korean mother, was no exception.

"You punk!" she yelled in Korean, her face red with anger. "How dare you say such a thing about your father! Your rudeness is through the roof! I should tell your father to kick you out of the house *now*. How can a son of mine be so rude? Maybe you're *not* my son. Maybe they switched you with another baby at the hospital."

"Mom, please calm down," he pleaded. "I was only asking because—"

She slapped the back of his head again. "How dare you interrupt me! That's why your father disciplines you. You have no manners. If Dad is not your father, then who is, huh? Who do you think feeds you, clothes you, and puts a roof over your head? How do you have a car and hang out with your crazy friends if not for Dad? Who bought your musical instruments and fancy golf clubs? What man does that for another man's son, especially for a son so disrespectful and lacking? And what are you saying about me? I had a son with another man? Why not send me to my grave now?"

He hung his head and walked out of the kitchen. No matter how bitterly his parents argued, he'd never heard them speak ill of each other. On the contrary, they always managed to present a united front. They wouldn't tolerate their children disrespecting each other.

Gun reached the park and paid the entrance fee, then found a spot along the banks of Onion Creek and cast his line in the water while Buddy sniffed and explored the ground around him. He shook his head, thinking back to that time. His mom had made such a fuss defending his father, but not long after, she filed for divorce and moved out of the house.

She and Juanita had been like busy worker bees right before she moved out, filling the refrigerators in the kitchen and the garage and stocking the kitchen pantry full of staples and their favorite snacks. He found all this activity suspicious and questioned her about it.

She waved away his queries. "You mind your own business. You ask too many questions, so you're always in trouble."

He hadn't been in the mood for another beating and was busy with the start of the school year, so he left it alone. He never knew what was going on in his mother's head.

Two weeks after school started, Gun came home and found his father's car in the driveway. His father was rarely home before seven p.m. Gun placed his hand on the door handle but hesitated before opening it because he couldn't calm his racing heart. He finally took a deep breath, opened the door, and found his father waiting in the entryway. His shirtsleeves were rolled up, and he held his trademark whiskey tumbler in his right hand.

His dad, never one for small talk, said, "Come into the family room. We're waiting for Luke."

Gun dropped his books and trumpet case on the entryway bench and stopped short. Where was his mother? Every day when he came home, his mother would yell at him to take his things upstairs. So why were there no sounds and smells coming from the kitchen? The house was eerily quiet. He entered the family room, where Sarah sat on the leather sofa with Roger, their yellow Lab. Her face looked pale, and her expression strained. She'd always been a lively little chatterbox, but that day, she was quiet and didn't bother to acknowledge him as he sat beside her. Roger was quiet, too, and must have sensed that things were not right.

"Dad, is Mom—" Gun had let the question hang, unable to verbalize his fear.

"No, no, your mother is fine. Let's wait for Luke, shall we?" He cleared his throat and took another sip of whiskey, clearly uncomfortable with the situation he found himself in, which was unusual. Their father had always been very sure of himself, always in command, and never at a loss for words.

A few minutes later, Luke came into the house. Their father went to meet him and brought him into the family room. Luke had come from football practice, and his hair was wet. He flung himself into the chair across from Gun and Sarah and shot Gun a look. "What's going on?" he mouthed.

Their father cleared his throat again and didn't pull any punches when he spoke. He told them their mother had moved out of the house today and served him with divorce papers.

Even after almost four decades, Gun could recall the emotions that ran through him. So many of his friends' parents had divorced, and he'd known it was only a matter of time before his parents would follow suit. Yet when it finally happened, it was shocking how hard the news had hit him, like having the wind knocked out of him. Sarah's face crumbled, and she broke into loud sobs. But it was Luke's reaction that surprised him. He bolted up from the chair, fists clenched, ready to fight.

"Daddy, what are you saying? Mom moved out of the house? Why? Did you ask her to leave?" Luke's booming voice sounded even louder than usual, and his tone was accusatory.

Gun had slid across the couch to comfort Sarah and looked up in surprise. Luke was closer to their dad than their mom and had always sided with him in their arguments. Although he'd never said so, Gun knew that Luke felt embarrassed by their mother's thick Korean accent and style. She stood out among their friends' socialite moms, and Luke hid whenever she showed up at their school.

Their father shook his head. "No, son, I most certainly did not ask your mother to leave—"

"Then why did she leave? Why didn't *you* move out? We've known for years now that y'all were headed for a divorce. It doesn't surprise us, but why didn't you let Mom stay with the house and with us? You're never home anyway."

Sarah stopped crying. She and Gun turned to look at their father for his reaction, then back at Luke. The two of them stood in a standoff. The young gunfighter challenging the old gunfighter. They'd seen it portrayed dozens of times in episodes of *Gunsmoke.*

"Now, hold on there, boy." Jack Donovan's smooth, erudite manner, which he used on his fancy Dallas clients, slipped, and he reverted to his native East Texas roots. "Yes, your mama and I have had our problems. I won't deny that. But I never once asked her to move out, nor did I ask for a divorce."

He took another sip of whiskey, and Gun found that ironic. Their father litigated multimillion-dollar cases but required liquid courage to speak to his children.

"If she had bothered to discuss it with me, I would have told her to stay in the house with you all, and I would have moved out. But your mama, well, she didn't give me a choice. She took matters into her own hands. I guess she couldn't stand to live with me anymore." He paused as if his statement's truth finally dawned on him. "I know y'all are worried about her, and rightly so, but don't forget your mama's a strong woman. After we married in Korea and I brought her to this country, she was just a young woman with a baby in one arm and another on the way. She had married a clueless young man fresh out of the Army who didn't even have a job. On top of all that, she didn't know much English or anything about this country, yet she raised you three just fine. Don't let her accent fool you. Your mama's one smart cookie."

Luke appeared to want to ask another question but thought better of it. They remained silent as their father relayed the information he knew. Their mother had moved into a house in North Dallas, and apart from the fact that she would no longer live with them, nothing else had changed. They knew that wasn't true, but they also knew better than to argue with their father. Everything had changed, and their world was now upside down. Gun sadly realized his suspicions about his mother's odd behavior were correct.

Her departure hit them hard.

Sarah stayed in her room crying with only Roger for companionship when she wasn't in school. Luke shut down and didn't speak, not even to Gun, whereas Gun couldn't get him to shut up before. They didn't congregate in the family room or fight over which television show to watch or whose turn to use the phone. During those first weeks after her departure, no one was in the mood to talk. The phone rang and rang until Luke unplugged it.

Juanita and Pedro were a source of comfort, especially in the early days. The news left them heartbroken. The couple had grown close to their mom and considered them like their children. Juanita wanted to stay with them in the evenings until their father came home, but he wouldn't hear of it. He insisted they were fine and there was no point in disrupting Juanita and Pedro's lives.

Their father continued spending most of his days and nights at the office. He went into their rooms each night to conduct a headcount but had little to say. He attended Luke's football games, but their camaraderie was gone. Gun was there, too, playing in the marching band, but he never received the same acclaim as Luke. The marching band was not an activity his father could brag about to the boys at the club.

In early October, after their mother had been gone for three weeks, Gun's dad called him into his study. As he had done each week since their mother left, he handed Gun an envelope filled with cash for their needs. However, this time, the envelope also contained a letter. Gun took it out, unfolded it, and discovered it wasn't a letter but a typed address and a phone number on his father's legal stationery. Barbara, his father's secretary, had probably typed it. She took care of everything for him. Gun glanced at his father, his eyebrows raised, not knowing why he'd given him this.

"That's your mother's new phone number and address in Lake Highlands," he said, pointing toward the letter with the same hand that held his whiskey. "Please take Sarah there this Saturday and let her spend the night."

"Yes, sir."

"Are y'all all right? Everything okay at school?"

"Yes, sir," Gun answered, wondering what his reaction would be if he'd told him they weren't all right.

"Good. Well, drop Little Sister off on Saturday. I know she'll be glad to see your mama."

His father walked to the wet bar to pour himself a drink, signaling Gun had been dismissed.

When Gun turned fifteen in July, his father signed for him to get a hardship driver's license and helped him buy a used Chevy Chevelle. The license and the Chevelle came with the proviso that Gun help with family errands. "I didn't buy you this car so you could go joyriding with your friends. Understand?" his father said.

So, it fell to Gun to drive Sarah to their mom's new house. Not that he minded. He was curious to see his mom's new home and what about it had enticed her to leave them. As the crow flies, their mother's house, located on the other side of Central Expressway, was not far from theirs, but it might have been on the other side of the world. Gun was surprised when he pulled into the driveway. He hadn't expected the house to be so comfortable, even if it wasn't as large or grand as their home.

Sarah, who prattled nonstop on the drive over, couldn't contain her excitement. She ran out of the car and danced around on the front porch as they waited for their mother to come to the door. When she opened it, Sarah threw herself into Mom's arms and cried. Gun couldn't believe the overwhelming relief he felt. He put his arms around them, and his eyes stung with tears.

Over the next few weeks, he deposited Sarah at their mom's house each weekend, and they finally began settling into a new routine. It wasn't ideal, of course, but better than before. Now, if only he could get his *hyung* to come around. Growing up two years apart, they had always been close, with hardly any secrets between them. But when their mother moved out, Luke shut out everyone but Janet, and he barely spoke to their father. Despite Gun's repeated requests, Luke refused to go with him to pick up Sarah. He didn't want to see or talk to their mom. Then, right before Halloween, Luke suddenly relented and agreed to a visit.

But during the drive to their mom's house, Luke sat in a brooding silence with his hands in his letterman's jacket, and Gun worried that the visit might not go well. However, when they arrived at the house, Luke looked all around at the home, representing their mom's new life. She had even set up a carved pumpkin display on the front porch, as she had done every October at their house. This was her home now, and she was not returning to theirs.

Sarah answered the door and shrieked at the sight of Luke.

"*Oppa*, you came!" She reached for his hand to pull him across the threshold. "Look at *Eomma's* cool house!"

Luke still hadn't spoken, but their mother came from the kitchen. Her eyes met Luke's as she dried her hands on her apron. She held her arms out, and he fell into them and sobbed.

"*Eomma, Eomma*," he said, unable to stop the tears.

"There, there, my baby," she said in Korean, patting his back while trying to soothe him. "It's all right. Everything's going to be all right. *Eomma* is sorry, my baby. *Eomma* is sorry."

The comfort of her embrace and her apology was the medicine Luke needed. He straightened up and wiped his eyes with the back of his hands. He'd forgotten about Gun and Sarah, but now the color on his face deepened. Gun pointed toward the restroom, and he hurried off to wash his face and gain his composure.

Gun smiled as he remembered that night. Since all her chicks were gathered under her roof, their mom had cooked all evening, and it had been a relief to see Luke acting like his former self again.

Buddy barked, and it jolted Gun back to the present. He turned around to see a Schnauzer passing by. "It's okay, Bud. That little fella's just exploring," he soothed, returning the friendly wave of the little dog's owners.

He hadn't thought about that time in decades and knew he had Greer to thank for his nostalgic musings. Her appearance in his life revived all the ghosts from his past—ones he thought and hoped were dead and buried. In the beginning, he fought them and resented her for it. Now, he realized he owed her a debt of gratitude. Thanks to Greer, he could finally see so many things, such as his father, who, while not perfect, was a good man. Gun had resented and blamed him for the direction of his life's path for most of his years. It had become his driving force. Every decision he made had been in defiance of his father, and now he realized how foolish he'd been. He was like a boxer taking jabs at the air against a nonexistent opponent.

He puffed his cheeks and let out an exasperated breath. He was almost fifty-two years old, and it was time to hang up his gloves. Long past time. Besides, the reasons for his resentment no longer existed. In hindsight, his father's meddling had worked for his benefit.

Buddy came and rested beside him, and together they watched the sunset. Gun felt peace in his soul for the first time in many years.

Gun thought about Greer as he drove home. She seemed to preoccupy his thoughts lately.

Ah, who was he kidding? She had for a long time now. As much as he cared for the Lees, his real reason for attending their party had been to conduct a reconnaissance mission. He wanted to know—*needed* to know—if Greer still felt the same about him or if her heart was with Jason now. Yet the sight of her almost caused him to abandon his mission. He hadn't been prepared for the strength of emotion that overcame him. Now that his eyes weren't clouded by bitterness, he felt as if he were seeing her for the first time. She'd looked stunning in her white dress and taken his breath away.

He'd expected her to give him the cold shoulder or display a complete lack of indifference. But she whipped around at the sound of his voice, and a half smile formed on her lips until she noticed Susie. Whoever said the eyes were the windows of the soul must have been talking about Greer. Her brown eyes were so expressive that there was never any doubt about what she was thinking. She revealed her feelings again on the dance floor when she demanded to know where he'd been. Her tone had been accusatory, and he felt like a husband caught sneaking into the house late at night. He chuckled again at the memory. So she'd been curious about him, had she?

He turned up the radio at the sound of George Jones's "He Stopped Loving Her Today," and then sucked in a breath as the song evoked a long-forgotten memory.

Several months after his mother left the house, he'd been in the kitchen late at night eating cereal. He padded in his bare feet to his father's study, hearing the faint sound of music. When he peeked through the crack in the door, his father sat slumped in his favorite winged-back chair with a whiskey tumbler in his hand. He sang along with George and looked old, tired, and defeated.

Gun smirked. It would serve him right to end up like that poor sap in the song who loved only one woman until he died. And it occurred to him that he'd finally found something he had in common with his old man.

# Chapter Fifteen

Greer deleted her third attempt to respond to Jason's text. Finally, after not hearing from him for several days, he texted her yesterday with the cryptic message, "I'm sorry about Saturday. Can we please meet?"

He was sorry? She hadn't wanted to attend the party in the first place, but he'd badgered her to go, only to ignore her. Then, to add insult to injury, anyone with eyes could see that Susie's appearance rattled him. The two of them needed to talk at some point, but right now, her mind felt like a tangled mess, and she didn't know how to untangle it.

She put her phone down at the knock on her office door. Before she could say, "Come in," the door opened, and a delivery man entered carrying an enormous flower bouquet. Following behind him were what looked like all the women in her office. The lawyers, paralegals, assistants, receptionists, and clerks were curious about the identity of the lucky recipient, so they followed him like children following the Pied Piper. Rita instructed him to set the arrangement on the coffee table.

Greer stood up, speechless at first. "What in the world is this? Whose flowers are these?"

"Whose do you think they are, silly?" Rita said. "They're for you."

Greer came from behind her desk and stood over the spring flowers arranged in a Korean Celadon vase while the women around her "Oohed" and "Aahed."

"Whoever sent this bouquet put a lot of deliberation into it," Molly observed. "Look at what's in here. Roses and tulips are a declaration of love. Daffodils represent new beginnings, and blue hydrangeas symbolize apology or regret. I think someone's trying to tell you something, Greer."

"The cost alone should tell her something," Megan laughed. "Whoever sent this is trying hard to impress her."

Greer continued staring at the bouquet in disbelief. It crossed her mind that Jason might've sent it as an apology, but it seemed too extravagant even for him. "But who is it from?"

Rita handed her a card—not a tiny florist card, but a regular-sized card in a red envelope made from heavy stock.

Greer opened it and read the handwritten inscription:

*Dear Greer,*

*If God were to grant my heart's desire, I would ask Him for this: to turn back the clock and start again. I would go back and undo the pain and hurt I have caused you. I know my actions and behavior have been inexcusable. I'm sorry. I sincerely apologize and hope you will find it in your heart to forgive me one day. And if that day should ever come, my greedy heart would ask for one more thing: the honor of knowing you. From the first moment I saw you, the beautiful girl with the dazzling smile, I knew my fate was in your hands.*

*Sincerely, Gun*

She stared at his writing, unable to speak.

Rita took the card from her and read it out loud. Everyone

squealed with excitement, and immediately, there arose two opposing camps. One wanted her to call Gun immediately and say all was forgiven, and the second wanted her to make him wait and sweat it out. They debated until Dianne broke up the party with, "All right, ladies. Time to get back to work."

They filed out of the office, leaving Greer alone with her bouquet. She didn't intend to respond to Gun, at least not immediately. She hadn't forgiven him for bringing Susie to the anniversary party, but that didn't mean she didn't love her bouquet. The vase looked real, and that would make it quite valuable. She took several pictures from different angles and re-read Gun's card—twice. He had terrible handwriting, but so did most men of her acquaintance. She found the wording curious but liked that he called her a beautiful girl. No one except Kerry Cunningham in the fifth grade had ever called her beautiful. And while not a girl, she liked that Gun still considered her youthful.

His line "from the first moment I saw you" confirmed that he, too, had felt something when they had met on the plane. It hadn't been one-sided after all. But she struggled with the part about his fate being in her hands. Hadn't he said—while sitting in her office—that he didn't believe in fate?

So, which was the truth?

Several days later, Greer found the courage to meet Jason over coffee. She didn't want to meet in the café, where too many people with prying eyes could be, so they met across the street at the iconic Driskill Hotel.

When she arrived, he pulled a chair for her at a round marble-top table. His manners were impeccable, but his smile appeared tense. It saddened her that their previous fun and easygoing relationship had become strained.

After ordering coffee, he struggled initially, but his story came rushing out. As she suspected, Susie was the woman he spoke of on their first date. Although he'd promised to wait for her, he'd met his now ex-wife while Susie was in New York. He admitted he'd always struggled with guilt for not waiting. He finished his story and shrugged, his mouth set in a grim line.

She longed to see his brilliant smile again, so she took pity on him and let him off the hook. "It's okay, Jason. You never lied to me or led me on, so I'm not hurt. I enjoyed our time together, but you have to follow your heart. It's not often we get a second chance in life."

Jason looked toward the ceiling and sighed. "Who's letting down who here? Would it have killed you to say you were a little hurt?"

Greer gasped. "Oh, Jason, I'm sorry! The truth is, I didn't want to make this hard for you. It does hurt a little. I liked you, and I still do. I hope you know that." She tried to smile, but her bottom lip quivered.

His million-dollar smile returned, and he placed his hand over hers. "That's better. So what are you going to do about Gun?"

"What do you mean?" She wasn't sure how much he knew about Gun's quest to ask her out, and she didn't want to pour salt on the wound.

He rolled his eyes. "Don't kid a kidder, my dear. You know what I mean. Gun and I have known each other our entire lives. We're always giving each other a hard time, but no matter what happens, he's still my brother. I know he asked you out."

Greer shrugged and looked away. "I don't know what I'm going to do. First, he sent flowers, and when I didn't acknowledge him, he called and texted, but I ignored him. Then he sent a gift card for an entire day at an exclusive spa and another card apologizing. When that didn't work, he started playing hardball. He had a fancy lunch delivered to the women on my team, and now they love him and are on his side. But I still haven't responded because I don't know how I feel."

"Greer, you know how you feel, and that's the problem. The first time we met at church, your eyes lit up when I mentioned Gun. Then, although I'd invited you, you were laser-focused on Gun at karaoke and followed him outside. You were even in the room with him at the hospital."

Greer looked back at Jason. It never occurred to her that any man would notice her, much less pay attention to her actions. However, if that were true, Jason wouldn't have asked her out in the first place. Ironically, she'd been too preoccupied with Gun to realize it. Before she could stop them, a few tears escaped from her eyes. "I'm sorry, Jason. I never meant to hurt you or use you—"

"Greer, don't apologize." He shook his head. "I'm not saying this to make you feel sorry or guilty. I like you and gave it a shot, but I'm a grown man. I'll live. Who knows, maybe I was trying to get Gun's goat." At her look of surprise, he continued, "I'm kidding. But if you're honest, you already know how you feel. It's how you've felt all along. So stop being afraid and don't waste any more time. Half of your lives are already behind you. What have you got to lose?"

Greer wanted to say her heart, but that would sound corny. She looked down, and that's when she noticed the time. "I'm sorry, Jason, I have to get back to work," she said in a panic.

They walked outside, and Jason hugged her. It was a bitter-sweet moment. She couldn't help but feel sad, and she kept telling herself not to cry. Then, like in the dramas, Jason raised a fist and said, "Fighting," for encouragement, which lightened the moment.

She drew a breath. "Jason, do you think I'm over the top?"

"Over the top? What do you mean?"

"In my love for K-dramas and Korean culture. Do I appear ridiculous? I'm a fifty-year-old woman, and I know I must come across as a silly fangirl."

"You enjoy it, don't you? The dramas, the culture, the people?"

She nodded.

"No, Greer, you're not over the top, and don't let anyone tell you otherwise. When it comes to pursuing your dreams, age doesn't matter. Doing the things you love is what matters. I think it's awesome. We might never have met otherwise."

Greer studied his handsome face with a tinge of sadness. She would miss him. When the dust settled, she hoped they could continue to be friends. Before she could stop, she stood on her tiptoes in the middle of the busy sidewalk and kissed him on the mouth. She'd always wanted to kiss him, but fear of her unresolved feelings for Gun held her back.

Someone walking by whistled.

Jason closed his eyes and took a deep breath. Then he stepped back, holding her at arm's length. When he regained his composure, he responded in typical fashion. "*Aigoo,* what timing. I'm not going to deny I enjoyed the kiss, but if you do that again, I'll have to punch Gun in the face and run away with you."

Gun texted again, asking her to call him. *Stop being so clingy!* Greer typed, then hit send before she had second thoughts. Yes, she liked him. There was no point in denying it any longer. But she had a lot to think about, such as whether she was ready for or even wanted a relationship. She hadn't had many good experiences. Most of the men she'd known had tried to control her, and that's what Gun's cajoling felt like, and it made her uneasy. Besides, she was set in her ways and liked her space. She wasn't sure she wanted to put someone else first, shave her legs every day, and always keep her house clean.

And what about Gun? Although he gave her the full-court press now, would he still be interested once the excitement of the chase was over? She'd never been a proponent of "better to have loved and lost." The pain wasn't worth it, and she wasn't a kid anymore. Would she be able to walk away in one piece?

While still mulling over her decision, Gun's nephew, Dylan, arrived at her house carrying a large square box. She understood why Gun asked if he could deliver it. It looked heavy. Dylan was polite and smiled easily, and from the moment he stepped inside, Kevin followed in lockstep while Sophie watched cautiously from a distance. Dylan placed the box on the round accent table in the living room and, before leaving, scratched Kevin on the chin. Surprisingly, Sophie stepped out of hiding, allowing him to scratch her chin too.

Greer stared at the plain brown box after he had gone, wondering what Gun had given her this time. This was his way of convincing her to go out with him? It didn't look very promising. She pulled back the flaps and found several bright-colored silk bags tied with a two-stranded beaded cord inside. She opened the first bag containing the original soundtrack CD to her first drama. That was the one that had begun her secret love affair with dramas, and the music was primarily responsible for that. She sucked in a breath and held it to her chest. How did Gun know? She'd diligently searched for the CD, like the pearl of great price, but couldn't find it.

In the next bag was a book by her favorite Korean actor, a collection of his photographs. His gorgeous face adorned the cover, and she squealed and kissed it. Underneath it was another book on speaking basic Korean in ninety days. She picked up speed as she opened each bag, like a kid ripping through wrapping paper on Christmas Day. A compact mirror with an exquisite, embroidered silk cover was in another bag. A large pink bag held a collection of K-beauty face masks, hand cream, and foot masks. There were also socks with various fun designs and several with cat motifs. Finally, the last bag had Korean snacks for her, Kevin, and Sophie.

As he had done with his other gifts, Gun included a card, which she found at the bottom of the box. The cover featured a painting of a Korean couple dressed in hanbok.

Greer opened the card and roared with laughter. He had written the message in *Hangul*.

# Chapter Sixteen

The evening temperature was a comfortable eighty degrees, a pleasant and unusual start to the beginning of June. At this time of year, temperatures typically hovered at the one-hundred-degree mark, even three weeks before the official start of summer. Texas, like its proud natives, had a mind of its own and did as it pleased, regardless of what the season dictated.

"What perfect weather for your date," Shannon Burns, Greer's friend who had come over to wish her luck, observed.

Standing in front of an oscillating fan in her dressing room in her underwear, Greer didn't comment. Despite the mild weather, she couldn't stop sweating and didn't know if it was due to a case of nerves or if she was having a hot flash.

Tonight was her first official date with Gun, and everything had to be perfect. With her friend's help, she decided on a pink summer dress with a deep scoop neckline. Shannon advised her to keep her jewelry simple, so she went with her pearl drop earrings but no necklace. Simple tan wedge sandals that were stylish but comfortable would keep her steady. Due to Gun's height, she could wear platforms if she wanted to, but with her record, she would likely fall flat on her face.

Shannon handed her two fingers of whiskey in a double old-fashioned and ordered her to drink it.

"No," Greer protested. "I don't want to get drunk because then I'll do something stupid."

"You won't get drunk," she insisted. "It isn't very strong. Stop worrying. You're gonna have fun tonight, I promise. It'll be awesome, and you better call me tomorrow and tell me all about it."

Shannon, a petite blonde who ran her own construction company, had missed her calling as a drill sergeant. She served as an expert consultant on several of Greer's matters, and Greer knew better than to disobey a direct order. She downed the drink under Shannon's watchful eye.

Gun arrived twenty minutes later, precisely on time, looking as handsome as ever. He wore a short-sleeved blue-and-white seersucker shirt and stone-colored chinos. Greer had worried her dress might be inappropriate for whatever Gun had planned, so it was a relief to see that she made the right choice and their outfits complemented each other. If they were in school, walking the halls, people would say they looked good together.

She introduced Kevin to Gun, and he picked him up, not caring if he had cat hair on his clothes. He held him the same way men held a football and bounced him up and down several times. "Hey, there, big guy. What do you weigh? Sixteen pounds? You and Bullet could work the offensive line on a feline football team." He patted Kevin's girth and set him down.

Sophie peered around the corner and approached slowly, one paw at a time. Gun squatted and waited for her to meet him on her terms. She sniffed his shoes, then his pant legs.

"Well, hello, little lady. Aren't you a pretty girl?" He fussed over her, and the little diva arched her back and preened for him. As with Dylan, she allowed Gun to scratch her chin.

They said goodbye to the kids, and he escorted her outside. A silver Mercedes sedan sat in the driveway.

"Is this yours?" Greer asked in surprise.

"No, it's my mom's. She was overjoyed to lend it to me when she heard we were going out tonight."

"Did something happen to your truck?"

"No, I didn't want you to climb into my truck if you wore a dress. And thank you."

"Are you thanking me for wearing a dress?"

"Yes, that, too. You look wonderful, by the way. I was thanking you for agreeing to go out with me."

She blushed and couldn't think of a response to that.

They drove south on I-35 to Wimberly, a town thirty-five minutes south of Austin, where Gun's clients owned a restaurant along Cibolo Creek. Gun was an excellent driver and didn't exhibit any signs of road rage, nor did he drive like an old grandpa. Greer had butterflies in her stomach, but he asked about her work and her cats and commented on the pleasant weather, nothing that required demanding conversation.

He exited off the highway and turned right on a county road, then drove for another mile before pulling into an empty parking lot recently paved and striped with parking lines. As a construction attorney, Greer had worked on cases involving paving disputes, so she noticed these things.

He came around to open her door, and she looked at him with a question.

"Is this the right place? There's no one here. It looks like it's closed."

Gun smiled. "We're at the right place."

They walked toward the building, where a green awning with the words *La Rivière* hung over the entrance. Gun opened the wooden door for her, and for a split second, it crossed her mind that he might be playing a joke on her. However, she realized it wasn't a joke once she crossed the threshold. They might be only twenty miles south of Austin, but she felt like she'd entered another world—like Dorothy when she stepped from Kansas's black-and-white world to the colorized world of Oz. Inside, she found a fascinating world of French countryside meets rural Central Texas.

There were classic but simple touches everywhere she looked. A distressed antique dresser used as a hostess stand at the entrance greeted them. A weathered stone pitcher holding Texas wildflowers sat on top of it. The dining room had been furnished with distressed tables and metal chairs, placed around the room to take advantage of the view from the wall-to-wall windows. However, more importantly than the ambiance, Greer's stomach awakened to the most delectable smells from the kitchen.

A pleasant-looking man emerged from behind the old-fashioned bar. He looked a little older than Gun. "Hey, Gun, good to see you. And this must be Greer."

Gun shook his hand and introduced Greer to Dave, the owner of the establishment and a friend.

"It's nice to meet you," she said. "You have an amazing place."

Dave smiled. "Well, thank you, Greer. I appreciate that. We put a lot of work into it and are proud of it. Come on, let me show y'all outside to your table." He walked them through the dining room and out a glass door leading to the deck.

The inside paled compared to the deck's view, and Greer couldn't contain her excitement. "This is incredible! I've never seen anything like this, at least not around here. But, Dave, where are all your customers?"

He laughed. "We're normally closed on Mondays, but Gun

helped us so much when we first opened that we owed him one. More than one. He told us he needed a special place for a special lady and asked if we could open it tonight. We're glad to be able to repay the favor finally, so tonight, the place is all yours."

Dave had opened the restaurant for the two of them? Gun must have done them some favor.

Gun pulled out a chair at a table with the best creek view, and Greer sat down. A woman wearing a chef's jacket brought an array of bite-size appetizers to their table, and he introduced her as Teresa, Dave's wife.

She was friendly and gregarious and waved away Greer's thanks for opening tonight. "We love Gun. We were thrilled he included us in your special night."

While she spoke, a young waiter filled their glasses with water. He returned shortly with a bottle of exquisite rosé wine. Although not a wine connoisseur, Greer recognized that it was excellent.

"Since it's a school night, I thought a tequila drink might be too much," Gun explained. "But of course, Dave will fix anything you'd like from the bar if you'd rather have something else."

Greer leaned back in her chair and took a sip of her wine. "No, this is perfect. Thank you."

The appetizers were savory, and she forgot to feel self-conscious. They'd just finished when Dave, accompanied by the waiter, appeared again. He served their dinner—lightly battered fish topped with jumbo shrimp and crab in a white wine caper sauce— inquired if they needed anything else and left them alone.

While they ate, Gun told her about the restaurant's farm-to-table philosophy and how seasonal items determined the menu. He explained that Teresa had grown up in Houston and trained to be a chef in Paris, but when she returned to Texas, she met Dave, and the rest was history. Teresa's training shined in her food. The fish, the flavorful rice, and the roasted summer vegetables were delicious. Greer especially loved the caper sauce. She could drink it by the gallon.

The sun began its evening descent into the horizon as they finished dinner, and the hundreds of white fairy lights wrapped around the broad oak trees illuminated the deck, enveloping it in soft light. Everything looked romantic in twilight. Michael Bublé's version of *"La Vie en Rose"* began to play through the speakers hanging on the building. She had always loved the Édith Piaf song, the ardor of her voice, accompanied by the lonely, sweet accordion, but she'd never bothered to look up the English lyrics before and had no idea they were so romantic.

The setting, the music, and the striking man sitting across from her felt like a dream or a scene from a movie, but she couldn't wrap her head around it. The last several months had been an emotional roller-coaster ride, and then overnight, they had morphed from adversaries to dating. It was mind-boggling. And suspicious. Tears slipped from her eyes, and she turned her head to wipe them away before Gun noticed.

But he had noticed—he noticed *everything*—and instantly knelt by her side. "Greer, what's wrong?"

She wanted to tell him to stand up, or he'd get his chinos dirty, but she couldn't speak. Then, to her shame, she began crying in earnest—ugly-crying—and fumbled in her purse for a tissue.

"Do you not like it here? Do you want to leave? Please tell me what I can do to help you." Gun sounded anxious, and she choked on her tears and gulped for breath.

He instructed her to take a deep breath and handed her the water glass. She took several gulps and calmed down, then turned her head away. She couldn't bear to face him looking like such a mess.

"Why did you take the trouble to do all this for me?" she managed. "Why would you send me flowers and gifts to convince me to go out with you? It wasn't that long ago that you acted like you hated me. I asked you once if I was a joke to you, and you didn't answer me. I guess I don't know what to think."

"Greer, I—I'm sorry. I've been selfish, and pressuring you into going out with me was unfair. You have every reason to feel upset and confused, but I want you to know I have *never* hated you. I've been angry with myself because of *my* shortcomings and took it out on you. I know it doesn't make sense, but it's the truth. You are not a joke, and I promise I'm not playing games with you. I asked you out tonight because I want to spend time with you and get to know you." He ran his fingers through his hair in frustration and said something in Korean. "I've been a jerk and an idiot, but I hope you'll forgive me and allow me another chance. Give me another chance to prove that I'm worthy of you."

It wasn't his apology but the desperation she heard in his voice that persuaded her to turn around. He appeared to be on the verge of tears, which moved her heart.

"Please," he pleaded. "Give me another chance. If you're not ready, I understand, and I will wait. I'll wait for you until you are ready to come to me. No matter how long it takes."

He would wait for her until she was ready to come to him? No man had ever given her that option. But did he mean it? She had been fooled so many times before.

She looked out at the creek and sighed. She hoped she wouldn't live to regret this. "Okay." She finally nodded, and Gun breathed a sigh of relief.

Teresa conveniently approached and asked if they needed anything before she served dessert.

Gun's face looked like he'd just been thrown a life preserver. "Would you please show Greer to the ladies' room?"

Greer was glad she'd listened to Shannon and brought a makeup bag, but it wouldn't help with her red, puffy eyes.

Teresa brought her a plastic bag filled with ice from the kitchen and put a comforting arm around her shoulders. "It's going to be okay."

"I'm sorry, Teresa," Greer said. "You and Dave were so kind to open for us on your day off, and I've ruined it."

She shook her head. "Nothing is ruined, so please don't worry about it. We like Gun, but even a good man is still a man and needs to be set straight. I was watching you from inside. Good for you for laying the groundwork from the beginning." She left Greer to finish refreshing her makeup and was told to come out when ready.

Greer walked back to the deck, half expecting that Gun had left her. Despite what he said about wanting a second chance, men didn't like drama.

He was still there, though, and his face relaxed. "I was afraid you might have called a cab and left me."

His honesty took her aback, and she realized she didn't know him well.

They walked to the edge of the deck and looked out over the creek in companionable silence, listening to the cicadas sing while lightning bugs presented them with a light show against the summer sky. She felt embarrassed and had little to say, but Gun carried the conversation for them both. He pointed out things along the creek that might interest her.

They returned to their table and shared a slice of a light, moist Chantilly cake with fresh berries and cream. A short while later, Gun suggested they leave.

Greer nodded. She felt exhausted after her breakdown, and

surely he regretted asking her out after she ruined the lovely evening he'd planned for her.

Dave and Teresa gave her a gift bag with a container of caper sauce and another slice of cake to remember their first date. Teresa insisted on taking their picture so that it would be something to look back on. Greer wanted to refuse, but Teresa and Dave were so kind that she didn't want to hurt their feelings. Unfortunately, the picture would be a painful reminder of their first and last date.

Once again, Gun carried the conversation while driving her home, but his voice sounded strained. He walked her to the front door, and she bit her lip to keep from crying. She had ruined their date and any chance of seeing him again.

"Thank you for agreeing to go out with me tonight, Greer. I enjoyed our evening together. Please get some rest."

He gave her a tender smile, but she had difficulty returning it. Finally, still unable to speak, she nodded and went inside.

After feeding Kevin and Sophie, she went to bed and cried. Gun had said nothing about calling her or seeing her again.

# Chapter Seventeen

The delivery of a single rose to Greer's office set everyone's tongues wagging the next day. They knew about her date but had obviously taken one look at her swollen eyes and prudently decided not to ask. Now, they insisted she spill and not leave out one detail. Her story left them awestruck, but they were proud of her for holding Gun's feet to the fire and equally impressed by his response.

Once alone, she opened the card and braced herself for the worst.

> Dear Greer,
> I enjoyed our evening together. Thank you for taking pity on an undeserving man. Yesterday was our Day One, and I look forward to the rest of our days together with happy anticipation.
> Gun

What? She'd expected an "On second thought, let's be friends" brush-off, not "Yesterday was our Day One." Referring to the Korean custom of marking the first day of a relationship, he sure knew her weak spots.

He called two days later and asked her out. She still felt embarrassed when Saturday night came, but Gun acted as if nothing had happened, so she followed his lead and allowed herself to enjoy the night. He'd planned a different date from their elaborate first one and took her for pizza and a movie as if they were teenagers. Then, even though they'd eaten, he bought popcorn and drinks at the movie theater, insisting it was part of the whole date-night experience.

They wore shorts because it was too hot to wear anything else, and Gun's left ankle rested on his right knee. She checked out his legs while they waited for the movie to start. They were long and tanned, and his calf muscles were well-defined. She sucked in a breath through her teeth.

"Is everything okay?" Gun asked.

He held the popcorn to his lips, and his bottom lip gleamed because of the butter. Cue the Barry White music. That bottom lip drove her crazy.

"Everything's fine. I'm just a little hot, that's all," she said and fanned herself.

The lights dimmed, and she focused on the coming attractions to get her mind out of the gutter. Her arm lay on the armrest between them, and Gun placed his hand on hers while glancing for her approval. Though not the first time they had touched, this time was different, and they knew it. Their eyes met in the dark theater. "Yes," she said.

He slipped his strong fingers between hers, brought her hand to his lips, and kissed it. His eyes were bright, and he gave her such a tender smile that her heart felt like it would burst out of her body.

Little by little, Gun became an ever-increasing presence in her life. He texted her while she worked to say hello and called her each night. After the first few nights, she would shower and change into her pajamas, anticipating his call. Then, she would lie across her bed while they talked. Remarkably, they never ran out of things to talk about. Gun was a fountain of knowledge, was witty and fun, and possessed a dry sense of humor. She often roared with laughter and kicked her feet in the air. It was an unexpected and enjoyable side of him. After their talks, she would go to bed feeling light-hearted and like she was sixteen again.

They had been going out for three weeks when Gun invited her to his house for dinner. She was excited but accepted his invitation with trepidation. An invitation to a man's house usually meant he wanted to take things to the next level, but she was reluctant to rush things. She was having the time of her life getting to know him. Every phone call and every date revealed something new and unexpected about him, and she wanted to stay in that euphoric phase of their relationship a little longer.

But if he did want to take things to the next level, why hadn't he kissed her yet? Didn't they say a man should kiss a woman after the third date? She and Gun had been on more than three, so was he having second thoughts? Did he not find her attractive? And who were "they," and how did they devise the three-date rule?

Gun insisted on picking her up, and when they arrived at his house, Buddy and Bullet were waiting for them. She greeted the loyal pair and was rewarded by the sight of two wagging tails.

He gave her a tour of his home, which was as impressive as the living area and kitchen. The primary bedroom and spa-style bath were on the first floor. His bedroom was nice but sparsely furnished, with only a king-sized bed, a nightstand, and a dresser.

"It's kind of small," she commented.

Like a typical man, he said, "But I only use it to sleep."

The en suite primary bath compensated for what the bedroom lacked. The entire bathroom, done in teak and soothing earth tones, had been super-sized for its large occupant. The shower looked like something out of a designer's showcase, with multiple shower heads with different functions and a skylight up above. A floor-to-ceiling window looked out to the backyard, bringing the outdoors inside.

"This is incredible! It's like a professional sauna."

"You're free to use it anytime," he offered slyly.

She blushed and remained silent. It was tempting.

Behind the staircase was his home office. He had a work desk in the center of the room and bookcases filled with books along an entire wall. There was also a wire rack holding rolls of blueprints, a printer, and all the electronics needed to run a business from home. Unlike her disorganized style, Gun was neat, and everything was in its place.

Just outside his office, she stopped to admire the many pictures in the hallway. They were mainly of Gun's family, including an adorable one of Gun and his two siblings. Gun and Luke wore white T-shirts and sported crew cuts. Luke was laughing, and Gun had a mischievous grin that displayed a missing tooth. They held Sarah, a chubby toddler, between them.

Another picture showed four boys—obviously Luke, Gun, Jason, and Justin—holding up their catch of fish. She moved in closer to get a better look. Something about it appeared familiar, but so did many pictures from that era. They all had that same sepia tone.

The house's second floor was nothing short of a sophisticated man cave and must have cost a fortune. A home theater with reclining leather seats and cupholders took up one section of the room. A pool table, foosball table, dartboard, and video game center were on the opposite side of the room. A refrigerator, wet bar, and cabinets lined a wall in between. The other two occupants of the house hadn't been forgotten. A sizeable cozy bed had been monogrammed with "Buddy," and a wide, comfy perch sat by the window for Bullet. Gun informed her he spent most of his free time here, and Greer could understand why.

The remaining rooms on the second floor were two guest bedrooms and a full bath. One of the bedrooms had two sets of bunk beds for his young nephews. Gun clearly loved his family and had designed his home to share it with them.

They returned to the kitchen, and he began to stir-fry beef bulgogi in a wok.

Greer's mouth watered when she took in a whiff of the marinated beef and onions. "What do you put in your marinade?"

He pointed to spices sitting on a Lazy Susan by the stove. "Soy sauce, sesame oil, garlic, onions, grated pear, and brown sugar. The sugar helps the meat develop a nice crust."

She inspected the spices, and when she smelled the sesame oil, she recognized it as the indiscernible smell at the Korean church.

He poured a thin, yellow batter filled with shrimp, scallions, and vegetables into a cast iron skillet for *pajeon*, a savory, crispy pancake. Did this man know the way to her heart or what? She loved *pajeon*. It was one of her favorite Korean dishes. Next, he opened a package of *ramyeon*, known to most people as ramen, and dumped the square of wavy noodles into the boiling water. Finally, he set out small plates of vegetable side dishes and bowls of white rice.

When they were ready to eat, Gun placed plates, napkins, and a pair of chopsticks on the granite island. She didn't see a fork and was embarrassed to ask for one. But before she said anything, he reached into a high cabinet, took out a small rectangular gift box, and set it before her.

"For me?" she asked.

He looked around the kitchen. "I don't see anyone else here, do you?"

She hesitated. "But shouldn't we eat first?"

His head cocked to the side. "That's what we're going to do. Please open the box. I'm hungry."

She slid off the pink bow and carefully peeled away the tape, careful not to tear the colorful paper. She would keep the wrapping paper as a memento, just like she kept everything he gave her. She lifted the lid and let out a cry. "You remembered!"

Nestled in tissue paper were pink children's training chopsticks. She had mentioned in passing during one of their nightly talks that she didn't know how to use them. Greer went around the island, threw herself at him, and kissed him, then pulled back, horrified. She covered her mouth with her hand. She couldn't believe she'd kissed him first. What if he didn't want—

Gun placed his arm across the small of her back and pulled her to him. He cradled her face to his with his other hand and kissed her. It was a quick, short kiss, but he kissed her again. This time, it was slower and deeper. His lips were soft and warm, better than she had imagined, and she liked his taste. She returned his kiss, and he groaned.

So, she had remembered how to do this after all. It had been so long that she worried she'd forgotten. Gun certainly knew what *he* was doing, and she started to feel weak in her knees.

Gun pulled his head back. His eyes were half-closed, and he breathed heavily. "Greer, you don't know how long I've wanted to do that. So, I'm having trouble believing I'm holding you in my arms. Thank you. Thank you for being here with me." He loosened his hold and let her go. "Come on, let's eat. I don't want you getting hangry on me."

They sat side by side at the island and dug into the delicious food. Gun showed her how to use the chopsticks, and by the time they finished eating, she was adept at using them.

When he drove her home a couple of hours later, he told her his entire family would be coming to town to celebrate the Fourth of July—well, everyone except his dad and his wife. "Is it okay to share your number with Sarah?" Gun said. "She wants to include you in the plans. But don't let her bully you, and feel free to say no to anything you're uncomfortable with. Or, if you prefer, we can spend the weekend alone, just the two of us. I'm good with that, too."

Greer spent most of her nonworking hours alone. She smiled. "Spending the Fourth with your family sounds like fun."

# Chapter Eighteen

The Donovan clan arrived in Austin for the Fourth of July weekend in two stages. First came Sarah, Scott, and their rambunctious crew of four boys ages sixteen to six: Sam, Ethan, Eli, and Mason. They arrived at Gun's house after lunch, carting monogrammed duffle bags and endless grocery bags. Sarah put away the groceries while Scott ordered the boys to carry their things upstairs.

Luke and Janet got into town late in the afternoon but went to Mrs. D's house first, where they would stay for the weekend. They arrived at Gun's house in the evening and comforted Sarah's boys, who anxiously awaited the pizza order. A mountain of pizza boxes finally arrived, looking like the opening scene in *Home Alone*. Janet looked at Greer's shocked face and assured her it wouldn't go to waste.

The kids ate upstairs in the game room while the adults sat outside. Thanks to several well-placed ceiling fans, the patio was comfortable, even on a hot July night. Gun also had a terrific audio system wired throughout the house. They could hear music in every room and outside on the patio. Sarah chose a playlist of seventies music, and Luke waxed nostalgic about their youth. Greer found their stories entertaining. She wished she'd met Mrs. D's family sooner.

They lost track of time until Sarah's youngest, Mason, came outside looking for his parents. He rubbed his eyes and told them his brothers were trying to cheat at foosball. Scott went upstairs to round up the boys for bed, and the party dispersed.

When Gun drove Greer home, he went inside with her. Kevin and Sophie greeted him, and he picked them up. He then held one in each arm as he walked through the house, checking for a breach in security, even though she had an alarm system. Finally, he set the kids down, and it was Greer's turn. She wrapped her arms around him and laid her head on his chest. She could hear his strong heartbeat.

"Thank you for tonight."

He leaned back to see her face and tucked her hair behind her ear. "What are you thanking me for? I didn't do anything."

"Yes, you did. You shared your family with me. Thank you for including me."

"You're welcome, but isn't that what you do in a relationship?"

Hearing him say out loud that they were in a relationship made her blush, but she loved hearing it.

"Silly girl," Gun said, then gave her a long, satisfying kiss.

Since their first kiss over a week ago, they'd been making up for lost time and doing lots of kissing. Not that Greer was complaining. His perfect lips weren't just for show. They locked perfectly with hers and created such a sensation within her.

"I better go now, or else I'll never leave," Gun said as he pulled away. He blew out his cheeks in frustration, kissed her head while telling her goodbye, and instructed her to lock the door.

She fed her kids a midnight snack and then went straight to bed. She slept soundly and did not wake up once.

⁓

She slept in the following day, which meant seven-thirty. An hour later, Gun texted, asking if she was awake and if he could call. Her friends had advised her not to be so easy and never respond immediately to a man's text, but she disregarded the advice. She was in the throes of new romance bliss and wanted to hear Gun's voice.

*I'm awake*, she texted back.

His finger must have been hovering on the call button because she'd scarcely hit send when her phone rang.

"Good morning," she answered, her voice still husky from sleep.

Gun sucked in his breath. "Love your sexy morning voice! Now I regret leaving last night." He chuckled. "I just wanted to let you know that my family's awake, and the group texts will be starting. My sister is sitting at the kitchen island drinking coffee. No doubt she'll start bugging you soon."

Greer laughed and assured him she could handle it.

Sure enough, Sarah and Janet began texting to coordinate the plans for the pool party that would be held at Greer's house. The two came over an hour before the rest of the gang so that Greer could give them a private tour of her home, free of husbands and kids. She thanked them for mentioning that the family had come to celebrate more than the July Fourth holiday. They would also celebrate Gun's birthday on July 5th, a minor detail Gun had failed to mention.

"Why do men act so strange about their birthdays?" Janet wondered aloud.

Shortly after noon, the rest of the family descended on her house, bringing enough food to feed an army. Janet arranged the food table and enlisted help from Darcy, her boyfriend Christopher, Dylan, and his buddy Michael.

The Donovans filled her house, which gratified her. Although she'd lived in the house for nine months, this was its inaugural party. Besides her extended family, she couldn't think of a better group to share the occasion with.

Gun and Luke arrived last. They brought the show's stars, the chicken and beef fajita meat, and Luke's famous pinto beans. Sarah had made Spanish rice, and Greer made her lauded guacamole. They had all the accouterments necessary for a fajita dinner: warm flour tortillas, grated cheddar cheese, sour cream, and pico de gallo. Not to mention enough drinks and desserts to last the entire weekend. The adults ate their lunch around the dining room table while the kids, including Darcy and Dylan and their friends, sat at the tables set up in the living room. The kids watched *The Goonies* as they ate, and Greer enjoyed hearing their laughter. Kevin mingled with them, and after her initial hesitation, Sophie joined them, too. The kids fussed over them, which warmed Greer's heart.

After the meal, everyone cleaned up and hurried to change into their swimsuits. But unlike the kids, Greer was not in any hurry to change. Today was the moment of truth, the first time Gun would see her in a swimsuit. She worried about what he would think of her fifty-year-old body. He had hugged her many times, so it wouldn't surprise him that she could stand to lose a few pounds. Still, a swimsuit could be unforgiving, so she'd looked for one that she hoped would cover a multitude of sins. After much deliberation, she'd bought a colorful tankini top with a V-shaped neckline. It revealed just enough cleavage to prevent it from looking like something from the Victorian era, yet it didn't show so much that it looked like something from Victoria's Secret. She paired it with a matching skort long enough to skim over the top of her thighs. She had been told she had nice legs but never liked her thighs. Finding a suit sexy enough for Gun to appreciate yet modest enough to wear around his family had been challenging. Still, she felt satisfied that she'd made the right choice.

When she walked out to the patio, the men were setting up the volleyball net in the pool. Gun was in the pool, and he took one end of the net from Luke and waded across with his arms above the water to hand it to Scott. When they were satisfied that it was secured, Gun climbed the pool steps and emerged looking like one of those men featured in the cologne commercials—the ones who emerged from the ocean with strategically placed water droplets dripping from their slick bodies.

The sight of his muscular, bare chest caused her to catch her breath, and she could hear the song "Oh Yeah," the one made famous in *Ferris Bueller's Day Off*, playing in her head. He walked to where she stood, preparing to join Sarah and Janet on the chaise lounges under the rectangular umbrellas, and she realized she was gawking.

Gun gave her the once-over with an enormous grin. "I like the suit. Is it my birthday gift?"

But she couldn't answer because she was mesmerized by a water droplet that trailed from the base of his throat, down his chest to the waistband of his navy swim trunks. Man, she was toast.

Gun, who had an uncanny ability to read her mind, laughed wickedly and caressed the top of her arms. "Exactly. Hold that thought for later," he said before jumping into the pool to join the others.

Greer gulped. She had to quash her desire to jump in after him to cool off.

Sarah declared that margaritas were in order since they'd decided to have a little gossip session. She made herself at home in Greer's kitchen and brought out a frozen drink for the three of them.

"Greer, I've meant to ask you. I heard you met Sunny. What

did you think of her?" Sarah asked before taking a long sip of her margarita.

"Uh, yeah, I did," Greer answered carefully. Where was Sarah going with this? She was on her side, wasn't she? "I met her at the hospital when Gun had his motorcycle accident."

"And?" Sarah prodded.

"Is this a trick question?"

Sarah and Janet laughed. "I haven't seen her in years, but it sounds like she's the same old Sunny," Janet said. "Let me guess. She came to the hospital proclaiming her love for Gun and calling him her husband."

Greer snorted. "That's exactly what she did. How did you know?"

Sarah shook her head. "Don't get me started. That woman has never loved my brother. She's always been after him for his money. I don't know why he puts up with her."

*Puts up with her.* Sarah spoke in the present tense—as if Gun and Sunny were still involved. Should she be worried? She needed to find out more.

"Our meeting was brief, but I didn't care for her very much. I'm curious why Gun would marry someone like her. I mean, she's attractive, but . . . he could've married anyone. So why did he pick her?"

Even behind their sunglasses, Greer could detect her companions' hesitant expressions.

Sarah swirled her margarita around in the glass, buying time. She finally spoke, weighing her words. "Well, when Gun met Sunny, he was going through a difficult time. I think he felt a little desperate, so he married the first girl that came along."

"Why would he have been desperate, though? I can't believe he didn't have tons of women chasing after him. He turns heads whenever we go out. More importantly, he's kind, smart, and funny."

Janet chuckled, and Sarah wagged her finger, reminding Greer of Mrs. D. "You're describing the man you know now. He didn't always look like this. Gun's always been handsome and super smart, but he was a late bloomer. In high school, he was a skinny band geek who wore glasses. Although he had tons of friends, he didn't have many girlfriends. He was the guy girls flirted with to get help with their calculus homework and then put in the friend zone."

Greer glanced over at Gun playing in the pool with his nephews. His biceps flexed as he lifted Eli to spike the ball over the net. "That's so hard to imagine, seeing him now."

"Oh, believe me, if you saw the pictures of what he looked like back then, you wouldn't recognize him," Sarah said. "He's gotten better looking with age."

"Really?" Greer said in disbelief. Come to think of it, none of the pictures Gun had displayed in his house were of his high school days. They were all pictures from his childhood or family photos. Now, she was curious to know what he'd looked like.

Janet murmured something in Korean to Sarah, who nodded. Greer guessed it must be highly sensitive intel. She would've insisted they share if she had been on her second margarita. Instead, she let it pass and asked Sarah to tell her more about how Gun and Sunny met.

Like her mom, Sarah liked having center stage. "Growing up, Gun *Oppa* and our dad didn't see eye-to-eye on many things. They argued when Gun quit the golf team in high school. Dad disapproved of Gun going to college out of state and, later, his decision to be an engineer. He wanted him to walk a certain path and put his talents to use. But that's not what my brother wanted. He's always had a mind of his own. Then, they had a *huge* falling out after Gun finished grad school. It had been simmering for years, and when it finally boiled over, Gun left for Korea to work for our uncle and ended up staying there for a couple of years."

"Is that when he met Sunny?"

"Yes. That nine-tailed fox dug her claws into him when he was far from home and feeling like a failure. She sucked the lifeblood out of him."

Greer titled her head, finding a disconnect in Sarah's tale. "Why did he feel like a failure? Didn't you say he had just finished grad school? That's quite an accomplishment."

"Watch out!" Scott yelled.

The volleyball bounced at Sarah's feet. She sprung from the chaise and served the ball into the pool with a strong arm. The interruption diverted their conversation, leading to a discussion of Sarah's days as co-captain of her high school volleyball team.

The men soon emerged from the pool to grab beers, and the older kids decided they'd had enough family time. They were eager to walk down the hill to Barton Springs Pool.

"Be back in a few hours, and you better respond to my texts!" Sarah called out after Sam. She then declared they needed another round of margaritas and went inside.

A few minutes later, Greer followed, walking in on Gun and Sarah deep in conversation. They spoke in Korean, and it sounded like Sarah was chastising him. Luke leaned against the kitchen counter, drinking a beer and shaking his head, while Scott snacked on tortilla chips and guacamole. She froze against the door, and they stopped talking.

Sarah poured a generous amount of tequila into the blender. "Sorry for the holdup on the margaritas," she said nervously. "I had to tell my brother something."

Whatever they'd discussed hadn't bothered Gun. He walked to where she stood and draped a long arm over her shoulder. "Gigi-ah, have we scared you off yet? Remember, we're Irish and Korean, so we're naturally loud and bossy, especially my little sister here. But this is your house, and we're the guests. So feel free to kick us out when you tire of us."

Everyone laughed, and Greer made her way to the bathroom. When she returned outside, a fresh margarita awaited her, and she leaned back on her chaise to relax. Sarah and Janet were in the pool with Sarah's boys.

Gun joined her, sitting on the chaise previously occupied by his sister. He picked up her hand, kissed it, and placed it on his toned abs. Then he sighed with contentment and closed his eyes. In no time, he was asleep, oblivious to his nephews' raucous shouting.

Greer's guests stayed a couple more hours before packing their belongings to return to Gun's house. The boys were hot, tired, and anxious for their uncle's air-conditioned game room. Luke and Janet had promised Mrs. D they would join her for dinner, and Sarah declared she was ready for a nap despite the late hour.

Gun kissed Greer goodbye on the lips, in full view of his family, and his nephews snickered. "Should I come back after dropping off this crew?" he whispered in her ear.

Greer, because she was at home and having fun, had allowed herself to indulge in one margarita too many. Consequently, she yawned in the face of the man she had gawked at only a few hours earlier. "Okay," she said, closing her eyes and resting her head on his chest. It would be wonderful to fall asleep while standing up against him.

Gun wrapped his arms around her to keep her from sliding down. He called to his family, "Hey, y'all, head to the house. I'll make sure Greer's okay and then walk back."

~

Greer woke up in her bed at midnight and looked around, confused. She vaguely recalled Gun helping her to her bedroom but remembered nothing afterward. She hoped she hadn't said or done anything embarrassing.

She got out of bed and walked through the dark house. The only light came from above the kitchen stove. Kevin and Sophie were curled in their beds in the living room, and while they lifted their heads for a moment, they went right back to sleep. They, too, had an exciting day. To her dismay, she realized she hadn't fed them. She returned to the kitchen, but their food and water bowls were half full. Then she noticed the note on her kitchen counter written in Gun's barely legible scrawl.

*Kids fed, litter box cleaned. I took your keys and locked your door. Call me in the morning, Sleepyhead. – G*

She picked up the note, held it to her lips, and smiled. She could not have been happier.

# Chapter Nineteen

On the Fourth of July, Greer sat beside Gun as they drove along Highway 290 to Dripping Springs, southwest of Austin. Gary Wilson, one of Gun's high school friends, and his wife, Michelle, owned a ranch there. Although eighty percent of the acres had been set aside as a nature and wildlife preserve, the rest was a working ranch with cattle-grazing leases. Five acres were used as a wedding venue, and every year, the Wilsons hosted a massive Fourth of July picnic there with food, games, a live band, and fireworks. It sounded like a lot of fun, but Greer was nervous to meet Gun's friends.

Gun reached over and squeezed her hand. "Don't worry, Gigi-ah. My friends are going to love you. And if they don't, to hell with them. Who needs friends with poor taste?"

Greer laughed, hoping he was right.

"There you go. But seriously, let me know if you feel uncomfortable about anything."

Gun parked in the dirt parking lot among several other trucks and SUVs. He held her hand as she stepped out of the truck and closed the passenger door as his friends rushed to meet them.

"Greer," Gary greeted her warmly. "We've waited so long to meet you and couldn't be happier. We've heard so much about you. We feel like we already know you."

She shook his hand but found his comments curious. She and Gun had been dating for only a month.

"I'm not shaking your hand," Michelle said, embracing her. "I know we are going to be great friends. Now y'all go mingle, and we'll catch up later."

Luke and his family were already there, visiting with the other guests. Gun escorted her around and introduced her, and although everyone was welcoming, she still felt relieved to have Gun by her side.

When Scott, Sarah, and their crew arrived, they went inside the multi-purpose venue where the food had been laid out to protect it from the heat. There was brisket, sausage, chicken, coleslaw, potato salad, and beans. In true Fourth of July tradition, they also served hot dogs. Everyone loaded their plates and found tables in the covered dance hall.

Greer ate almost everything on her plate, and Gun finished the rest. She washed it all down with ice-cold sweet tea with a squeeze of lemon. Her soul and belly felt content and satisfied. She'd eaten one of her favorite meals while seated beside her favorite guy.

Gun put his arm around her and leaned his head against hers. "Happy, my Gigi-ah?"

She was, indeed. Life was good.

Their brief idyll was interrupted when Gary and Michelle approached their table. "Gun, I'm stealing your girl for a tour of the ranch," Michelle said. "You and Gary can go play horseshoes with the guys."

Not waiting for her consent, Michelle led Greer outside to a golf cart, telling her that although they weren't going far, it was too hot to walk. The cart whirred as she backed up and followed a wide dirt road behind the venue. Soon, a hacienda-style stone church with a bell tower appeared.

Michelle came in hot and parked in front of the chapel. Built of Texas limestone, a red roof covered its bell tower. The kind of bell people in the movies rang to warn the villagers of impending danger. Hopefully, she wasn't in any.

They climbed the stone steps to the archway, and Greer craned her neck up and around, trying to take it all in. Inside, thick oak beams crisscrossed the ceiling, and stone benches sat on either side of the center aisle. At the front stood a stone altar with a simple wooden cross. It felt reverential and serene.

"We built the chapel away from the other amenities to preserve its sanctity," Michelle said. "It deserves to stand alone. Now, there's one more place I want to show you."

They returned to the golf cart, and Michelle drove up a hill until they leveled out on a cliff overlooking rolling hills and the creek below. "The view from this ridge is magnificent in the spring and late fall," she said.

It looked gorgeous now, so Greer could only imagine what it would look like in those months when God's handiwork was fully displayed.

"We're in high demand throughout the year and booked one, sometimes two years in advance. But we'll always make accommodations for you and Gun, so let us know when y'all are ready." She grinned. "Judging by how you two look at each other, I'd say it won't be long now."

Ready for what? Ready for *marriage*? Greer observed Michelle closely as they walked back to the golf cart, checking for signs of a heat stroke. But Michelle appeared fine and returned Greer's look with a genuine smile. Wasn't she putting the cart before the horse? She and Gun hadn't been dating long enough to talk about marriage.

*Wait a minute.* Greer stopped in her tracks. What was *she* thinking? Why was she even *entertaining* the thought of marriage? The brisket and the romantic wedding venue must be playing with her emotions.

They returned to the venue, and she and Janet partnered for the three-legged race and came in third. She cheered for Sarah's boys, Sam and Ethan, as they hopped to victory in the sack race, then played bean bag toss with Eli and Mason. She watched Gun and Scott compete in a game of giant Jenga and consoled Gun with a kiss when Scott pulled out a win. Later, as the band was warming up, Greer sat to enjoy the show, but Gun grabbed her hand and pulled her to her feet. "I lost track of time," he said. "We'd better go, or we'll be late."

Greer's eyebrows rose. "Late for what? Where are we going? Can I say goodbye to Gary and Michelle? What about your family?"

"You'll see my family tomorrow at my mom's house, and here are Gary and Michelle."

The couple approached carrying two brown paper bags. They hugged Greer goodbye and handed Gun the bags filled with several food containers.

He briskly led her to his truck, and she'd barely snapped in her seat belt when Gun peeled out of the parking lot and onto Highway 290 North toward Austin.

"Gun, where are we going in such a hurry?"

He looked confused. "Your parents' condo. Didn't they invite us to watch the fireworks from their balcony?"

Greer bit her lip. Oh, yeah. That. She'd forgotten about relaying her parents' invitation to Gun. He'd appeared enthusiastic, but she didn't think he would remember—or, more precisely, she'd *hoped* he wouldn't. She was nervous about introducing him to them, like how Baby felt about introducing Johnny Castle to her dad in *Dirty Dancing*.

When she'd finally found the courage to tell them about

Gun and that he was Asian, her father stared at her, speechless. "What did you say?" he finally said, shaking his head. "I can't believe what I'm hearing. You can't be serious."

"That's okay, that's all right. We're all God's children," her mother said to keep the peace. Her response was better, but it wasn't a ringing endorsement.

So Greer hadn't pushed tonight's visit. Her mom would be okay, but her dad was a different story. He could be rude, and Gun didn't deserve to be treated that way, especially a day before his birthday.

They arrived at the condo, and while they waited for her parents to come to the door, she held her breath. *Please let tonight go well.*

The deadbolt clicked.

*Please, please.*

Her parents opened the door, and she finally exhaled when she saw their smiling faces. Her mother and Gun looked at each other in surprise, and her mother said, "Oh my goodness! It's you!"

"Hello, ma'am. How are you?"

Greer looked from one to the other. "What's going on?"

Her mother beamed. "Remember I used to tell you about the handsome young Oriental man at the grocery store? Even though he was just a customer, he was kind and helpful. I can't believe it, but it's him! It's Gun! Talk about a small world!"

Greer winced. She remembered her mother telling her about the kind young *Asian* man at the grocery store. He helped her reach for things too high on the shelves and even took her cart to the cart return. "He's so friendly," her mother would comment. But she wished her mother hadn't used the word *Oriental*. She glanced at Gun, but he didn't seem offended.

Never in a million years would she have dreamed that

"young man" was Gun. Maybe Mrs. D was right about fate. All their fates appeared entwined.

She introduced Gun to her father and wanted to cover her eyes with her hands. *Please, please.*

Gun extended his hand and, in his most respectful voice, said, "Hello, sir. It's a pleasure to meet you finally. Thank you for the invitation."

To her great relief, her father didn't rebuff Gun's gesture. Instead, he shook his hand, and his smile appeared genuine. "Gun, it's good to meet you. We've heard a lot about you. Come on in, make yourself at home. Although it sounds like you and my wife are already buddies."

Gun held up the brown bags and explained they'd brought barbecue and all the fixings. He apologized for the late hour but suggested it would make some excellent leftovers. They assured him it was fine—it smelled mouthwatering, so they'd try some now—and led them to the dining table, where a beautiful chocolate cake covered with strawberries awaited.

"Greer said it's your birthday tomorrow, but I didn't know what kind of cake to get," her mother said, looking at him as if waiting for his approval.

"This is perfect! How did you know I love chocolate?" Gun put his arm around her mother.

She hugged him back, and her affection seemed genuine.

They gathered around the dining room table while her parents sampled the barbecue. Her father tried to get along. "Gun, do you follow NASCAR?"

"Well, sir, I don't follow it closely, but my brother is a fan," he said. "So I know the drivers in the race for the cup. Didn't they race in Daytona on Saturday?"

Greer breathed easier. Gun just scored a hundred points.

They cut the cake, but after only a couple of bites, they

abandoned their plates and ran out to the balcony at the sound of the first pop of fireworks. Gun reached for her hand and smiled brightly. He didn't appear upset about being here instead of with his family and friends, and Greer sent up a silent prayer of thanks. So far, so good.

The Fourth of July celebration wasn't finished. They spent the next day, Gun's birthday, at Mrs. D's house, where she prepared a Korean feast of Gun's favorites. It was Greer's first time inside, and she enjoyed looking around. Mrs. D had lived in the United States for over fifty years, yet her house held many reminders of her home country.

Greer figured she would do the same if she were an ex-pat. She helped in the kitchen until Mrs. D ran her out, then she retreated to the living room and found a photo album of Gun's baby pictures on a shelf. He'd been an adorable baby, and she studied his pictures wistfully. She would have loved to have a baby that looked like him.

She snapped the album shut when Sarah's youngest, Mason, climbed into her lap. His brothers, Ethan and Eli, joined them and explained their latest video game to her.

Over lunch, Mrs. D, beside herself with happiness, proclaimed that she always knew Gun and Greer were meant to be together. Then she thanked Darcy for setting the wheels in motion by taking the picture at the airport.

Darcy laughed. "Uncle Gun was so funny! I told him to talk to Greer, but he said she'd think he was some creepy stalker. I took her picture so he'd remember the one that got away."

It may have been Greer's imagination, but the adults—except for Mrs. D—seemed uneasy as they exchanged glances.

Greer wished they would let her in on their secret. Was there a woman from Gun's past, the so-called one that got away? And if there was, should she be concerned?

# Chapter Twenty

After the Fourth of July weekend, the summer flew by. Greer and Gun saw each other daily as their lives became more entwined.

They grocery-shopped, cooked, and split their time between each other's houses. Gun watched the dramas with Greer and explained the things lost in translation, and his colorful commentaries kept her in stitches. Since they'd discovered they'd both gone there as kids, they went to Sandy's Hamburger's and got their famous frozen custard cones. Like when they were kids, they ate them at the picnic tables in the back, hurrying to finish before the creamy custard melted down the cone and onto their hands.

When Gun left for Korea at the end of July, Greer used the time to get reacquainted with her pie-baking skills. It had been over twenty-five years since she'd made a pie from scratch. Still, she taught Darcy, Christopher, and Dylan—who had returned to town early for the fall semester—and they surprised Gun with homemade peach cobbler and strawberry pie upon his return. Greer even surprised her parents and the people at her office with pies. She enjoyed cooking and baking again and liked having the kids over. They were lively and pleasant company and were good with Kevin and Sophie. She'd always wanted a house full of kids and was finally living her dream.

However, the time she loved the most was their nightly walks with Buddy. She and Gun walked him after dark every night so the sizzling asphalt would not burn his paws. As they walked, it felt as if they were the only two people in the world, with Greer's hand resting inside the crook of Gun's elbow, talking about their day, sharing intimate secrets only lovers share. It had been years since Greer had an intellectual and emotional connection with a man, and she hadn't realized how much she'd missed it.

But as much as she enjoyed doing things together, she was reluctant when Gun suggested they take a moonlit motorcycle ride.

"Babe, I know. It can be scary," he said. "But I promise I won't let anything happen to you. Do you trust me?"

She was still afraid, but she knew he would care for her when she looked into his eyes. "Yes, I trust you."

The bike's powerful engine roared as he pulled into her driveway the night of their ride.

She met him outside and eyed it warily. "Are you sure it's safe for me to ride? You wouldn't lie to me, right?"

"I promise it's safe. *I'll* keep you safe." He smiled, but his eyes were strangely serious. "Gigi-ah, maybe we should talk. There's something I need to tell you—"

Greer's chest tightened. This didn't sound good. "Gun, we better get going before I chicken out," she said in a rush, unprepared and afraid to hear what came next.

He put his hands in his pockets and looked down at the driveway, deep in thought. After a few seconds, he nodded and looked up. "You're right. We can talk later."

She had been granted a reprieve. For now. She'd been holding her breath and exhaled with relief.

He made her wear a jacket and a helmet and told her to hold on tight. He lifted the side stand with his foot, fiddled with a few things she didn't understand, squeezed the clutch lever, and started the engine. "All right, Gigi-ah!" he said over the noise. "Let's go!"

She was surprised when "Mixed Emotions" by the Rolling Stones blasted from the stereo as he rolled down the street. She had no idea motorcycle sound systems were so fancy, but then again, she knew nothing about them. She hugged him tightly and laid her head on his back. Her boyfriend was so cool. And so freaking hot.

Gun drove slowly through their neighborhood, but even so, the hilly Barton Skyway made her stomach clench, and she shut her eyes and held on tighter. He turned right on Lamar and picked up speed as he headed toward US Highway 290, but several traffic lights caused them to stop. They finally reached the "Y" in Oak Hill, where US Highway 290 meets US Highway 71, and although there were fewer traffic signals, he continued at a moderate pace, which she felt was for her benefit. The four-lane highway was smooth but wound up, down, and around the rolling hills.

Greer finally overcame her fear and lifted her head from Gun's back. Everything looked different from the back of the bike. With the wind in her face and without the confines of a car, she felt a freedom she hadn't known in years.

They drove for half an hour, taking Highway 71 West through Bee Caves, past Hamilton Pool Road and the community of Spicewood. Occasionally, he'd look back and shout, "How are you doing? Are you okay?"

He pulled into a gas station parking lot before they reached the Blanco County line, stopped, and then turned around. "What do you think so far? Are you having fun?"

She nodded. "I love it! I don't know why I was so afraid."

Gun got off the bike. "That's my girl." He offered his hand. "Come on, let's stretch before heading back. I don't want to overdo it on your first ride."

They headed home, but not before stopping at Kerbey Lane Café for a midnight snack of pancakes. They talked until the early morning hours, and she didn't want their time together to end when they reached her house. They kissed on her porch, and she curled his silky hair around her fingers and gave it a gentle tug. She couldn't get enough of him. Likewise, his kiss felt urgent, seeking, and his left hand rested on her neck at the back of her hair. After their exhilarating night, this would be the perfect time to invite him to stay.

She pulled away, trying to catch her breath. "Gun—"

"Gigi," he said breathlessly, reaching for her again.

"Do you want to—"

*Maybe we should talk. There's something I need to tell you.*

"Yes?" he said, covering her face with kisses.

She put her hand on his chest and gently pushed him away. "I'm sorry, I didn't mean to . . ." She drew a breath. "I think it's time we called it a night."

"What?" Gun looked like someone had thrown a bucket of cold water on him, and his breathing was heavy. "Oh, right. Okay."

She wished someone had poured cold water on her. The hurt and confusion in his eyes killed her, but she had so many doubts and questions.

He went inside and checked the house, then leaned in and kissed her cheek before leaving. "Goodnight, Gigi-ah. I'll call you later today."

She changed into a nightgown, sat on the edge of her bed, and looked at the clock. Ugh. Two fifteen. Although exhausted, her mind raced. She hadn't meant to lead Gun on. Last week, when she caught herself singing Madonna's "Crazy for You," it hit her like a ton of bricks that she had fallen for him. But what if Gun didn't feel the same way? She knew he cared for her, but he'd never told her he loved her, and she didn't believe that was a detail to overlook. She'd made that mistake before and didn't want to repeat it.

But the real reason for her hesitation was the little voice in her head that wouldn't be silenced. It kept warning her that their relationship wouldn't last. And tonight, that little voice had reared its ugly head again. *Maybe we should talk. There's something I need to tell you.* That was never a good conversation starter, and she didn't want anything interrupting her happiness, however temporary it might be. She knew she was overreacting, but there were other signs.

Why had Sarah talked about Sunny as if she was still in Gun's life? Had Gun had a change of heart about Sunny since the night at the hospital? To Greer's knowledge, Sunny hadn't contacted Gun since then, but would Gun tell her if she had? During her marriage, Beau had been in touch with his old girlfriends but kept it hidden. He'd told her his private life was none of her business.

Then, there were the furtive glances between Gun and his siblings at Darcy's mention of "the one that got away." Most likely, it wasn't Sunny, but was there someone else from Gun's past? Several times, she had caught Gun with a quiet, faraway look in his eyes, and once, she'd asked him if something was wrong. He'd brushed away her concerns and said he was thinking about a problem on one of his uncle's projects. But he usually discussed those problems with her during their walks, so she wondered if he was honest with her.

~

In mid-July, her best friend Maggie had resurfaced, and Greer wanted to cry with relief. Maggie's twins, Madison and Maxwell, were at a two-week Spanish immersion camp in Costa Rica, so Greer and Maggie met for lunch. "I finally get to have an uninterrupted adult conversation," Maggie said. As much as Greer loved the twins, she was relieved to have one-on-one time with Maggie. She had a lot to share.

"What? You're *dating?*" Maggie shrieked. "Why am I just hearing about this? Why didn't you call me?"

"Because you're so busy chauffeuring the twins, attending your various mother's groups, or you and Bob are doing things with other couples, you never answer your phone. At least not for me. I tried calling you—several times—but it always went to voicemail. I didn't feel like sharing the news—*my* news—by text. I wanted to hear the excitement in your voice when I told you."

Maggie had the grace to look sheepish. "I'm sorry I haven't been there for you. I haven't been a very good friend."

"It's not an indictment, Mags. It's just the way of the world, right?"

Maggie smiled. "Well, show me a picture. I'm dying to see what he looks like."

Greer held up her phone with Gun's picture, and Maggie looked taken aback.

"He's hot, but you've always dated such waspy guys. When did you become attracted to Asian men?"

"Emm, sometime around the fifth grade, I think. It's funny, but I can't remember exactly when."

"And your parents are okay with this?" she asked.

Greer shrugged. "They seem to be. I think they genuinely like him."

And when she and Gun went to dinner at Maggie and her

husband Bob's house the following week, Maggie liked him too. While alone in the kitchen preparing dessert, Maggie whispered to Greer, "I think he's a keeper." That was high praise since she hadn't liked Greer's former boyfriends, including Jake, and she detested Beau.

So, now, after her motorcycle ride with Gun, Greer was relieved Maggie was back in the loop. Who better to confide in about her sense of foreboding? They talked on the phone while Maggie took what she described as a mental health break with her favorite Merlot.

"It's like in the dramas," Greer said, trying to explain. "Everything is going well for the lead couple, but then the scene cuts to the arrival of a mysterious person at the airport. I don't know why it's always the airport, but it is, and you know that person's arrival signals the beginning of the end."

Maggie, who'd never watched a K-drama before, obviously had no idea what Greer was talking about. "That's absurd. I think you're watching too much television," she said between prolonged sips of the Merlot. "Life doesn't always imitate art and vice versa. I've seen you together, and Gun cares for you. I'd go so far as to say he's falling in love with you. No one is going to come between the two of you. Stop thinking that way. I think you're scared because of your past relationships."

Greer considered that. Perhaps Maggie was right. Was it possible she was subconsciously self-sabotaging the relationship out of fear of being hurt again? She had nothing concrete to support her doubts. It was just a gut feeling, but her instincts were rarely wrong.

Time would tell.

That time came sooner than she expected.

"Babe, I'm sorry to spring this on you, but I'm flying to Korea tomorrow evening," Gun said when they walked Buddy the following Thursday. "Uncle In-Bae has asked me to review a construction project that's behind schedule due to the monsoon season. Would you drive me to the airport? I want to spend as much time with you as possible."

Greer felt a pit in her stomach. She found the trip's timing suspicious, coming so soon after she hit the brakes on their intimacy.

Gun grinned. "Aww, Gigi-ah, what's wrong? Do you miss me already?"

"Yeah," she admitted with a forced laugh, but she couldn't shake the dread that came upon her. He'd left for a week in July and returned to her. Why would this time be different?

On Friday afternoon, Gun gave her a satisfying, long kiss when she arrived at his house, which made her wonder if her instincts were malfunctioning. He certainly didn't behave as if anything was wrong. They said goodbye to Dylan and the boys and left for the airport.

Gun leaned back in the passenger's seat. "I'm sorry for the sudden trip. You know I wouldn't go if it wasn't urgent." He snapped his fingers. "I almost forgot. I printed a hard copy of my flight itinerary for you. I know you're inundated with emails."

His backpack sat on the floorboard between his feet, and he reached down and unzipped the front pocket right as his phone rang. He rolled his eyes and showed the phone to Greer. It was his mother, and he answered and switched to Korean. Whatever she said to him had him digging in his backpack again, and he hung up after a few minutes.

"Your client is relentless," he teased. "She wanted to be sure I had the documents she asked me to give to my uncle. I don't know why she won't let me email them to him. She's just old school, I guess."

Greer did not comment. She kept her eyes glued to the road and gripped the steering wheel so tight that her knuckles turned white. Although prone to having a lead foot, she doggedly observed the speed limit while cars rushed past her. She detected Gun looking at her sideways and knew he was wondering what had gotten into her. They reached the Spirit of Texas exit, and her stomach tightened. The next exit would lead them to the airport. She couldn't go any slower, or they would be rear-ended. Even with her attempts to delay, they arrived sooner than she would have liked. She pulled into the passenger drop-off lane and began to tremble, feeling like Marsha Mason's character in *The Goodbye Girl*. Maybe she did watch too much television, but no matter what Maggie or anyone else said, she suddenly knew with absolute certainty that things were about to change.

Gun came around the car, and she threw her arms around him, grabbing handfuls of his shirt.

"My poor Gigi-ah. You were quiet on the drive over." Gun leaned back and held her face in his hands. "Please tell me what's the matter."

She thought her heart would rip at his tender look. "Nothing's the matter. I just . . . I love you, Gun." She hadn't meant to say that, but she panicked and what if she never got another chance to tell him how she felt?

Gun's face fell. "Oh, Greer. What timing. I . . . well, there's something I've been wanting to tell you."

And there it was. Her instincts had been right. Only she had been the one to cause their demise.

The police officer directing traffic blew his whistle and ordered her to move her car. Feeling mortified by her impromptu confession, she pulled away from him and hurried back inside her car.

"Greer, wait!" Gun called out. He tapped on the window of her door. "Greer! Park the car. Let's talk."

She couldn't bear to face him, much less talk. She shifted to Drive just as he approached the passenger side and hit the gas pedal as if her life depended on it, barely missing the pedestrians in the crosswalk. She exited the airport and drove home on autopilot, oblivious to her surroundings. Once in the safety of her own home, she dropped to the floor and let out a wail from the deepest part of her soul.

~

*November 1989*
*Dallas, Texas*

Greer sat on the edge of her seat and put her hands on her knees to keep her legs from shaking. She looked up at the clock on the wall, waiting for the click of the small hand landing firmly on the two, signaling the end of class. Without waiting for Professor Banks to announce class dismissed, she slipped on her backpack and shot out of the classroom like the space shuttle blasting off after ignition. Charlie called after her, but she didn't stop. She'd been fighting back tears for the past hour and couldn't hold them back any longer.

She sprinted across the Quad and took a right toward the university campus, not wanting to be anywhere her friends could find her. Once she cleared the Quad, she slowed down and walked along the crowded sidewalks filled with undergraduate students on their way to class. She kept her head down to hide the hot tears that wouldn't stop and racked her brain for a place to hide. Then she remembered the hidden garden. When she discovered it, she couldn't believe such an exquisite and peaceful place existed in the middle of campus.

She flopped on the curved stone bench and dropped her backpack on the gravel path, her back to the garden entrance. The large angel with perfectly symmetrical wings stood before her, her head tilted slightly, and her arms outstretched. Even with a stone face, she appeared sympathetic.

Today had been Greer's turn in Civil Procedure. She read the assignment twice and thought she understood it. But Professor Banks had shown her otherwise.

"Ms. Garza!" he barked, pointing his finger at her, demanding her answer. Except she kept drawing a blank. She looked down at her textbook, frantically searching her notes and the highlighted portions, but the words on the page ran together. She'd sputtered phrases, attempting to answer, only to have him ruthlessly cut her off.

"Did you even read the assignment? Don't waste my and your colleagues' time coming to class unprepared. Mr. Walker, help Ms. Garza out."

Professor Banks had humiliated her and exposed her as a fraud, someone unworthy of being here, in front of everyone. She couldn't imagine what her classmates thought of her. From the start, she'd never been confident she had what it took. Her father had pushed her, and she didn't dare fight him. It had been almost three months since the start of the semester. Each day, she increasingly doubted that she was smart enough or capable enough to endure this path. Today's utter failure proved that law school and the legal profession weren't for her. Apart from the friends she'd made, she hated everything about it and wanted to give up.

She started to sob, then hiccuped to a sputtering stop at the sound of crunching footsteps on the gravel path. Someone had found her.

"Please," she said shakily. "I'd like to be alone."

But the footsteps grew louder until the person was right

behind her. He said nothing but offered a white handkerchief over her left shoulder. The simple act of kindness made her cry harder.

He squeezed the same shoulder for encouragement. She couldn't look at him but turned her head, her gaze so low that only her benefactor's torso was visible. He wore a UT sweatshirt and jeans, which narrowed his identity to about a quarter of the guys in her class.

"Thank you," she said as he walked away.

She blew her nose and folded the handkerchief. The other side was monogrammed with a navy block letter "J." She sniffled and ran her fingers along the stitching. Who had given her the handkerchief? Her friends Jim Monroe and Jared Healey were the first to come to mind. Jim lived on the Inn's second floor, and they liked to sit in his room drinking beer and wine coolers while listening to Bonnie Raitt's *Nick of Time* album.

Jared also lived on the second floor, but their shared interest was food. He knew all the good restaurants around Dallas and took her and Carole Anne to his favorites. Another possibility was David Jones, who was in her study group. But Jim had gone to college in Maryland, Jared to Baylor, and David to Texas A&M. None of those guys would be caught dead in a UT sweatshirt. So, who was the "J" who had gone to UT and knew her well enough to follow her? She caught her breath when she realized who fit the profile, then grabbed her backpack and ran toward the Quad.

Jake stood on the sidewalk by Lawyer's Inn at the point where it branched in two different directions, like a fork in the road. He wore the UT sweatshirt and jeans, and his eyes widened when he saw her. "Greer, are you okay?"

Without thinking, she ran to him and wrapped her arms around him. "Yes. No. I don't know. I don't know if I'm okay, but thank you, Jake."

"What's this all about? I didn't do anything," he said above her head.

"Yes, you did. You were there for me when I needed a friend."

"Well, I . . . you're welcome. I guess. But what happened that has you so upset?"

She told him the awful story as he escorted her to the steps on the south side of the Inn. He didn't criticize, and his steady voice comforted her. Although he was late for class, he stayed with her until she calmed down. He also told her about his experience in criminal law, which sounded worse than hers. She doubted it was as bad as he made it seem, but she was grateful for his attempts to ease her shame. He assured her that no one would remember or judge her since they were all in the same boat.

She stood on the Inn's bottom step, making them almost eye level. He took her hand, something he'd never done before, and his green eyes held such tenderness that she believed him. Her doubts about him being cold and distant began to fade at that moment, and she saw him in a new light. Although he was not the affectionate type, he was a good person. A kind person. And she knew she could trust him.

# Chapter Twenty-One

Gun called several times Friday evening, probably while on his layover at the DFW Airport, but Greer refused to answer her phone. He then switched to texting, begging her to call him so they could talk. But she wasn't ready to hear what he had to say. It couldn't be anything good.

She stayed in the house all weekend, watching tearjerker movies and listening to sad music. She didn't have an appetite, not even for the Blue Bell Rocky Road ice cream she kept for emergencies. Except for her daily call to her parents, she made no contact with the outside world. She felt guilty for not checking in on Dylan as he house-sat for Gun, but the connection was too close.

On Monday morning, getting out of bed and ready for work was an effort, but she did it. She considered calling in sick—she'd accrued years of vacation time and sick leave—but she didn't want to be home alone with her depressing thoughts.

However, she couldn't focus and made careless mistakes. She'd never relied on anyone to do her work and felt uncomfortable asking for help now. Work had always been her refuge, but she could no longer hide in its shelter. Unable to work but reluctant to go home, she sat behind her desk and stared at the wall, immobilized by grief.

Her team realized something was wrong, and Rita took matters into her own hands. She marched into Greer's office and took the files from her desk. Seconds later, Greer heard her assigning them to Megan and Molly. After a while, Greer heard muffled voices, and a few minutes later, Giles Hudson entered Greer's office. "You mean a lot to us, Greer, so go home and take all the time you need," he said. "I hope everything is okay. Please let us know what we can do to help."

His kind words caused the tears to flow again, to her shame. Since she was in no position to argue with him due to his seniority and her mental state, she did as he said.

Once at home, she let her purse fall to the floor and dropped face-down on the sectional without changing her work clothes. Her babies jumped onto the sectional, seeming to sense their mommy's hurt. Kevin lay at her head and Sophie at her feet, guarding her at both ends.

She had prayed fervently since Gun left. Yet, instead of receiving an answer, she'd dreamt about Jake again. It made no sense. Why was this happening to her? What was she doing wrong?

"Please help me, God," she whispered desperately before falling into a troubled sleep.

Her ringing phone woke her. Although groggy and with a terrible headache, she lifted her head and fumbled inside her purse. She squinted at the screen. Had she slept for two hours? An unknown Dallas number showed on the screen. She was about to let it go to voicemail but changed her mind and swiped the white button with her index finger.

"Hello?" she said.

"Hello, Greer?"

Nearly two decades had passed since she'd heard that voice, but she recognized it immediately. "Yes?"

"I'm not sure you'll remember me because this is going way back, but—"

"Jake," she said breathlessly, unable to believe it herself. She'd hardly slept or had a thing to eat or drink in three days, so she might be delirious. She pushed herself up and sat with one leg tucked under her.

"I'm surprised you remembered my voice after all these years."

She wanted to tell him it wasn't so difficult, especially since they used to speak every day. "I remember it."

"Oh. Well, my colleagues and I are in town preparing for a trial that starts on Wednesday. Would you want to catch up over dinner?" He sounded so nonchalant, as if they'd kept in touch and spoken only last week.

Surely, she was dreaming. After all, Jake had invaded her dreams for the past eight months. Nevertheless, she agreed to pick him up tomorrow night at his hotel.

As soon as she hung up, she texted Maggie, Carole Anne, and Charlie. Maybe if she shared the news, it would seem real to her. They responded immediately, expressing their disbelief. Charlie warned her she'd better not fall back in love with Jake, or he would never speak to her again.

She laughed at the absurdity of his comment. She no longer harbored any feelings for Jake.

Greer didn't go to work on Tuesday but spent the day preparing for her dinner with Jake. She needed to look her best tonight. She didn't want him to think her life had gone to hell in a handbasket since the last time she'd seen him, even if it was true.

She washed her hair for the first time in four days, got her nails done, and then went to the mall to look for something to wear. Never mind that she had a closet full of clothes, the excursion made her feel better. She continued checking her phone, but there was nothing from Gun. That was disappointing.

When it came time to pick up Jake at the Four Seasons Hotel, she was so nervous she couldn't stop shaking. How much had he changed, and would she recognize him? What would he think of her now? The last time they'd seen each other was about twenty years ago.

She parked along the hotel's circular drive and waited outside her car. A few men of similar ages and looks walked out, but they passed on by. Finally, a man wearing a T-shirt and jeans emerged from the revolving doors, and she recognized him immediately. Jake hadn't changed at all, and once again, she felt like she was in a time warp.

He recognized her too and smiled and waved. She held her arms out to hug him as she did all her friends, but he put his hands up and stepped back, making her feel embarrassed and foolish. They settled in her car and began the usual polite but mundane conversation of colleagues.

She turned right on San Jacinto Boulevard and drove eastbound on Cesar Chavez Street to I-35 South. Driving with Jake so close wasn't easy, and she kept glancing at him, telling herself this wasn't a dream. What a strange twist of fate to have him sitting in the passenger seat of her car when, less than a week ago, Gun had sat there, and Jake was the furthest person from her mind.

They were seated immediately at the restaurant, and her hand shook as she reached for the water glass. He was sitting so close, too close, and she couldn't help but think of Gloria Estefan's "Here We Are." But unlike the song, sadly, they were distant acquaintances at best, not even friends anymore.

Typical of when she felt nervous, she began to ramble. She recapitulated her life over the last twenty years in less time than it took to order dinner. Jake smiled and nodded while he looked over the menu, not seeming to find her ramblings strange. She'd forgotten how patient, calm, and always willing to listen he was. They'd grown close after their rough start, becoming confidants and best friends who spent all their time together outside of class, sharing their fears and dreams and learning everything about each other. She had fallen crazy, madly, stupidly in love with him.

As they talked, the years began to melt away, and she felt the same surge of emotion for him as she had then. No wonder Charlie had warned her against falling in love with him again. "When did you get into town?" she asked, trying to reign in her traitorous emotions.

"The litigation team drove down together on Sunday night, but I couldn't get away until yesterday, so I flew down."

So he'd called her the day he got into town. Was his call premeditated or spontaneous?

She asked about his wife and whether they had any kids. Their last communication had been when he invited her to his wedding, so she knew nothing about his family life. On the inside of the invitation, he wrote, *I hope you can come. We need to talk.* She didn't need to think twice about either answer. *No,* and *no.*

Strangely, he hesitated but then informed her that he and his wife had been married for seventeen years and had two girls. He was a partner at his firm and doing well, but he sometimes felt bored and stuck in a rut. He rattled off these facts like he was reading a book report, but she wasn't fooled. His life sounded idyllic, and she felt envious. *Does your house have a white picket fence?* She wanted to ask. If things had turned out differently, that would have been her life, too.

He then began reminiscing about their time together, and she was surprised that he remembered so many things about her. "What? How do you remember that?" she asked. "I'd forgotten all about that."

"Greer, I remember everything about you. About us."

She searched his face, wondering if he was sincere. He returned her gaze with the green eyes she'd always found disarming. She looked down at the black napkin on her lap and bit her lip. No, he was not going to do this to her. He'd led her down this emotional road once too often, only for her to arrive at a dead end every time. How did he still have this effect on her after so many years? She lifted her head. "Speaking of that time in our lives, do you keep up with anyone from school?"

It was the perfect diversion. From there, they moved on to the safe topics of unusual cases and demanding clients. There was so much she wanted to say and so many unanswered questions she wanted to ask, but what would it matter now? It was all water under the bridge, and he was married.

As if to drive home this point, he looked at his watch. "We'd better get going. I promised my wife I'd call her before ten."

She wondered if his wife knew about their meeting. Probably not.

Once they were back in her car, she still couldn't shake off her nerves and fumbled with her seatbelt strap. When she turned around, Jake handed her an envelope. "Here you go," he said.

She thanked him but stuck the envelope in her purse because she had no emotional strength to open it now. Not if she wanted to maintain her dignity and not break down into a crying, emotional wreck. She'd been doing that too often lately.

They returned to the hotel just as a white truck that looked and sounded like Dylan's pulled out of the drive. But what would Dylan be doing here? She shook her head. Nothing made sense anymore.

She stepped out of the car with Jake. They'd never said goodbye, never properly ended their relationship, and she doubted she would ever see him again, so this was her chance. "I'm glad you called. It was good seeing you again, and I'm glad you're happy. I'd always hoped that you were. Good luck with the trial, and goodbye, Jake."

She didn't attempt to hug him again but offered her hand.

This time, Jake took her in his arms and held her much longer than appropriate for a friendly hug. She sucked in a breath and hugged him back, fighting back tears. *Oh, Jake, why did you come back and do this to me again? Why now?*

"Greer," he whispered in her ear. "Greer, I wish I could . . . well. Please take care of yourself, okay?" He held her for a moment more before letting her go, then waved goodbye and walked into the hotel.

For many years, Greer had hoped to see Jake again for closure. However, seeing him last night had the opposite effect, leaving her shaken. So much that she'd forgotten about Gun for a little while. However, the collision of both events in a matter of days was like a battering of emotional body blows. She felt bruised and beaten.

She returned to work on Wednesday, and her team warmly welcomed her. She still didn't feel quite like herself but needed to return to her routine. It would help her peace of mind. The things she had feared—that Gun would be controlling and suffocating—never materialized. Gun was none of those things. He was kind, helpful, encouraging, and playful. He'd become her best friend and confidant, and her heart ached for him.

Sitting at her desk in her office, she smiled bitterly, finally understanding those corny wedding invitations she'd always made fun of. But what about Gun? Had everything he said and done been a lie? Or had he been looking for companionship without wanting to bring love into the equation? She supposed that was possible. Tina Turner sang a song about that. Yet, even if Gun didn't reciprocate her feelings, she believed him to be honorable. Could he not at least have shared his true feelings and let her down easily?

She sighed. That's probably what he'd been trying to tell her. Only she hadn't allowed him to do it.

She wondered what he was doing now. During the airport drive, he said he'd printed out his itinerary but failed to give it to her. Now, she was utterly cut off from him.

Speaking of hard copies, Jake had handed her an envelope, but she'd forgotten all about it. She opened her bottom desk drawer, dug it out of her purse, and studied it, unsure if she was prepared to handle its contents. Had he written her a letter? She couldn't take any more surprises.

He'd written "G" on the outside, but it could be mistaken for a "6". Like Gun, he had terrible penmanship. The envelope was made of high-quality linen, and she rubbed her fingers against the grain, then realized whatever was inside wasn't flat. She lifted a corner of the flap and carefully ran her fingernail under it across the length of the envelope.

There was no letter inside, only a USB thumb drive. Why had Jake given her this? She plugged it into the side of her laptop and double-clicked on the file "1989." Then, she stared at the screen, unable to comprehend what she was looking at.

# Chapter Twenty-Two

K ang Sun Ni, known to her American friends as Sunny Kang, tapped her newly acquired nail fills on the arm of the chair. She sat in the spa at the Four Seasons Hotel, treating herself to a manicure and pedicure, having flown in from California last night to see Gun. Yet when she had reached his house, Gun's pimple-faced nephew had informed her that Gun was not home—that he was in Korea. To make matters worse, that punk Dylan had treated her like a stranger and not allowed her inside the house. Since she'd dismissed her Uber, Dylan offered to drive her to the hotel in his tacky pickup truck. She accepted because she was running short on money and didn't know when Gun would return.

To her horror, Dylan whistled for Gun's dog. "Come on, Buddy. Wanna go for a ride?"

The dog's tail wagged a mile a minute at the prospect of a ride. Then he turned vicious and growled at her. They walked outside to Dylan's truck, and he placed her luggage in the back. Even though the truck lacked running boards, Dylan didn't offer her help. She had to lift her dress and hold onto the grab handle to hoist herself into the monstrosity.

He started the engine, and country music blasted from the radio at a decibel that would wake the dead. The dog poked his head between the bucket seats, and Dylan said, "Are you ready, boy? Let's go!"

He didn't bother asking *her* if she was ready. She also detected a strong Southern accent from the boy. The entire family spoke with a Southern accent, but Luke's was the most pronounced. The apple did not fall far from the tree. She sneered with distaste, having never understood why a wealthy family like Gun's insisted on acting so countrified.

It was half past nine at night but still ninety degrees outside. Despite the heat, they drove with the windows down for the dog's benefit. Sunny had always hated Texas in the summer, and sweat ran down her back while the wind disheveled her signature chignon. She might as well have been in hell with the heat, the dog, and the truck.

When they reached the hotel, the roar of the truck's diesel engine caused everyone to turn and stare, and she nearly fell backward in her haste to get out. She pulled her dress down and looked around, hoping no one had seen that.

Dylan grabbed her luggage from the back and announced in his loud, country voice, "Here you go, ma'am. I'm sorry I couldn't let you in the house, but my uncle gave me strict orders not to let anyone in except his girlfriend. Are you going to be okay?"

She snatched the luggage from his hand and hurried inside the lobby without answering.

Once in her hotel room, she changed out of her dress, now covered in dog hair, and plotted her next move. Her credit cards would max out if she stayed at the hotel for long. She would have to work fast.

She called Gun several times, but he didn't answer his phone. It was morning in Korea, so he was awake and ignoring her. She then called Jason, one of the few in Gun's circles who treated her kindly. His tone had been friendly, but he had no idea about Gun's return to the States and wished her well.

She exhaled in frustration. She had to think of something. The gossip had reached her in California. Gun's mother was bragging that her son was dating a *byeonhosa*, and she expected them to announce news of their marriage any day now. Sunny could not let that happen and had come to Austin to break them up. She relied on Gun to help her whenever she was in financial trouble, and she was not about to let him go.

Sunny knew that little troll was trouble from the moment she saw her. She'd peeped in the door at the hospital and observed her with Gun. He had a look on his face she'd never seen before, not even during their marriage's early, blissful days.

She bolted upright in the salon chair as an idea occurred to her. "Sorry," she apologized to the nail technician doing her pedicure.

Gun's homely girlfriend would know when Gun was coming back from Korea! Now, all she had to do was find her. What was her name again? Grunge? It was something odd like that. If she found Grunge, she could kill two birds with one stone. She would learn about Gun's return and hint that she and Gun had been planning a secret rendezvous. She smiled with pleasure at her devious plan. She would love to see Grunge's face when she dropped that bomb.

Now, how would she go about finding her? Grunge was a lawyer, so she should not be hard to find. Sunny bristled. She knew Gun liked intelligent women, but what a strange choice for him.

She asked the nail tech for more wine and sat back in her chair, reflecting on her past with Gun. They had met twenty-six years ago at a tent ramen shop in Seoul where Sunny worked as a waitress while she waited for fate to change her fortune. Gun came in one cold January night and sat at a table for hours, drinking himself drunk. Something about the sad young man with the mop of hair caused her to have a rare pang of empathy. Maybe because, unlike many of the other male customers, he wasn't pawing at her but kept to himself. He stayed until closing, and since he could barely walk, she had put him in a cab with instructions to the driver to take him home.

After that night, he returned to the restaurant, looking for her, to thank her for her help. "Were you the one who called a cab for me the other night?" he asked in perfect Korean.

She was surprised to see him, and his kindness piqued her curiosity. He returned several more times after that, and she learned more about him. He was an American who had fled to Korea to work for his uncle and escape his father's wrath. She suspected there was more to his story but didn't push. Her suspicions were confirmed one night when he fumbled through his wallet to pay his tab, and a picture of a girl popped out. She was smiling, and her dark hair partially covered her face. Gun stared sorrowfully at the picture for so long that she feared he might break down and cry.

"Do you believe in fate, Miss Kang Su Ni?" Gun said.

Sunny took a seat with him at the table. "As in, do I believe two people are meant to be? No, I do not."

Gun's face became crestfallen.

"I believe life is what you make of it," Sunny continued. "Many people will come and go from our lives, some good, some bad, without explanation. I do not waste my time mourning the ones who leave. I have too much to accomplish in this short life we are given."

Gun tilted his head to the side, and he studied her momentarily. She saw the uncertainty in his eyes.

"I don't believe in fate nor regret. I believe that all that matters is the here and now. Whose face is in front of you now."

Sunny covered his hand with hers and smiled, and his body relaxed. She never told Gun that she had lied to him that night. She *did* believe in fate. She believed the girl in the picture had lost her opportunity, and fate had brought Gun to her. She guessed that he came from a family of means based on how he dressed and the money he carried with him. But she had no idea just how much until after they began dating. They married less than a year later, and as Gun's wife, she had more money than she had dared to dream.

But her joy at her newfound luck was short-lived when Gun lost interest in her after only a year of marriage. Although she had not married for love, it hurt her pride, so she consoled herself by using their time apart to travel and party with her friends. Shortly after Gun turned away from her, she took up with a younger lover. He was everything Gun was not. Exciting, dangerous, and broke.

Shifting in the manicure chair, Sunny let out a deep breath. Gun owed her, and he owed her big. He was a lost young man when he ran away to Korea to escape his family and heal his broken heart. She accepted and never questioned him about the girl he held in his heart or demanded acceptance from his family. She was the one who helped him laugh again, but he never acknowledged her role in helping him put his life back together. Now, she would show Gun *and* his little troll that they could not throw her out like dirty dishwater. She was not going anywhere.

# Chapter Twenty-Three

S unny returned to her hotel room and slipped on a little black dress that showed her figure to its best advantage. Since she had no idea when Gun would return, she might as well have a little fun while she waited.

Downstairs in the hotel lobby, she sat in one of the wing-backed chairs to get a lay of the land. Crossing one shapely leg over the other, she gave the men who walked past a preview of things to come. Receiving so many admiring glances was gratifying, but no one appeared promising.

She was about to try her chances at the bar when a woman wearing a white T-shirt and khaki shorts walked through the front door with her hair in disarray. She looked familiar, but Sunny was not sure why. She would never keep company with someone who would show up at the Four Seasons looking so slovenly.

*Omo*, she remembered how she knew her. It was Grunge, Gun's girlfriend! However, she did not remember her looking quite so terrible when they met at the hospital. She snorted. That was what dating Gun did to a woman. Being with him had almost caused her downfall, too.

She stood, ready to confront the troll, but then sat back down. What was Grunge doing at the hotel if Gun was in Korea?

Her question was answered when a handsome man with glasses walked up behind Grunge. He touched her arm, and she spun around in surprise like a nervous cat, but she did appear to know him. The man said something, but Sunny was too far away, and the hotel lobby was too noisy for her to hear what he said. They started walking toward the hotel's other side, and she followed them but maintained a discreet distance. Something told her this would be more rewarding than meeting someone at the bar.

The man led Grunge to an area near the meeting rooms that was not used at night. An assortment of chairs, tables, and plants decorated the area with a lovely courtyard view. With the sunset, it was dim and afforded privacy and discretion. The man pulled his chair close to Grunge, and his knees practically touched hers. Sunny sat behind them, hidden by an indoor Rubber Tree but close enough to hear them.

The man spoke first. His voice was deep and measured. "Greer, what's going on? Why did you want to see me?"

Greer! That was her name! Sunny remembered it being something awful.

"Because of this," Greer said, handing him an envelope.

"What is it?"

"Please don't act like you don't know," she said. "I've hardly slept in days and am too tired and old to play games anymore."

"I—I don't know what you're talking about," the man stammered.

"Open it! Open the envelope."

He did as she asked, but Sunny could not see what was inside.

"A thumb drive? Am I supposed to know what this is about?"

Greer huffed. "Jake, please. Of course, you know what it's about! You gave it to me after our dinner last night."

Sunny grinned. This was getting interesting. Had they gone to dinner last night? Judging by their informal language, it did not sound like a business dinner. Ha. When the cat's away . . .

"Greer, I'm sorry, but I didn't give this to you," Jake said, then paused. "Wait, was this the envelope I found in your car and handed to you?"

"Yes! Now do you remember?"

"Yeah, I do, and I remember handing it to you, but I didn't know what was in it. It's not from me. I found the envelope in your car on the passenger seat floor. I thought it might be important and didn't want you to lose it."

Greer ran her hand through her messy hair. "This *isn't* from you? But it must be! No one else could have given it to me. And how did it end up in my car if it isn't from you?"

"Well, first of all, do you know what's on it?"

"It's a playlist of songs. Songs that were popular in 1989, our first year of law school."

Jake looked puzzled and pushed his glasses farther back on his nose. "Other than the fact that I was the one who handed you the envelope, why did you think it was from me?"

"Because of the mixtape you gave me. Do you remember that? I found it on my desk in my dorm room. You must have left it there during one of our Inn parties. It was so long ago that I'd forgotten about it. But from what I remember, many of the songs on that mixtape and this thumb drive are the same."

He brought his fingertips together under his chin. "Greer, I can confidently say that I have never given you, or anybody else, a mixtape. I'm confident because I've never made a mixtape in my entire life. I wouldn't even know how to make one."

"Then who gave it to me?" she exclaimed. "The song selection can't be a mere coincidence. The person who gave me the mixtape and the person who gave me the thumb drive must be the same. Logically, the only person who that could be is you. How else can you explain that you and an item from our past reappeared simultaneously? You were always doing thoughtful things like this for me."

He shook his head. "I hear what you're saying, but I'm sorry, Greer. It wasn't me. You always gave me too much credit. Who else has been in your car?"

"Only one other person, and—" She sucked in her breath.

"Who?" Jake prompted.

"It couldn't be him. I suppose if they were random songs, maybe. But how could he duplicate the songs from a twenty-seven-year-old tape? I didn't know him back then, and it's not like he could've found the tape at my house and duplicated it. I don't have it anymore."

Jake paused momentarily and then said, "Greer, I'm sorry I can't help you, but I'm glad this gave us another opportunity to talk. I want to tell you I'm sorry, not just about the tape but about, well—"

Greer shook her head and looked down while grabbing a handful of her hair above her head. "I cherished that tape for years. Do you realize it was the *only* gift you had ever given me —or so I believed? But I was wrong about that, too, just like I was wrong about so many things. Was anything about us real? Did you even care for me?"

"I did care," he insisted. "Why do you think I wanted to see you again?"

Greer lifted her head. "You cared for *me*?"

Jake nodded but looked away from her.

"Then why did you string me along for years, during law school and for years afterward, throwing crumbs my way? Why did you hint at a future together and give me false hope? Was that your way of caring?"

Sunny leaned in closer. Like Greer, she was waiting for Jake's answer. This conversation had become quite interesting, like a Korean melodrama.

"Greer, you're the one who said we needed a break!" Jake's voice rose defensively.

"Yes, but only because we weren't going anywhere. I'd hoped you might realize I meant something to you, but you met your wife instead."

Jake rubbed his hands on his pants. "I'm sorry. I never meant to string you along or give you false hope. I liked you, but there could never be a future for us. That didn't mean I didn't care. Didn't you know that?"

"No, and how was I supposed to know since you never said anything? And now, after all these years, you claim you *liked* me, but we couldn't have a future. How does that make any sense?"

He sighed. "You're right, it doesn't make any sense, but it's true. Greer, I didn't just care for you. I loved you but couldn't go against my parents' wishes. They had no objection to our dating. They said you were a nice girl, but marriage would have been different. Don't you remember? Mixed marriages were frowned upon back then. My dad was a judge and someone in the public eye, and I couldn't embarrass my family. It was selfish. I know that now. I loved you, and I wanted to keep you by my side, but I guess I didn't—"

"Love me enough?" Greer finished for him. "That is if you loved me at all. What you're describing doesn't sound like love. You enjoyed being with me if it was convenient and didn't require any sacrifice. In other words, you used me, knowing you would never marry me." She paused and took a deep breath. "You said you didn't want to embarrass your family, but isn't it time you stopped hiding behind them? They were a convenient excuse when the truth was, *you* didn't think I was worth fighting for. Wasn't that the real reason, Jake?"

"Greer." His words faltered, and he hung his head.

Greer pulled a tissue from her pocket and dabbed her eyes.

Jake grabbed her other hand and held it. "Greer, I'm so sorry. I never meant to hurt you."

"I'm not going to lie or try to act brave anymore to spare your feelings. It does hurt," she said through tears. "It feels like a dagger in my heart. All this time, I've revered your memory as holy ground. You were the great love of my life, the one who got away, and I mourned losing you for years, always wondering what I had done wrong, why I wasn't good enough. Yet deep down, I always knew the truth, but I didn't want to believe it. I needed to hear it from you. And now that I have, I know that everything I've convinced myself about us was true—our story—was nothing more than an illusion."

Sunny could not believe her good fortune. This was not a business meeting but a meeting between two former lovers. Greer was made of sterner stuff than Sunny had realized, and she felt a slight admiration for her. She had the guts to confront this man, and judging by the anguish in their voices, this talk had been long overdue.

Still, Sunny could not let the opportunity go to waste. She had silenced her phone and took pictures as leverage as they talked. She selected the most incriminating ones and sent them to Gun as text messages. He would not ignore her now. Then she slid away undetected and walked to the bar with a spring in her step. It was eight at night in Texas, so it was ten in the morning in Korea. Yes, Gun would be awake, and she would bet a first-class plane ticket back to California that he would respond.

Gun's phone pinged every few seconds, alerting him that he had new text messages. Someone had their skivvies in a bind, and he was willing to bet that someone was Sunny. Dylan had told him she'd shown up at his house last night, and shortly thereafter, she began burning up his phone with calls and texts. But he was consumed with completing a hotel project and didn't have time for her nonsense. Besides, he already knew why she was calling. It was the same reason she always called—she wanted money.

He glanced at his phone as one text after another came through, realizing she was sending pictures. Now, what did she want? If he had to guess, it was the latest handbag, or she wanted him to pay off her credit cards. The woman had no shame. They had divorced over twenty years ago, yet she still came to him for money when she was between boyfriends.

Okay, he would take the bait. But only because he needed to give his brain a break from looking at the endless vendor spreadsheets.

He tapped on the first picture. To his shock, it was not a picture of Sunny's never-ending wish list but a picture of Greer sitting with a man, and their faces were much too close for his liking. He spread the image with his fingers to enlarge it. The man held Greer's hand, and another picture showed him caressing her shoulder.

He couldn't believe what he was seeing. There had to be some mistake. The last picture captured the man's face, and Gun remembered seeing him somewhere before. His mind raced with possibilities, but he couldn't think of any scenario to calm his fears. He had no choice but to call Sunny.

"*Yeoboseyo*," Sunny answered after the fifth ring. She was enjoying this.

"Cut the crap, Sunny," he growled into the phone. "You know it's me and why I'm calling."

"Ah, Gun-ah-ssi," she said in a deceptively sweet tone. "You got the pictures of your little girlfriend, Grunge? It's such an awful name, but it suits her, especially today. She looks terrible. Doesn't she know a woman should always try to look her best, especially when meeting an old lover?"

By sheer willpower that surprised even him, Gun remained calm. Sunny would pay for this latest stunt, but right now, he needed her to give him more information. "Where did you get these pictures? Did you pay someone to follow her?"

"Gun-ah-ssi, would I ever waste money on someone else? They fell into my lap like a gift from the heavens, so I shared them with you."

"Fell into your lap? Give me a break. Where are you?"

"At the Four Seasons Hotel. Since you won't allow me to stay at your house, I have no choice but to stay here."

"The Four Seasons?" he barked, forgetting his resolve to remain calm. "You ran into Greer at a *hotel*?"

"Oh yes. I ran into Grunge here at the hotel. Well, I didn't exactly run into her. I was sitting in the hotel lobby, minding my business, when she came in. That man was waiting for her, and he took her off to a secluded place where they could be alone. As you can see from the pictures, they seem quite close. I didn't know Grunge had it in her."

Gun ignored her jab. "So you followed them and took the pictures?"

"Yes, I followed them. It was my duty to you as my ex-husband. You should know your little girlfriend is not as innocent as she leads everyone to believe. I'd hate for anyone to make a fool out of you."

"What were they talking about? I know you must've eavesdropped on their conversation."

"Well, I didn't mean to overhear, but they weren't exactly quiet or trying to hide."

"Just tell me. What did you hear?" Gun closed his eyes as if preparing to be punched.

"They were confessing their love for one another. Grunge told him he was the great love of her life. They were also talking about songs on some tape, but I don't know what that was about."

Gun massaged his throbbing temple. He couldn't believe it, even though the proof was in the pictures. He'd been an idiot to leave Greer hanging, but he thought he had time to fix things. Instead, in less than a week, history had repeated itself, and he'd screwed everything up again. Only this time, he'd probably lost her for good.

"Did you hear what Greer called him?" he asked. "Did you get his name?"

"Yes, she called him Jake."

He nodded. She hadn't needed to tell him. He'd already known.

# Chapter Twenty-Four

The next day, as Greer sat in her office, she replayed her conversation with Jake. Like a chronic inflammatory disorder, her feelings for him had attacked her mind, body, and soul and colored the way she looked at the world for twenty-seven years. Hearing the truth from him was a painful but necessary medicine and a conversation they should have had long ago. Jake confessed that their relationship had always weighed heavily on him. The trial had given him an excuse to come to Austin, but he couldn't bring himself to say the words he wanted and needed to say. Without her discovering the thumb drive, they might never have had an opportunity to lay the past to rest.

Now, the question on her mind was the mysterious thumb drive's connection to the mixtape. She knew it was the key to making sense of everything. Gun was the only other person who'd been in her car, the only one who could have left it there. But how had he matched the songs on the thumb drive, almost song for song, to the mixtape? She'd listened to that tape hundreds of times until it had worn out, and from what she remembered, many of the songs were the same except for a few new additions. The probability of Gun picking the same ones was about a gazillion to one.

And why would he prepare a playlist of romantic songs for her if he didn't share her feelings? That was if the thumb drive was meant for her. She'd assumed it was because of its similarities to the mixtape, but since it fell out of Gun's backpack, was its intended recipient a woman in Korea?

She plugged it in and listened to it for the nth time since first discovering it. Chicago's "Will You Still Love Me?" was the first song on the list. She'd always loved that song, and there was that pesky word *destiny* again. She rubbed her forehead. *Wait.* Hadn't she dreamt about this song in one of her Jake dreams?

She brushed it aside and closed her laptop when Mrs. Yoon, the Korean interpreter and translator, arrived. Greer had worked with her for several years, having her translate documents for her Korean clients, who preferred reading them in their native language. Mrs. Yoon was normally chipper but didn't look like herself today.

"Are you all right?" Greer asked. "Would you like a cup of tea?"

"No tea for me today, but my weekend was difficult," she confided. "The police had me contact a university student's parents in South Korea. The young woman was struggling with her doctoral dissertation and had been unable to find a job, and she overdosed on pills to take her own life. Fortunately, her roommate found her in time and called 9-1-1."

Greer gasped. "What a tragedy! Is she going to be okay?"

"Yes, but naturally, her parents took the news quite hard. They are on their way from Korea to see her." She sighed. "You see, education is of utmost importance for my people. Parents place a high premium on their children earning a degree and finding a job. There is no room for failure."

Greer had heard this before, but it still came as a shock to her. Even during her first year of law school, when every day was a struggle, she'd never considered taking her own life. That poor young woman must've felt desperate and out of options to go to such extremes.

Mrs. Yoon handed her a translated earnest money contract for her client, John Kim, who was purchasing a block of duplex homes. After she left, Greer gave the contract to Molly with instructions to email it to Mr. Kim for review.

Greer returned to her desk to resume listening to the music, but she was interrupted again when Dianne called to tell her she had a visitor. Greer's heart leaped at the possibility that it might be Gun. "Who is it, Dianne?"

"It's Jampa, the young man from the café. Do you have time to see him?"

Jampa? He had never come to her office before. She hoped everything was all right. "Yes, please send him back."

She checked her makeup in the mirror she kept in her desk drawer, rose from her chair, and opened the door right before he knocked. "Jampa! What a nice surprise. What are you doing here?"

She'd never seen him in anything but his barista uniform. Today, he wore a colorful paisley, short-sleeved button-down shirt. It was tucked into his jeans, showing off his flat stomach. Talk about a looker.

He smiled as he looked around her office. "I always wondered what your office looks like. It's nice, and it suits you. I like your law license—big and hard to miss." He turned and fixed her with his candid gaze. "Sorry for dropping by unannounced, but I haven't seen you lately and want to say goodbye. I got another job."

"Another job? May I ask where?"

"For a construction company. I'm going to be a project manager's apprentice. The company will pay my tuition so I can finish college, and afterward, they'll hire me as a full-time employee."

"Oh my goodness, Jampa! That's wonderful. How did you find that job?"

He hesitated, looking uneasy. "Well, I don't know if I should be telling you this, but Gun introduced me to the owner and set up the interview. Remember that day when your ex-husband showed up in the café? Gun said he noticed my work ethic and that I would be a good fit for his friend's company. He said everyone my age is entering the tech industry—that no one wants to do the jobs they consider manual labor, even though this is an office job."

Wait, what? "But why didn't Gun tell me?"

"He wanted to surprise you. He asked me to wait until it was confirmed I got the job, but that was on Monday, and I know Gun is in Korea."

"How do you know that? Did he call you?" She was desperate for any word about Gun.

"No, but he gave me his business card, and I texted him to let him know. I was wrong about him. He's a nice guy."

Gun's business card? He was a businessman, so it made sense that he would have one. But why had she never seen it? Her Spidey senses tingled. "I know you're going to think this is strange, but can I see the card?"

Jampa fished out the card from his wallet and handed it to her.

She took the ivory-colored card with trembling hands and read the name on the card: "J. Gun Donovan."

She leaned against her desk and gripped the edge with both hands while holding onto the card.

~

Greer stood at the top of a stepladder and reached for the floral box hidden in the back of her closet shelf. Once she was back on solid ground, she dusted off the cover and opened it. Inside were precious mementos from her previous life. Pictures. A small stuffed teddy bear from her high school boyfriend. Cards she'd received from various boyfriends. Love letters from her college boyfriend in Virginia. The handkerchief Jake had given her in the garden, preserved in a baggie.

Although seemingly unrelated, she knew the playlist, Mrs. Yoon's tragic story, and the name John Kim were clues to the answers she sought. But why? It didn't make sense, but that changed when Jampa showed her Gun's card, and she knew where to look for her answer.

At the bottom of her collection of mementos lay the missing clue, which would confirm or dispel the irrational and improbable scenarios in her head. Yet she could scarcely believe it. Hadn't everyone told her that life doesn't imitate art? These kinds of coincidences only happened in K-dramas or telenovelas. Not in real life.

But sometimes, the truth *was* stranger than fiction. She took a deep breath and thumbed through the First-Year Law Student Directory.

# Chapter Twenty-Five

G un arrived home in the early evening. After fussing over Buddy and Bullet, he jumped in the shower to wash away the last forty-eight hours. He had to see Greer immediately and find out if there was any hope of salvaging the mess he'd made. He expected the worst but hoped for the best.

Ever since the airport fiasco, he'd counted the hours and minutes until he could get back to her. He called her several times, but when she didn't answer, he knew she had jumped to the wrong conclusion. Not that he could blame her. While waiting at DFW Airport for his flight to Incheon, he called Sarah, and she let him have it. "I've been warning you to tell her the truth!" she exploded. "How could you leave her hanging like that? I'm telling you, *Oppa*, you better not blow it with Greer, or you'll have to answer to both me *and* Mom."

Sarah was right, but how could he have told Greer the truth over the phone or by text? He'd considered postponing his flight, but his uncle was counting on him. So, as much as it pained him, he had to wait until he could see Greer. This was a story he needed to tell in person. A punishment he had to accept face-to-face. He'd worked nonstop since his arrival in Korea to finish the project and get home to her. He hoped he wasn't too late.

Gun was just about to leave his house when the doorbell rang. He opened the door to find Greer standing there. Despite her tan, her face looked thin and pale, and she had dark circles under her eyes.

"Greer! I can't believe you're here. I was on my way to see you. Please, come in—"

She shook her head. "I don't want to come inside. Since last night, I've been driving by your house, wondering when you were coming home, and today I saw your truck in the driveway. I know you don't share my feelings, and I can accept that, but there's a question I've got to ask you."

"No, that's not true. You've got it all wrong. I was coming to see you, so come inside and talk. There's something I need to tell you, something I should have told you from the beginning." He reached for her hand, but she stepped back and folded her arms.

"Greer, please. I know you're upset and have every right to be, but we need to talk. Please give me a chance to explain what happened at the airport—"

She shook her head. "I don't care about what happened at the airport. Not anymore. You don't have to explain because your silence was enough. I'm only here because there's something I need to know." She ran her hand through her hair. "I feel like I'm going crazy."

He wanted to hug her so bad that it hurt. This was his fault. He'd let things get out of control. So what did she want to ask him? Or was she going to tell him she was back with Jake? He braced himself for whatever she threw at him. "Okay, I'm listening. What do you want to know?"

"Did you ever go by the name James Kim? Did we go to law school together?"

Her question knocked the wind out of him. He didn't know how she'd found out, but it was finally time to come clean. He let out a deep sigh. "Yes. We first met in law school, and I used the name James Kim then."

She covered her mouth with her hand to stifle her cry. "Why didn't you ever tell me? All this time . . . And when did you first realize it? When did you recognize me?"

A lump formed in his throat. This wasn't how he'd imagined this moment playing out in his head. And now that he had a chance to tell her the whole story, he was at a loss for words.

Greer looked anguished, and she was silently crying. "No wonder. So many times, I couldn't understand why I felt so close to you, why you seemed familiar. I thought it was because of my feelings for you, but now I know why." She swallowed. "That's why you hated me! When did your feelings for me change? Or did they change? Was this your way of revenge? Did you plan to make me fall in love with you so you could get back at me?"

"What? No! Greer, you've got it all wrong—" He exhaled in frustration.

She shook her head. "What an idiot I've been. I can't believe I didn't recognize you. What must you think of me?"

"Come inside, and let's talk," he said again.

She shook her head and wiped the tears from her face. "I can't do this right now. I shouldn't have come." She walked down the steps to her car, her shoulders slumped and shaking.

He stood immobilized in his doorway. He didn't want to upset her further, but if they didn't clear the air now, they might never be able to put this behind them. He ran after her, the hot stone steps burning his bare feet, but she drove away. He ran back up the steps, stuffed his feet into the sneakers by the door, and hollered for Dylan.

"Hey, Bubba, stay another night with the boys, will you? I may be out all night."

He jumped in his truck and drove to Greer's house, but she wasn't there. He waited an hour and worried when she didn't come home. She wasn't answering his calls or texts, and he had no idea where she may have gone. He went to her office building and drove through every parking garage level. There were only a few cars on a Friday evening, but Greer's SUV was not one of them. Next, he went to her parents' condo. Once again, he scoured the parking garage without any luck. He didn't want to alarm her parents, so he didn't stop.

He finally drove back to Greer's house around eight o'clock. They had exchanged keys and alarm codes for each other's homes weeks ago. He texted her to tell her he was going inside, then did so, turning on the lights. He fed Kevin and Sophie, who brushed against him and let him pet them. He stayed with them for a few minutes, assuring them their mama would be home soon, then refilled their food and water bowls and cleaned the litter box.

He parked his truck up the hill from her house to await her return. She shouldn't have been driving in her state. He hadn't slept in over fifty hours, and his eyelids grew heavy as he waited.

~

*August 1989*
*Dallas, Texas*

Gun wiped the sweat off his brow as he walked through the center of campus. It was August in Texas, so the sweltering heat didn't surprise him. But it did exacerbate his misery. He could scarcely believe he would be starting his first semester of law school in a couple of days.

*Law school.* Those two words made him sick. After earning a civil engineering degree and an MBA, he'd looked forward to starting his career this fall. He'd received several offers, including one from his uncle's company in Korea, but his father, unable to stop meddling in Gun's life, had other plans.

"Is this what you want to do with your life, son?" Dad asked. "Work for someone else? Why don't you go to law school and use your engineering degree to become a patent attorney? Then you can join my firm and write your own ticket."

Yes, being an engineer was what he wanted to do with his life. He had no desire to be a patent attorney or any other type of attorney, especially not at his father's firm. He'd always known the law wasn't for him. He wasn't wired that way. So why couldn't his dad understand or accept his decision? Luke had graduated from law school a year ago and worked as an associate in their father's firm. That should've been enough family legal dynasty to please the old man.

Gun still couldn't believe he'd allowed his father to badger him to attend, yet here he was. He acquiesced under two conditions. First, he would limit his tenure to one year. If he didn't like it, he could drop out. Second, he would register under a pseudonym. The law school was his father's alma mater, and his father was well-known in Dallas legal circles. The last thing he wanted was to be known as Jack Donovan's son or Luke Donovan's brother, for the inevitable comparisons would follow.

Their father made generous contributions to the school, so he arranged with the registrar to allow Gun to enroll under James Kim. That had been simple enough. James was his first name, and Kim was his mother's family name. The registrar had agreed but told them he would have to use his full legal name for the background check and other official documents.

Unable to put off the inevitable, Gun went to the university bookstore in the morning before the crowd and explored the campus, looking for a secluded place to hide between classes. Everyone hung out in the Quad, but he couldn't envision hanging out with a bunch of law students. He wanted nothing to do with those people and was counting the days until next May.

His venture paid off when he stumbled upon a gravel path that led to a small garden hidden behind the Meadows School of the Arts. It was well cared for and had stone benches and a giant statue of an angel, and he doubted it would attract many students. They were too busy with Greek life and football games. He sat on a shaded bench while finishing his second Big Gulp he'd bought at the 7-Eleven across the street.

After cooling off, he left the garden to return to the Quad when a girl walking ahead caught his eye. Her dark hair was in a ponytail, swinging back and forth as she walked. She wore a yellow T-shirt and white shorts that showed off her tanned legs. Admiring the legs and other assets, he picked up his pace to discover if her front looked as good as the back.

As he got closer, he noticed her struggle under a load of books. They wobbled in her arms until she dropped them all over the sidewalk. Another girl and a guy he recognized from First-Year Orientation walked with her. The girl stopped, but the guy went on ahead.

The girl in the ponytail turned around, and she looked even better than he'd imagined. She was beautiful. She flipped her bangs away from her face and smiled the most glorious smile he'd ever seen. Her lips were full and nicely shaped, and her teeth were perfect. Had she worn a retainer for years as he had? His heart began to race. He continued walking toward her, but then she and her friend laughed. He stopped. It made him uneasy when girls laughed in groups. He was never sure if they were laughing at him or something else.

The girls left the books behind and continued walking

toward the Quad. He picked them up and almost caught up with them, but they beat him by a nose and went inside Lawyer's Inn. He set the books on one of the patio tables and waited for the girl to come out, but to his annoyance, the Big Gulps kicked in. He went inside the Inn, but just his luck, the bathroom was being cleaned. He ran to the one located inside the law library across the Quad. After finishing his business, he returned to the Inn, hoping he hadn't missed her.

The girl came back outside as he reached the front steps, but another guy stood beside the books. The girl smiled at him as if she'd received the best news of her life, and he heard her say, "Hi Jake, I'm Greer."

Greer. That was the name of the dark-haired girl with the ponytail. It was an unusual name—not that he had any room to talk about names—but it suited her because nothing was ordinary about her. Maybe the whole law school thing wouldn't be so bad if he could see Greer.

By some miracle of fate, they were assigned to the same first-year section. That meant they shared all the same classes, and he could see her five days a week. He had become friends with Danny Hill, another misfit who felt he didn't belong there.

When the seating charts were passed around, they picked seats with the best view of Greer. He paid more attention to her than to the professors' lectures. He loved watching her flip her hair back when she laughed or was nervous. He found everything about her charming and waited for the right opportunity to meet her.

Danny called him crazy and said Greer was out of his league. But Gun wasn't discouraged. His mom was always talking about fate, so maybe that was why he was in law school, to meet Greer. He knew he would never be a lawyer.

He finally met her at a Student Bar Association happy hour when Danny, acting as his wingman, approached her and smoothly roped Gun into the conversation. He wasn't disappointed. In addition to her beauty, she was friendly, had a lovely voice, and laughed at his jokes. She was his fantasy come true.

"I like you. You're funny," she told him and flipped her hair back.

He felt as if he had conquered the world.

After that happy hour, she would greet him with a wave and one of her gorgeous smiles whenever she saw him in class or around campus. They met at several social events together, and while she was friendly enough, he couldn't make any headway with her. His friends grew tired of his moping.

"Give it up, man," they told him. "Our sources tell us that girl is *crazy* over that dude Jake."

Jake Sutton. Yeah, he knew who they were talking about. He was the same rude jerk who had taken credit for carrying Greer's books. He'd seen Greer chasing after Jake, and it annoyed him. Not because he was jealous but because Greer deserved better. Anyone could see that Jake didn't share her feelings.

He attended the happy hours held at Lawyer's Inn, always hoping to talk to her. He stood outside her room the night she ran out, calling after Jake. But Jake was too stupid to realize what he had in Greer—or worse, he didn't care. He embarrassed her in front of Kie and that skinny girl, Tracy. Anger burned in Gun's heart. He called out to help her save face, pretending they had a date. The relief on her face was palpable, while Jake looked irritated.

"Ready to go?" he said and offered her his arm.

She took it without missing a beat. She held her head high as they walked to the stairwell, down the stairs, and outside to the porch. Then she sat in one of the wrought iron chairs and turned her head while discreetly wiping away tears.

"Are you hungry?" he asked. "Where should we go eat?"

"We don't have to go eat. I know you were being nice and helping me out up there." She wouldn't meet his eyes.

"Well, I'm hungry and could use something to eat. Do you mind keeping me company, even if you're not hungry?"

She smiled in the dark. "I'm always hungry but didn't bring my purse."

"No problem, it's on me."

"But—"

"Come on, girl. Is this the thanks I get? After helping you out, will you make me eat by myself?"

Greer laughed. "Well, okay then. I'd love to come."

They went to Snuffer's on Lower Greenville, a popular hangout for university students, ordered burgers, and shared a basket of chili cheese fries. Greer tried to put on a good front, but he could see the sadness on her face. Jake's asinine behavior hurt her.

Gun hoped that night would be a turning point in their friendship, and it did change, but the needle didn't move in his direction. Strangely, Greer paid him less attention. His friends might've been right about her only having eyes for Jake, but he was unwilling to give up.

Out of desperation, he confided in his sister. Sarah, a sophomore at Texas Christian University across the metroplex in Fort Worth, was delighted to help. She suggested he give Greer a mixtape of love songs, but he cringed at the idea.

"A mixtape? Isn't that too sappy?" he asked.

"*Oppa*, girls love sappy. Trust me, she'll love it."

"Is it too strong? I don't want to scare her off."

"Write her a note and tell her you're her secret admirer," Sarah told him.

She helped him with the tape by suggesting several songs, but he insisted on having input. He'd overheard Greer say she liked the song "Will You Still Love Me?" because it mentioned the word *destiny*. It had to be the very first song on the mixtape. The next song he picked was "When I See You Smile," the new song by Bad English. He thought of Greer every time it played on the radio. It perfectly captured his feelings for her. Then he added Sarah's suggestions.

He left the tape in Greer's room during the Inn's November keg party when everyone was at the other end of the hall, and the door was wide open. He snuck in and placed the tape and a note on her desk, then afterward regretted leaving the anonymous letter. He hoped she would not jump to the wrong conclusion and think it was from Jake.

Why hadn't he thought of that sooner?

A few days later, while watching her in Civil Procedure, he debated telling her the truth about the tape. Her face was animated, and her hands moved while she shared some story that caused Charlie Bell to roar with laughter. Then Professor Banks walked into the room and cleared his throat, and the room grew quiet. Had Gun known that everything would change then, he would have jumped over the rows of students and rushed to Greer's side to confess.

Banks called her name, and the color drained from her face. Over the hour, he brutally interrogated her and the other two students, giving no quarter. Banks was especially tough on Greer, as if trying to break her. Gun watched her struggle and clenched his fists in frustration.

As soon as class ended, she shot out of the classroom. He followed her as she ran across the Quad and, to his surprise, the garden. He'd never seen her there before. He didn't want to embarrass her, so he stood at a distance and listened to her cry. When he couldn't take it any longer, he walked along the path to where she sat on the stone bench. His shoes crunched on the gravel beneath them, and Greer stopped crying. He reached in his backpack for the handkerchief he carried. A young associate at his dad's firm—who didn't know him well or that he went by Gun, not James—had given him the monogrammed set when he graduated from business school.

Poor Greer started crying even harder. Not sure how to comfort her, he gave her the handkerchief, squeezed her shoulder, and left to give her privacy when she asked to be alone.

He was waiting for her on the steps of the Inn when she finally started making her way back. He stood to meet her, but Jake intercepted her from the parking lot. He stood on one path and Jake on the other. Greer stood where the two sidewalks merged at the literal and proverbial fork in the road. She never saw him waiting for her because she only had eyes for Jake. It was then that he realized that she would never come to him.

Their grades were based on one final exam at the end of the semester, but their Torts professor gave them a midterm to serve as a warm-up. He received a "B." Although he had never made anything less than an "A" in his academic career, this didn't come as a surprise. He wasn't adjusting to the study of law. It was for people of a certain mindset that he did not possess. He was disenchanted with law school and everything associated with it.

As he prepared for the final exams, he realized he couldn't keep his promise to his father. Over Thanksgiving, his dad peppered him with questions about his progress. He replied with vague answers. Although there would be hell to pay, he'd had enough. If things had worked out with Greer, it might have motivated him to stick it out for the rest of the year. But he supposed things worked out the way they were meant to. Gun couldn't endure three years of this mess, and she wouldn't want to date a law school dropout. Greer was destined for a different life. She would finish law school, become a lawyer, and marry Jake.

Gun bought a one-way plane ticket to Korea to leave after

finals. There was no point in sticking around for Christmas. Even Luke warned him he better get out of Dodge before their dad found out. Gun cleared his apartment, and Luke and Janet assured him they would take care of whatever he left behind. They didn't know about Greer since he had always kept things close to his chest, but they knew something had happened to make him unhappy.

But even then, Gun hated giving up on Greer, so he went by her room one last time. He knocked on her door, but her friend Carole Anne came down the hall and informed him that Greer wasn't there. She had gone home for the weekend to study. During their final in Contracts, he tried to say goodbye, but too many people were around her. He looked up her phone number in the First-Year Law Student Directory, a little tan booklet containing all their pictures and phone numbers, and left a message on her answering machine, telling her he had enjoyed getting to know her but was leaving school. He left his number, but she never called back.

Luke drove him to DFW Airport on a cold, wet December night two days later. Gun had graduated with honors from Georgia Tech and the UT School of Business but felt like a total failure. He was leaving Dallas as an unemployed disgrace to run and hide with his mother's family in Korea. He'd tried to pursue the girl of his dreams, but she never noticed him. Danny had taken a picture of her and given it to him, and it was the only thing he had to remember her by. He would never again believe in fate.

"Gun-ah, don't stay away too long, bro," Luke said when he pulled up to the sidewalk at the airport. "Just give it a little time. Let Dad cool off. Everything will be okay." He got out of his Jeep and came around to hug him. "I'll always have your back, Gun. Always. Merry Christmas, my *deongsang*."

# Chapter Twenty-Six

G reer walked into her shower and switched on the rain setting, then stood under the shower head and let the water wash over her with its warm simulated raindrops. It was comforting but not enough to wash away her guilt. When she found the student directory, she frantically flipped through its pages until she found Gun's picture—or James Kim's—and gasped. Although it was an old-school photocopy with poor image quality, she could still make out his face. She rubbed her finger over the picture. Sarah had been right. James Kim had been handsome—he looked like the young K-drama actors she admired—but he didn't look like the Gun she knew now. She'd stared at the picture in disbelief, wondering how she hadn't put two and two together.

She started to remember now and recalled James as a tall, friendly guy with shiny black hair that glistened in the autumn sun. She liked the way he brushed it away from his eyes. He also had a brilliant smile and a great laugh. She closed her eyes and remembered his voice calling her as she walked across campus. Unlike Jake, James had always called out to her first and looked out for her several times. He had treated her kindly, much better than Jake, but she hadn't repaid his kindness.

Her classmates teased her that he had a crush on her, and she secretly believed they were right, but she'd always denied it. She'd heard their derision uttered behind his back and was afraid they'd turn against her, too.

They belittled his intelligence when he was called upon in class. "Well, of course, he knew the answer. He's Asian," they snickered. "What do you expect from Confucius?"

They mocked his hair and glasses. "Could he be more of a dork?"

They criticized him for having two degrees and pursuing yet another. "What is it with these Asians and their endless degrees?" Tiffany Smith remarked. "At USC, they're professional students pursuing one degree after another. I'm so sick of them."

Little did they know that James didn't conform to their bigoted stereotype. He exuded confidence and hadn't been afraid to stand up to Jake on the night of the dorm party. His chivalry impressed her. She'd felt comforted by the strength and sturdiness in his arm as he led her away from the fray. He was no wimp. Then, to her surprise, she enjoyed their time at Snuffer's. James was kind and did his best to cheer her up. He was funny, too. She took a good look at him when he removed his glasses to clean them on his sweater. Although she never told anyone, she liked Asian guys and realized James was cuter than she thought. Maybe she should get to know him better. She would have to tread carefully, though. She didn't want to use or lead him on when unsure of her feelings. Not to mention, she would be teased mercilessly.

However, she never got to know him because the situation was wrenched from her hands. She knew she was in trouble when Trent Hughes, a snarky busybody, ambushed her as she walked across the Quad. "I saw you eating with Jim Kim. *Everyone* saw you. What were you thinking? I can understand ditching Jake. He's so dull and backward. But are you so desperate that you settled for the —?"

"Don't call him that!" she'd exclaimed, referring to the hateful racial slur.

Trent clicked his tongue. "My, my. Aren't we touchy? You better watch out, Greer. No White guy will ever want to date you if they think you have a penchant for those people. You'll be seen as damaged goods."

Like the snake taunting Eve in the Garden of Eden, Trent's words struck the heart of her vulnerability. She liked James but didn't want to become a social outcast for his sake. Law school was hard enough. Besides, she'd convinced herself that she did not like James in *that way*. She still liked Jake. To quell the rumors, she avoided James as much as possible. She still waved a discreet hello when she saw him but ran in the other direction if their paths were about to cross. She hated doing that to him but felt she had no choice.

When James left school, she felt ashamed of how she treated him and sad because she knew she had lost out on having a good friend. She thought about him for several years afterward, but that was before the internet, so she had no way of looking him up. She'd never known his reasons for leaving and wondered if she had influenced his decision.

She finally understood the reason behind her dreams. She'd thought they were a premonition of Jake's reappearance in her life, but now she knew they were pointing her to the truth about Gun.

After leaving Gun's house, she needed time alone and didn't know where to go where he wouldn't find her. She turned left onto Barton Springs Road, then realized she shouldn't be driving. She eased into the first left turn lane she saw and drove into Zilker Park. It would soon be dusk, so several cars were leaving, and she found a parking spot near the playground. Once her tears were under control, she got out of her car and walked around. Although she had loved coming here as a child to play with her cousins and later as a teen to swim in Barton Springs Pool, it had been years since she'd been here, even though it was a mere five-minute drive from her house.

She walked to the playground and sat on a swing. The playground had been modernized, so it wasn't the same swing set she had played in all those years ago when she had pumped her legs to swing as high as she could.

"Don't go so high, or you'll fall," her mother and aunts would caution. But she and her cousins would laugh and keep pumping, seeing who could go the highest. They had no fear.

When had that changed? When had her heart grown fearful, and the opinions of others began controlling the way she lived her life? Whose approval had she sought? Her parents and extended family? Her friends?

She dug her feet into the ground, bringing the swing to a halt as realization dawned on her. The person she had tried to please, the illusive acceptance and favor she sought but could never gain, was hers. Her constant striving—in life, school, and work—had been to prove that every label ascribed to her—that she wasn't smart, talented, pretty, or good enough— was untrue. She was a workaholic, not solely because she enjoyed her work but to prove that she was indispensable.

Likewise, she had sought a romantic partner who, by association, would make her feel approvable. Someone who would bolster her street cred. Outwardly, Jake checked all the boxes, and she had sold out on a chance of happiness in favor of acceptance. She ruled out James Kim as a prospective love interest, not because she didn't like him—she hadn't known him well enough to know that—but because dating someone that society writ large deemed "unacceptable" would've proved the labels she desperately tried to shake off true.

Would she and Gun have spent the last twenty-five years happily married if she had not wasted time chasing after the wind? Would she be teaching their children how to make pies alongside their cousins? She couldn't answer that but shuddered to think about the opportunities she had given up. And it begged the question: did she deserve to be with Gun now when it cost her nothing? No, she didn't. She hoped that Gun could forgive her, but she would accept his decision if he did not. She stood from the swing and returned to her car. It was time to stop hiding and face the music.

When she arrived home, Gun was asleep in his truck, which was just as well. She was emotionally drained and too tired to talk. She called him and told him to go home. She waved from her driveway, and he waved back but didn't leave until she was inside the house. It hadn't surprised her that he'd fed Kevin and Sophie. He was always doing thoughtful, helpful things for her.

Now, no sooner had she gotten out of the shower than Gun texted her that he was outside with breakfast tacos. She invited him in, but the atmosphere was tense, and she'd lost her courage from last night. They sat on the banquette in the kitchen breakfast nook, and after a few bites of the potato, egg, and cheese taco, she told him about Jake's visit.

Gun nodded. "Uh, I know. Sunny is staying at the Four Seasons and saw the two of you."

Greer exhaled loudly. "I don't appreciate Sunny spying on me, but I'm glad you know. It's one less secret between us."

After breakfast, they moved to the living room, with Kevin and Sophie accompanying them. They sat apart on the sectional. Greer tucked one leg under her and hugged an accent pillow.

"I'm sorry," they apologized in unison after a brief hesitation.

Gun looked puzzled. "What are *you* apologizing for? I'm the one who kept the truth from you."

Greer shook her head. "That's nothing compared to what I've done. When I realized who you are, I felt so ashamed."

He shrugged. "Ashamed of what? You didn't do anything wrong. You liked Jake. It wasn't your fault you weren't interested in me."

"No, you don't understand. It's more than that. There's something I need to tell you. Something I must confess. I've never told you before because I didn't want to hurt you."

She looked down, searching for the right words. *Just tell him the truth.*

"Until very recently, I would've never dated an Asian man. Because of how things were when I was growing up, I didn't think anyone would approve, and I was afraid. So, I've always kept the attraction under wraps. Isn't that crazy? Me, the K-drama fanatic, has been afraid to admit she likes Asian guys."

"I'm not sure I like where this story is going," he said with mock anger. "Who are these Asian guys you like?"

"Gun, please be serious! This isn't easy. The ugly truth I'm trying to admit is that I wouldn't have given you a chance even if Jake hadn't been in the picture. I remember thinking you were cute and a nice guy. I suspected you had a crush on me but deliberately ignored it because I was a coward who was too afraid of what others would think. It's so unbelievable to me now, and the irony is that I rejected you for the same reasons Jake rejected me. And speaking of Jake, I was blinded by what I wanted to believe, and I was . . ."

She stopped, and her eyes met his. "Oh, my goodness. I can't believe . . . how did I not see this before? It was you, wasn't it? *You* made the mixtape, and *you* were the one who comforted me in the prayer garden. The handkerchief with the monogrammed 'J' belonged to you."

Gun nodded but didn't say anything.

She covered her eyes with her hand. "What a blind fool I've been! I've lived my entire life worrying about what others think of me. And for what? All it's gotten me is a life full of regret for making poor choices. Yet, the worst choice was not choosing you. I don't know how you'll ever be able to forgive me or if you *can* forgive me."

Gun moved several spots closer and took her hand in his. "Greer, look at me. You have no reason to hide. And I have something to say. I love you. *Saranghae.*" And when she gasped, he said, "Do you like that? I knew you'd believe me if I said it in Korean, and it's true. I love you. It feels so good to tell you finally. I've wanted to tell you since the night of our first date— longer than that—but I needed to come clean about the past. That terrible day at the airport, your confession caught me off guard. I didn't know how to tell you I loved you without first revealing my identity. Sarah has been badgering me to tell you the truth, but I was ashamed and afraid. So, if anyone has been a coward, it's been me."

Kevin jumped on his lap, and he petted his head.

"I don't care what your reasons were back then. I don't want to waste one more minute on regret. I only care about how you feel now. If you love me, that's all that matters to me."

"But—"

He put his finger to her lips. "Hold on. I'm not done. What I wrote on the card about you holding my destiny in your hands, I didn't mean when we met on the plane. I meant long before that —when you dropped your books on the sidewalk. I saw you and Carole Anne together and carried your books to the Inn. You captured my attention and heart from that moment, and I've been carrying you in my heart all this time. Without you, something was missing. I didn't know what it was, so I've spent the last quarter of a century chasing the wrong dream. But now I know what I've been searching for."

Tears of joy came to her eyes. Was this really happening? Was her incredible, handsome Gun giving her a love confession from his heart? "I love you too, Gun. I've been lonely all my life, even when surrounded by people, because I was searching for my true friend. Now I know my heart was searching for you."

Gun wiped away her tears. "Oh, Gigi-ah. I am humbled and grateful for your love. I don't deserve it. But please don't cry, my Gigi-ah. It hurts to see you cry."

She sniffled, and Gun handed her a Kleenex from the coffee table. "But when did you first realize it was me? Did you recognize me on the plane? You gave me a strange look at the baggage claim like you were trying to recognize me."

She had been sincere, but he laughed. That great laugh she had feared she would never hear again.

"I didn't recognize you then, but I remember having a strange sense of déjà vu. I think it was your eyes that drew me in. I hadn't checked any luggage, but I was trying to work up the courage to talk to you. That's why I went with you to baggage claim."

"I knew it! But when did you realize it was me?"

He sucked in a breath. "That day my mom took me to your office. When you stepped out to help Mr. Hudson, I was nosey and began looking around. My mom has always called you Lawyer Garza, and that day, she had her head in the clouds talking about destiny, and she forgot to introduce us. But when I saw your name on your diploma and law license, I knew it had to be you. There's only one Greer."

"When did the others know? That night at karaoke—"

"No, they had no idea that night. I told them later." He gently removed an indignant Kevin from his lap and moved closer to kiss her, but she raised her hand and stopped him.

"Wait. There's something else we need to talk about. You called and left a message when you left school, but I didn't call you back. I was afraid to call because I didn't know what to say, but for years I felt guilty. I wasn't very nice to you back then, and if I could do it all over again . . . well, I'd do many things differently." She bit her lip. "Is that why you were so angry when you recognized me? Because of how I treated you?"

Gun sighed. "Once I realized it was you, I was shocked and then angry. After my anger subsided, I intended to call you, but you surprised me by showing up as Jason's karaoke date. Then I was angry because you didn't wait for me again. I know it's irrational, but I felt like history repeated itself." He shook his head. "As for your treatment of me, I don't think you've remembered the past correctly. The truth is you were always nice to me. Your liking Jake was partly the result of bad timing and my failure to make a move. Later, as the anger and bitterness loosened their grip on my heart, I began to remember your kindness. Your friendly smile and the time you lent me a pen in class. You returned the umbrella I had lent you and insisted on buying lunch to thank me. Then I made an interesting discovery."

"What?"

"Luke and Janet found an old box from my apartment during law school. Inside was a copy of the mixtape I made for you. That's how I put the same songs from the mixtape on the thumb drive. I carried it with me so I could give it to you when the time was right, but it must have fallen out of my backpack on the way to the airport."

Realization dawned. "So that's how you copied the same songs."

He pointed his index finger at her. "Yes, but there's more.

Also in the box was my old answering machine, and unbelievably, it still works after all these years. The last message on the machine was left on the day I left for Korea, but I'd never listened to it until you dissed me at Walgreens."

She rolled her eyes. "I didn't diss you."

"Hey, who's telling this story? Care to guess who the message was from?"

"Who? Me? No way! I don't remember that!"

"Yes, you. Yes, way. Don't you find it fascinating that you and that box of hidden secrets from my past should reappear simultaneously? It's eerie. One could almost call it *unmyeong*."

Greer was astounded. First, her dreams, then Gun, Jake, and the tapes—they'd all appeared in her life at the same time. She had first believed it to be a strange coincidence, but now she knew otherwise. It wasn't *unmyeong* in the mystical sense, but Providence, as in the hand of God, directed this glorious tale. She smiled in wonderment.

"There's that beautiful smile!" Gun grinned back. "But Gigi-ah, can you please kiss me and revive a dying man?"

How could she turn down that request? She had missed those lips and the beautiful person attached to them. She tossed the pillow to the floor and wrapped her arms around his neck. Several minutes later, they lay on the sectional, wrapped in each other's arms, grateful to be together. Finding each other again and in midlife, no less, was miraculous.

Greer studied the face of the man she loved and ran her fingers over his brows. She traced the bridge of his nose and his perfect lips that excelled at kissing.

He took her finger between his teeth and gently bit it. "My dear Gigi-ah, I have an important question to ask you," he said, suddenly serious.

She held her breath.

"As you know, in the dramas, the couples always separate

for a year before getting back together. Since you love dramas, do you think we should do the same? Should we separate for a year?"

She tapped his chest with her finger. "Listen here, my Kimchi Cowboy. I love my dramas, but you have another thing coming if you think you'll keep this Texas girl waiting."

Gun laughed. "That's exactly what I wanted to hear. Gigi-ah?"

"Yes, Gun-ah-ssi?"

He slid off the sectional and got down on one knee. "I've discussed it with Kevin, Sophie, Buddy, and Bullet. They're agreeable to blending our two families. So now it's up to you. Will you marry me?"

This time, her heart performed the entire gymnastics floor routine. There was only one acceptable response to his question. "Yes!"

# Chapter Twenty-Seven

Ms. Greer Garza and Mr. J. Gun Donovan married on a brisk mid-November afternoon as the sun descended toward the horizon. They spoke their sacred vows against the gleaming gold and red cliffs of Gary and Michelle's ranch, witnessed by hundreds of family and friends.

From the moment Greer had said, "I do," Gun insisted on paying the entire wedding tab. He wouldn't hear of it whenever she attempted to cut corners and was adamant that she picked whatever she liked, no matter the cost.

Sarah had also encouraged her. "Gun *Oppa* loves you and wants to spoil you. He's rich, so don't worry about it."

Greer had only three months to plan their wedding, and her friend Shannon insisted that she hire a wedding planner. Greer knew better than to cross Shannon, so she did as she suggested and also enlisted the help of her family and friends, who were all eager to be involved.

First things first, she had to find the dress. She and Maggie drove to Dallas to meet with Sarah, Janet, and Carole Anne. Sarah suggested a shop in Koreatown, and there, she fell in love with an exquisite sequined dress that incorporated elements of the modern hanbok. She'd been unsure how she would look in hanbok since that dress style wasn't designed for curvy figures, but the moment she tried it on, she knew she'd made the right choice. Her friends would tease her for wearing white, but her life with Gun represented a new start, so why not?

Gun hadn't spared any expense on her engagement ring. It was a stunning diamond solitaire with a diamond platinum band in a classic setting. She'd never owned anything so precious, and she couldn't stop admiring how it looked on her hand. The women at her office whooped with glee when she walked in wearing it.

"I bet that ring cost as much as my car!" Rita exclaimed.

Besides the excitement of preparing for the ceremony, Greer and Gun still had a few loose ends to tie up. Sunny hadn't returned to California, and through the grapevine, they learned that she was considering relocating to Austin. Greer had Sunny meet at her office two months before the big day, then handed her a check and the business card of one of her California clients, Blane Murphy. Blane was a polished, well-preserved man in his early sixties who'd made a fortune in a Silicon Valley startup. He'd noticed the picture of her and Gun displayed on her desk and remarked that he liked the Korean people. Greer told him about Sunny and hoped she was not throwing him to the wolves, but he winked and assured Greer he could handle Sunny.

"The check is for your ticket back to California and other expenses," Greer informed Sunny. "It's from my account, not Gun's. Blane is expecting your call, and if I were you, I wouldn't pass up this opportunity. Gun and I wish you well, Sunny."

Sunny glared at her. She opened her mouth as if to fire a parting shot but made no comment, took the card and the check, and left.

Greer reduced her workload for the first time since she

began practicing. The wedding took up much of her time, not that she had any complaints. She counted these days as some of the happiest of her life. Therefore, she had no reservations about assigning several new clients to Megan. She had proven herself to be meticulous and good at client relations, and with Molly to help her, their clients were in good hands.

The firm had built a firewall around Beau to prevent a conflict of interest, but Rita confided that Beau was a difficult client and Nick Taylor regretted courting him. He'd been over-heard saying the fees were not worth it. "Everyone's now saying they should have listened to you," Rita told her.

Greer resisted an overwhelming urge to gloat at the next shareholder meeting.

She and Gun met with Jason before the wedding, and he agreed to act as master of ceremonies and had some good news of his own. Susie was back in New York, arranging her move to Texas.

"Good. I hope you and Susie will also be walking down the aisle soon," Greer told him.

Upon hearing the news of their engagement, Gun's father and his wife, Barbara, drove to Austin to meet Greer. Barbara was soft-spoken and easy to talk to, but Greer felt intimidated by Gun's father. Yet, despite his commanding presence and erudite manner, he was down-to-earth. He bore a strong resemblance to Luke, but there was also a likeness between him and Gun, and she said so.

"Really?" both Gun and his father said in surprise.

She nodded. "You have the same expressions and manner-isms, especially when telling a story. Gun has your smile, and y'all have the same nice hands."

Her future father-in-law took a drink of his whiskey and studied her without saying a word, but she could tell it pleased him. "Son, where you been hidin' this girl? Not only is she pretty, but she's pretty darn smart too! I'm delighted I'll soon be able to call her my daughter-in-law."

Gun squeezed her hand and grinned, and the rest of the evening went well. It was heartwarming to see Gun and his father getting along.

A month before the wedding, Gun convinced Greer to take a short break and took her to the state fair. They were joined by Luke, Sarah, and their families. They spent the day looking at the exhibits and eating fair food while the kids enjoyed the rides. Gun bought her a funnel cake, and they sampled the fried butter Luke insisted they try.

After that short respite, the wedding was soon upon them. Gun was determined to share their happiness with everyone, so they had an enormous guest list. His uncle from Seoul, Kim In-Bae, was in attendance. He wore black-rimmed glasses, looked remarkably like Mrs. D, and greeted Greer with, "So you're the young lady taking my nephew away from me."

Greer had prepared for this moment. She bowed politely and disarmed him with, "*Samchon, annyeonghaseyo.* Hello, Uncle. It's a pleasure to meet you, too."

He laughed and waved his hand at her while saying something in Korean. Gun gave her the thumbs-up sign, and she placed her hand on her stomach with relief.

Gun had, of course, invited Juanita and Pedro.

"*Mijo!*" Juanita greeted Gun with a hug at the rehearsal dinner. "Aye, my handsome boy."

A woman in her late sixties, Juanita had salt-and-pepper hair and reminded Greer of her aunts. Pedro was quiet but had a pleasant face. When he shook Greer's hands, she noted that his hands were rough. They embraced her like old friends.

"Lucas could never settle down. He was like a wild colt," Juanita told her. "But Gun, he was always a good boy. My *mijo* was just a dreamer, that's all. You could see in his eyes that he wanted more. I'm glad *mijo* found someone like you. He deserves a good woman, and he deserves to be happy."

The morning of the wedding dawned cool and bright. Maggie, Sarah, and Janet had spent the night with her, and they made breakfast, brought it to her in bed, and helped pack everything she needed to take to the wedding venue. Sarah clipped a small burgundy bow on Sophie's head and slipped a tuxedo shirt on Kevin.

"How were you able to do that?" Greer asked in amazement.

"It's called bribery, *Unni*, in the form of treats," Sarah said while she and Maggie lifted the cats onto the bed. "Now, let's take a picture with Mommy on her wedding day. *Hana, dul, set.*"

Greer was a bundle of nerves as they drove to the ranch. She'd heard a glitch was inevitable in every wedding, and thus far, theirs had gone without one. She really had to stop waiting for the next shoe to drop.

Carole Anne and Donnie had driven down from Irving, and Carole Anne came to the bride's room and embraced her, careful not to mess up her makeup. She dabbed at the corners of her eyes and claimed credit for the day. "See, Gigi, you *were* meant to catch the bouquet at my wedding! It was prophecy!"

Greer and Gun decided to start the ceremony by entering together. They weren't kids who lived in their parents' homes and were entering this union as clear-eyed, mature adults. Gun came to the bridal room to collect her and stood in the doorway admiring his bride. His eyes were bright, and his face was full of love. "Am I dreaming?" he said, slapping his cheek, imitating her. Then he walked to where she waited and took her hands in his. "'You are altogether beautiful, my love; there is no flaw in you.'" They'd read the Song of Solomon together in preparation for their wedding vows.

Greer glowed with happiness. "'This is my beloved, and this is my friend.'"

He smiled widely. "Come on, Gigi-ah, let's do this. Let's walk this path together for the rest of our lives."

As the master of ceremonies, Jason announced the bride and groom's entry. Everyone stood as the orchestra began to play, and all eyes were on the bridal couple.

It was a packed house. Greer recognized the many faces of her relatives in the crowd—people she'd known and loved her entire life—and her friends who'd always wished the best for her.

Charlie was one of them. He waved to her, calling out, "Dang, girl!"

Tammy, her college roommate from Virginia, and her two sisters, who were more like family than friends, were also there.

Greer's parents sat in the front row on the left. Her father looked dapper in his tuxedo, and although he smiled, she noticed tears in his eyes. Her mother wore a burgundy-colored floor-length dress and looked elegant. "Oh, *mija,*" she said, smiling through her tears.

Mrs. D, in a dark blue hanbok traditionally worn by the groom's mother, couldn't stop grinning and whispered loudly to a beautifully coifed Barbara, "I knew it was fate."

Tall and dashing in a tuxedo, Gun's father looked upon his son with pride.

Luke, Sarah, and their families sat up front, too. Her niece and nephews—Darcy, Dylan, and Sarah's boys—had all dressed for the occasion. Luke and Sarah were the brother and sister Greer had always wanted. She could hardly believe she was marrying into this wonderful family.

At the end of the ceremony, after their kiss, the pastor introduced them as Mr. and Mrs. James Gun Donovan, and Greer turned to her handsome new husband. "This isn't a dream, right?"

Gun kissed her again, and the crowd whooped. "Yes. It's a dream come true."

But this wasn't an ordinary dream. It was her heart's dream and desire, and it was real. Everything that had happened to her in the past year led her to this moment. That night in her Dallas hotel room, she'd whispered a prayer for God to give her a glorious, romantic adventure. To bring her the man she dreamed of but didn't dare to believe existed. God had answered her prayer far more than she could ever ask or think. He'd written her story better than any drama writer could ever imagine. He was, after all, the Author of romance.

They didn't go on a honeymoon immediately, instead spending the holidays with their families. They spent Thanksgiving with her parents and Mrs. D, then hosted everyone, including Gun's father and Barbara, for Christmas. It was the most exciting and fun-filled holiday season in Greer's memory. Then, after Christmas and right before the New Year, Gun took her on a month-long honeymoon.

They snuggled together, lovey-dovey newlyweds in first class. "Is this really where you wanted to go?" Gun asked. "It's going to be cold."

Greer kissed him on the lips. "I know, but as the Dean Martin song says, our love will keep us warm."

Fourteen hours later, they looked out the window at the snow-capped mountains before touching down at Incheon Airport. Gun kissed her and said, "Welcome to South Korea, Mrs. Donovan."

# Epilogue

## July 1975
## Austin, Texas

T he Zilker Park train blew its whistle upon returning to the station. The line of children waiting for the train's next trip jumped up and down, unable to contain themselves. As the previous passengers disembarked, the waiting children rushed to the train to find a seat. Among them was a girl with a ponytail and twelve of her cousins playing at the park. The small carriage cars were made for two, and the girl was the unlucky number thirteen who had to sit alone. She looked at her mother, standing with her aunts and the other parents.

"It's okay," her mother encouraged her with a smile. "You'll still have fun."

"Hey, can I sit with you?"

The girl turned the other way to see who was talking to her. A tall Asian boy stood by the side of the train, his hand on the carriage door. He had straight, shiny bangs and wore braces. He smiled and looked nice.

"Sure." She grinned back as he climbed into the car with

her, glad she would not have to ride alone. "Are you here by yourself?"

"No, I'm with my brother, sister, and friends."

He pointed, and the girl turned around. Sitting behind them was another boy about her age who waved with his arm, and beside him was a younger boy who laughed and stuck his tongue out at her. An older boy wearing a baseball cap sat behind them. He looked like he was in junior high and seemed bored as he sat next to a little girl whose ponytails stuck out from her head. She was missing a front tooth.

"Aww, I like your little sister. She's cute," the girl said.

"Sometimes she's cute. When she's not being a pest."

They giggled, and the boy said, "My name is Gun. What's your name?"

"You mean like the guns they use in *Starsky and Hutch?*"

He nodded.

"That's so cool! My name is Greer, but I don't like that name, so my family calls me Gigi."

"Hey, both are names start with a 'G'!"

They laughed.

"I turned eleven last week, and I'm going to be in sixth grade," Gun said. "How old are you?"

Gigi's eyes grew wide. "You're older than me by a whole year and two months! I'll be ten in September and starting fifth grade in Mrs. Vaughn's class."

Gun looked down at the transistor radio she held in her lap. "I like your radio. Can I see it?"

She handed it to him.

He flipped the switch, and Elton John's "Your Song" filled their carriage car.

"You listen to KNOW radio station? I do, too!"

They laughed again, happy to have found another thing in common.

The man wearing the conductor's hat walked along the train's side, ensuring their doors were securely closed. He announced in a loud voice that the train would start soon and warned everyone to keep their hands inside their compartments and not hang out over the side of the train.

He sat up front, blew the whistle, and the train shifted. The children let out a collective shout. Finally, the train left the station by Barton Springs Pool to begin its journey around the park.

Once they were moving, the warm breeze blew the hair from their faces and swayed the overhead branches. Despite the conductor's warning, they stuck their hands out of the train to touch the branches as they passed.

When "Magic" by the group Pilot came on the radio, Gigi said, "Hey, I like this song."

Gun turned the radio volume up, and he and Gigi sang along. They shook their heads from side to side, like the *Peanuts* gang danced. When the song ended, they continued gabbing like two magpies and giggled when Gigi's cousin turned around and teased her because she was sitting next to a boy.

The ride was over too soon, and the train returned to the station.

Gun jumped out and held the door open, and Gigi followed, jumping onto the gravel. He handed the radio back to her. "Bye, Gigi. Thanks for letting me sit with you. It was fun. Maybe I'll see you again."

"You're welcome. I had fun, too."

Gigi watched him run to meet his family. Two women wrangled the kids together and spoke a language she'd never heard before. One of the women wore a beehive hairdo and oversized round dark sunglasses. She turned and looked at Gigi, then lifted her sunglasses and smiled. She waved at the woman and joined her mom, aunts, and cousins, who waited for her.

"Did you have fun?" her mother asked.

She nodded. "I did! And I met a nice boy!"

"I saw you talking to him. I told you it would be fun."

Gigi smiled. That boy Gun had been nice. She hoped she would see him again one day.

## THE END

# *Acknowledgments*

"Now to him who is able to do above and beyond all that we ask or think according to the power that works in us—to him be glory in the church and in Christ Jesus to all generations, forever and ever. Amen."
Ephesians 3:20-21

I began this journey nine years ago with no knowledge of the writing and publishing industry. All I knew was that I had a story to tell. Many people along the way encouraged, prayed for, and supported me, generously sharing their time and expertise. I still have much to learn, but I wouldn't have come this far without their help.

To my incredibly kind beta readers—Brittany B., Sheila B., Holly G., Linda G., Carol H., Jill K., Sarah L., Kim M., Michelle P., Phaedra R., Jill S., and Collin S.—thank you for your support of the manuscript during its early stages. Your feedback was both helpful and encouraging.

I want to thank my wonderful friend, Elise G., for letting me use her beautiful and peaceful home as a writer's retreat.

I owe a debt of gratitude to my kind Korean American friends and sensitivity readers, Oksun C. and Johnny T. I would also like to thank Oksun for reviewing the glossary to ensure the accuracy of my definitions. Any mistakes or misspellings are my own.

Christy Distler: Thank you for encouraging me to think

outside the box. The story is significantly stronger due to the insightful questions you posed and your expert editing.

When I panicked and needed a final proofreader, Cathy H. adjusted her busy schedule to help me. Thank you, Cathy!

Thank you, Gretchen of GSB!ackburn Design, for your stunning artwork and cover. You transformed my ideas into something even more beautiful than I could have imagined.

Aiden at Indian Motorcycle Austin patiently answered my numerous questions about motorcycles with grace.

Special thanks to the bar manager at the Ritz-Carlton Hotel in Dallas for kindly letting me view the ballroom.

To Johnny and Richard at State House Printing: thank you for printing my countless drafts!

I also want to express my gratitude to my parents, who have offered their love and support through all the ups and downs, the countless rejections, and the moments I wanted to give up.

Finally, all praise, honor, and glory to my Lord and Savior, Jesus Christ, who made this possible. I don't deserve such mercy and grace. "For from him and through him and to him are all things. To him be the glory forever. Amen." – Romans 11:36

# Author's Note

Like Greer's character, I am captivated by Korean dramas and culture, having visited South Korea in 2019. When I first began writing this book in 2016—before Parasite and Squid Game—very few streaming platforms offered K-dramas. Whenever I mentioned them to people, they would ask, "What's a K-drama?" Therefore, one of my goals in writing this book was to introduce readers to the wonderful world of dramas and Korean culture. I had no idea their popularity would surge as it did, especially during the pandemic. However, I'm glad they are now appreciated and enjoyed worldwide. If you are unfamiliar with K-dramas, I hope this book piques your curiosity and encourages you to watch one or more. You will not be disappointed. But be forewarned: they are addictive.

While some locales mentioned in the story are real—I have many happy childhood memories of the summers I spent at Zilker Park playing with my cousins—I have taken considerable artistic license. The rotunda in the middle of the SMU Law School Quadrangle and its inscription are genuine, but to my knowledge, the SMU campus does not have a secret garden. Coincidentally, there is a Greer Garson Theatre—the actress after whom Greer is named—located in the Owen Art Center on the SMU campus. I did not intend to besmirch the Office of the SMU Dedman School of Law Registrar; I needed a plausible explanation for the plot twist, so my apologies to the Registrar! Austin does not have a Waterloo Golf Course. There is an

Asian American Resource Center in Austin, but it does not resemble the center in my story; that place is fictional. Also, my apologies to the beautiful Four Seasons Hotel in Austin. The hotel did not have a spa at the time when the story was set.

# About the Author

Sandra L. Moreno, an attorney and cat mom to Spencer and Domino, is a proud fifth-generation Texan and a third-generation resident of Austin, Texas. She enjoyed growing up in the 1970s—when Austin was a weird yet cool college town—and thinks the 1980s were a blast. She comes from a large Hispanic family where everyone is in each other's business, and food plays a central role in their gatherings. Think of *My Big Fat Greek Wedding*, and you'll get the idea. Although she has been writing fiction since the first grade, *More Than I Dreamed* is her debut novel.

www.ingramcontent.com/pod-product-compliance
Lightning Source LLC
Chambersburg PA
CBHW071913210626
46818CB00015BA/2888